From The Women's Press Ltd
34 Great Sutton Street, London EC1V 0DX

F/327086

Stevie Davies   Photo: William Hunter

Stevie Davies was born in 1946. From 1971–84 she taught
English Literature at Manchester University, before becoming a
full-time writer. She is author of a number of non-fiction works,
Emily Bronte: The Artist as a Free Woman, *Images of Kingship in
'Paradise Lost'*, and *The Idea of Woman in Renaissance
Literature: The Feminine Reclaimed*, and has edited *The Bronte
Sisters: Selected Poems* and *Renaissance Views of Man*. This is
her first published novel.

STEVIE DAVIES

Boy Blue

The Women's Press

First published by The Women's Press Limited
A member of the Namara Group
34 Great Sutton Street, London EC1V 0DX

British Library Cataloguing in Publication Data

Davies, Stevie
  Boy blue.
  I. Title
  823'.914[F]   PR6054.A8915

ISBN 0-7043-5013-0
ISBN 0-7043-4031-3 Pbk

Phototypeset by AKM Associates (UK) Ltd
Ajmal House, Hayes Road, Southall, London
Printed and bound in Great Britain by
Hazell, Watson and Viney Ltd, Aylesbury, Bucks

To Rosalie
for the joy of our friendship

Part One

Part One

One

The Air Force base at Old Sarum lay petrified under sheets of ice. In the black air the fighting men's breath fumed out like clouds of cigarette smoke as they worked to retrieve the runway. The clang and ring of their shovels carried like the toll of bells for many miles across the plain. The stations at Lark Hill and Boscombe Down were also deeply snowbound, their attentions temporarily diverted from the enemy to the weather. It was December of 1944. The V1 rockets had ceased to clatter on their manic, raucous flight across the Channel, like mad birds haywire with solitude; but the silent V2s still nosed across in their place, and wherever they fell vast craters opened, pitting the landscape till it impersonated the surface of the moon. The plain was now a sea of blank lunar light, visibility perfect, so that the mounds of the old hillforts round Salisbury stood out like islands – Figsbury Ring, Clearbury Ring, Old Sarum hillfort itself – fortifications built by an older warrior culture, now extinguished.

When Christina's young man first came out of Wales to Old Sarum, to be trained and drilled into a fully fledged airman, he had at once noticed the mounds and taken an interest in them.

'I've read up all the gen in an old book,' he told her. 'And it seems they were originally to do with mother-cults, not meant as forts – you can see that by their shape – like a womb, do you see, or like breasts?'

But Christina, being only eighteen and shy to the marrow of her being, coloured up and averted her eyes, giving no answer. Then he came to her and said, 'I'm posted to Italy.' They were married; they made a baby; he flew off, all in three days. The cold set in.

Christina's father was on the night shift at the railway that night. The points had frozen over, and the men were working to free the iced metal, so as to let the lightless trains slide through to their destination. No one spoke. The railway track burned blue black

3

within the limits of the hurricane lamp; it continued in a silver ribbon toward London in the analytic moonlight. The wrenches clinked against iron. At home, in the tiny terraced house close by the station, Christina's mother was fast asleep. Christina's rocking horse stood alongside her rocking duck, with a streak of moonlight along the former's wooden mane, the latter's pleasant head and bill. Father had constructed these strangely twinned creatures with homely art at weekends a decade ago, with Christina and her two elder sisters and the one brother looking on in quiet rapture, their young eyes mesmerised by the brisk motion of the lathe, the fall of soft filaments of shaven wood. The rocking horse and the rocking duck were only Christina's by virtue of the fact that she called them so in her mind. And as the youngest of the children, she had been the last to sit astride their backs, and travel by fractions of an inch upon the epic journey to the window, where in amity they were now stabled in the moonlight. In the next room, Christina's mother was just a rounded bulk under the pinkish-grey sheen of a bulbous quilt. She dreamed of a house where there was no carbolic, only scented soap, and she washed her hands in a baroque pastel bowl; the butler flung open doors to an immense and delightful rainbow troupe of persons who were all welcomed graciously into the warm and glossy interior; and where you were not constrained to the narrow compass of your terraced home by a husband's inveterate shyness – a shyness which was growing so intense with age that he could only bring himself to answer the door with his cap pulled down over his eyes and his collar up as if to guard against draughts. Out of this armour, his eyes gleamed, soft and terrified, as through a visor. But, in the dream house, there was space and largesse and liberality of trust, and the teeming people, cleansed as if with linguistic soap of the Wiltshire burr in their dialect, flowed and pooled freely. In the dream house, the world came in to Christina's mother, and she met it with royal ease.

Out in the countryside, on the London line, Christina's father and the other men finished their work on the points, and stood back from the line to watch the first train through. The world was a livid white in the moonlight; their breath rose in pools like milk; their boots crunched on the frosted snow layers and they beat the fist of one gloved hand into the cupped palm of the other for warmth. Someone got out a flask of tea, and the steam entered the atmosphere, and hung transiently like a cloud of incense. There was no call for incense in that penitential landscape. Henry

Gartery's subsistence life went on in a shadow as chill as that cast by the grinding, reluctant train as its iron-black sides went slowly past him high as a house, causing, as it blanked out the moonlight, a sensation of terminal cold. The heavens stretched above Salisbury Plain like a lake of blue-black ink soaking into blotting paper. As the train loomed past, snorting out random bursts of steam and smoke in the manner of one who is gripped by a very bad cold, Henry, because he came of a family prone on the male side to motiveless suicide and because he was always conscious of this inheritance, thought once more of ending it all, and did not stir. When the train had gone through they all turned for home and, waving to the woman in the signal box (who did a good job, Henry felt, at standing in for her conscripted male predecessor), began tramping up the line across the resentful snows that creaked and tore under their soles.

He had been born the seventh in a family of twelve children, bred up in hideous poverty in a terraced house two streets away from his married home. His father too had been a railwayman, a dour man, free with his fists. Henry could not remember a time when he had not felt crushed by the superfluity of people jostling around him. He had been the runt of the litter, pathetic and maudlin, so that one would have laid odds against his survival. Words came late (he was five before his utterances could be understood), and were still hard to find. He thrashed about in his mind when called upon to reply to the simplest 'Good morning', or 'How are you keeping then, Henry?' But he grew up tall and handsome, to his family's surprise, a head higher than his tallest siblings. In young manhood, he grew very fetching moustachios, which he preened and fostered, curling the ends between thumb and finger. He was thought a good catch as a husband, if you went by physical beauty alone and did not mind the prospect of living with a sad sack, crippled with shyness and prone to doleful fits of silent head-shaking.

'Bear up, Henry! Be a man!' his sisters and wife and multitudinous cousins used to implore him. His shoulders drooped at the world's insistence that he should look lively, keep his heart up. He was happy when people left him alone, he smoked his pipe, he ate his quiet meal.

In general the presence of his children depressed him beyond words. He would sit in his armchair of an evening and count them over, and though there were only the four, a comparatively modest number considering the numerous litter into which he had been

5

born, he could not somehow accept the multiplicity of selves for whom he was forced to fend. Their identities punched holes in the thin shell of his personality. Their noise got into his head. But he did not shout at them or lambast them. Henry's manners were insanely mild. He put up the newspaper between himself and them, and studied the form so that he could bet on the gee gees.

But there were obstacles to a complete withdrawal. The worst was the exaction of his overwhelming love for Christina, his youngest girl. It did not let him rest. If he had won a little money at the racecourse, he would come in to find her playing with her doll at the hearth, and, smiling, he would sweep her up like winnings, and sit her in his lap, allowing her every licence.

'*Why* is your face often so sad, Dada? What are you thinking about?' She cross-questioned him from her privileged position.

'Don't ask questions, my girl. I just think, that's all.'

'But what about?'

'About bad girls who keep bothering me with questions.'

Christina wrinkled her forehead as she stared at him, searching out clues to the sources of their life's communal unease.

'Is it my fault, Dada? Do I make you so sad?'

He pulled his cap further down over his eyes, shaking his head furtively. For she was not wrong, it was in some sense her fault, in that she obliged him to love her, forcing him to stay alive, stripping him of choice. He felt more comfortable with her elder sister Lilian, the thumping great girl, athletic, brawny, independent, who had never called forth the slightest affection from him: more like a boy than a girl. She was off climbing trees, playing football. She didn't trouble him. As in the case of the only boy, George, so dull and stolid there was nothing at all to be said about him, he felt he could ignore Lilian, not take the fret of responsibility.

Minnie was even less trouble, for she was entirely negligible: a homespun, basic girl with a lugubrious, sallow face and greasy hair. One could spend all day in a room with Minnie and Chrissie together, and scarcely register Minnie's existence. She appeared to accept her insignificance with a good grace.

As a child Christina would go to bed and brood on the sadness she felt she evoked in her father. She hated Lilian for Dada's apparent preference for her. Lilian was broad and buxom. She had a hearty, insensitive manner, and a foghorning voice which the fastidious Christina was ashamed to hear.

'You are not a proper girl,' said Christina to Lilian. They were

6

forced to share a room, all three sisters, so that Christina was constantly maddened by Minnie's and Lilian's untidy ways.

'How do you work that out, Lady Muck?'

'You throw your clothes in a heap on the floor when you take them off. You don't care how you look. You fight boys. You are too tall. You are loud mouthed. You'll never get yourself a husband *that* way.' Christina was eleven years old. 'It's true, you know it is.'

'Hear that, Min? Little Miss Superior says I'm not a proper girl. I'll throttle you one day, I'll squash you like a bug, I'll cause you to have a severe downfall. What have you got against me, Chrissie, anyhow? What harm have I ever done you? Come on now, tell me.'

Lilian sat plump down on Christina's bed, wearing a baggy green nightgown and a hairnet, to Christina's censorious eye a grotesque figure. And yet Lily's face was invariably forgiving and humorously inclined, even when she threatened to trample you underfoot or have you for dinner. Christina faltered, morally uncertain.

'Well you are a bit rough, Lily – uncouth is the word. Not ladylike. You must admit.'

'Little sister, I'm just me. You'll have to accept me, warts and all. What are you in a state about?'

Christina's lip trembled.

'Dada likes you better than me!' she wailed. 'He does! He does so! And it isn't fair!' She burst out crying.

'Dada doesn't have to worry about me, that's the point, Chrissie. You seem to bother him somehow, you're too soft, too thin skinned and in need of protection.' She stroked, ruefully, the delicate blond skin of Christina's thin arms. 'Do you think I wouldn't have liked to have been vulnerable like you, and so sweet with people, and so meek, and have held them all on a short rein like you do, Chrissie?'

Christina didn't comprehend. But for a while she let Lilian love her and be close to her, before she elbowed her surreptitiously away again. But she never in future allowed herself to indulge in fits of outspokenness. She got far more by smiles and soft speech. Besides, as she grew up, all roughness and violence shocked her deeply. Men alarmed her, with their bristly chins and loud mouths. The boys at school made her spine creep with their gross language and the way they had of cannoning into you and felling you in the playground. Then the war came, which was also her flowering

7

time. 'Really, Chrissie, you ought to be a model,' people said, in admiration. Even in her hated grey gymslip, belted at the hips to hold in the bulging cloth, it was obvious that Christina was blossoming wildly. Her body was lissom and tall, her hair a soft wavy cloud, her eyes the true colour of violets. Her manner was ductile and modest but her upright carriage called attention to the proud quality of her beauty, so that it was clear to those around her that she was cut out for fine things, beyond the range of Salisbury altogether. It was a shock when Christina's call-up papers came and she was sent away to the munitions factory in Bristol. Somehow, she had never taken the inevitability of this at all seriously. Something would happen to prevent it. Europe would end its quarrel, America would close its great fist around the enemy and squeeze it into nothing, the men would come home, all before Christina's eighteenth birthday. She did not say a word when the call came, but shut her eyes tight for a moment, tears breaking out, rocking herself in her own arms. Her father and mother stood by and watched her awful pain at having to go out into the alien world of machines and factory people. She had heard that only a very low type of woman from the slums, with dirty hair, and also Irishwomen who were not nice, worked there.

'But Chrissie it is our patriotic duty to work in the war effort,' said her mother helplessly. 'It may not be so bad. There are bound to be some decent girls for you to make friends with.'

'Yes Mum. I know I've got to go.' She was smoothing and folding her few dresses, ready to pack.

'Don't take it so bad then, my love.'

'I can't help it, Mum.' Christina was whispering, her back turned to her parents. 'It isn't feminine, it's degrading. I don't want to go, I don't.'

She was utterly frightened. When she got to Bristol the fear increased. The blaring noise of the machinery went on and on, raping the ear-drums. She had to handle the cylindrical bodies of shells, icy to her fingers; then she was set to manufacture parts for tanks, to kill people. The work was back-breakingly heavy, she was on twelve-hour shifts, it was all death. She cried herself to sleep at night, out of homesickness, exhaustion and an oppressive horror which never left her at the significance of the work she was doing. None of the other girls seemed to be troubled by this.

They cheerfully cursed over their work, but they accepted it as necessary. Their chief grievances seemed to be concerned with the lack of time they were given to do their shopping, which they remedied by taking turns to feign illness; and the dearth of men, along with the poor quality of males available. They made obscene jokes at the expense of the foreman, who lorded it over them, cock-of-the-walk, they said, ruling the roost with his pot belly stuck out before him as he waddled by, like an advertisement for the charms beneath. He spotted Christina immediately as an unusual beauty, and the oily little man – half a head the shorter, with his few hairs highly combed and trained across his shiny dome – made opportunities to tutor her in depth, wedging his body against hers at the capstan. Christina was so shocked at the work she was being made to do that she hardly noticed the hot-breathing ardour of her initiator. 'Come on, be kind to me,' he whispered to her in the canteen corridor, sliding a hand into her blouse. In her infinite shock and mortification, she lashed out blindly, knocking him off balance so that when he returned to the factory floor, his bald head had grown a little blue-black egg where it had contacted the fire extinguisher. 'Filthy little slut,' he hissed as he passed her, and gave her a wide berth. She laboured on with the metal weapons under the echoing roar of the machines. One night she dreamed of being pregnant; of giving birth to a ten-pound bomb, which slid out from between her legs in a trail of cold slime, and when she touched it the skin of her hand stuck to the freezing body. She woke the other girls in the dormitory with her screams. She would not survive. She realised this.

Then Christina came home one weekend. There was the dance at the town hall which the airmen from Sarum and Lark Hill attended en masse. There was Jim. There was shelter, marriage, a baby. She came indoors from the public outside world of the factory and the war. The exposure to noise, to strangers' eyes, to brutal manufacture, ceased, and she came home to Dada and the peace and quiet of his endless dolour. She herself had changed in many ways. She did not now ask, 'Why are you so sad?' Not only was it a taboo question, but in a way she felt she knew without asking. Catching other people's stray remarks, she began to gather the fact that Dada had on several occasions since the beginning of the war attempted suicide, by drowning. The womenfolk kept their corporate eye on him; they warned him, 'Bear up now, Henry. Be a man.' Squadrons of aunts and second cousins were put on the alert, vigilantly trailing him if he were late home of an evening.

'You won't do it again now, Henry, will you?' said Mother, categorically.

'Can't very well now, can I? There's Chrissie's blasted baby on the way.' He sighed. Another tie to fix him to mortality. He could not in all honour elope into the next world, with Chrissie expecting.

'He's a morbid old sod,' said Lilian to Minnie, in Christina's hearing. 'He needs to do exercises or something, to get his blood circulating round his brain-box.'

No, he's sensitive, thought Chrissie. He hates the war, that's all, he hates it like me so that the whole world is his enemy; but he hasn't resources to fight, stand up for himself. But Jim is going to change it all.

Jim was Welsh, and warm, and loving, and jaunty. He had words that overflowed torrentially, words full of bubbles as if he poured his nature out quickly, and it all ran away foaming like beer from the keg; but there was plenty more where that came from. He was Henry Gartery's opposite. He never took no for an answer: he had the habit of joy, and found the habit next to impossible to grow out of. When Jim had flown into Old Sarum in the early spring of 1944 for special training, he didn't expect anything but the usual bunk in a barrack, drill, exercises, perhaps the odd evening touring the pubs. He expected nothing out of the ordinary but found, instead, a miracle. He had brought with him a religious tempera-ment, nurtured in the Bethesda chapels of his mother country, and although he had ditched the dogma that went with the tempera-ment long ago, he could not help seeing his meeting with Christina as meant; an intention in Somebody's mind; an act of Grace. He called it his 'pure buckshee good luck'. Threading through the smooching girls and men on the smoky dance floor, the local band attempting a bumpkin impersonation of Glen Miller, he looked casually round at the girls. He carried his pint in one hand, his fag in the other, and he was in uniform, forage cap tucked under one epaulette. He wasn't easy with girls, inclining to be shy and foolishly reverential in their company. As he wended through the labyrinth of swaying bodies, guarding his pint against his chest, he saw the tall still figure of a thoughtful girl standing against the wall, isolated. A crowd of new dancers took the floor, censoring his view. The band went into 'Don't sit under the apple tree', and the dancers began to jive, American servicemen spinning their chosen girls about with rubber-limbed, solemn virtuosity. Jim got out of the crush and found her still there, the quiet-faced person with

10

head averted so that her features were shadowed, her hair lit radiantly from the spotlight behind her. As he stepped up to her and she turned her head to him, he saw that she was lovely. He asked for a dance. Her arms were bare and golden, braceleted. Her dress was pale cotton, slenderly fitting to her body. As they danced, and they smiled fugitively, and looked away, a transaction of the utmost complexity and weighty implication went on under the surface of their few words. It was negotiated outside the limitations of the clock and the shallowness of the occasion. Matters of life and death had to be determined on the spot these days; you might not get another chance. Neither of them was surprised or disquieted. By the time he accompanied her home through the ancient streets of the town, it was understood between them that they would soon be married. Embarking for Italy, he left his baby in her body, his spirit lodged within the walls of her mind for safe keeping. Love-letters flew between them, passionate and gauche. They expressed on paper a craving and wanton abandonment they would not have dreamed of saying out loud.

Christina, in her parents' house, lived for these letters. She loitered at the postbox and caught the mail as it fell. Then she would run upstairs with the precious letter clutched to her smock, shut herself in the bedroom and read it over and over with hammering heart. When there was no letter, she placed the other mail in a tidy pile, went out of doors and walked, her face white. Secretly she distrusted the postwoman, whom she suspected of inefficiency, though she smiled at her beseechingly whenever they came face to face. She needed the letters absolutely, as later she needed the pregnancy, as verifications of Jim's existence. It was hard to believe she had met him at all, it seemed so brief. He was like a joyous ghost or a jubilant dream. She feared to awaken. When the letter said, 'I love you Chrissie, I adore and worship you, I want you so badly, you are more than God to me,' the sacrilegious words were holy wine, they streamed in her veins, she fainted away from the dull mediocrity of her household and was not made of matter at all, but all spirit and light. She tried to credit Jim with immortality. Nothing must happen to him, ever. At first her pregnancy seemed in doubt, for she bled at the times when she would normally have expected her periods. So she said nothing to him at all of the baby until the fifth month when the bleeding stopped. The pregnancy stabilised, she became fit and hale, her hair silky and bright, and everyone said 'Oh Chrissie don't you look radiant!' though Lilian would keep spoiling things by feigning astonishment at Christina's girth, saying, 'What a size you're getting. What you got in there then, our Chrissie, a whale?' A god, thought Christina, a beautiful god, that's what I'm carrying, and she flounced away tossing her curls in scorn.

She wrote to break the news to Jim, eagerly awaiting his response. But at about this time some hitch occurred with their letters. She was still hearing from him by most available posts, but his letters were heavily censored, and he was not allowed to tell her his exact whereabouts. He was not hearing from her at all, he said, but he hoped and trusted she was well and he knew she was thinking of him. Obviously he was still in Italy, since she had received a photograph of Jim and an Army friend standing with their hands in their pockets, forage caps tilted at an angle, in attitudes of modest self-importance in St Peter's Square, Rome, and another of the two standing likewise in Pompeii, the city of the dead. She carried them about with her, and at odd moments got them out to study, with her eyes screwed up close to the images, as if she were near-sighted, sometimes shedding a few tears. If her mother caught her, she said, 'Now then girl, give over that blubbering,' bending in her comprehensive floral apron at the grate, sweeping ashes into the pan, slightly caustic with those who had spare time for the luxury of a good weep. Then Christina riposted that she didn't blubber, she cried. When he heard this kind of thing, Chrissie riding her high horse, Mother trying to bring her down to earth, Henry couldn't help but smile to himself behind his newspaper at Christina's insistence on the dignity of her nineteen years, and a housewife's status now without a house to queen it in. As she came nearer and nearer to her time, she weighed on him more painfully. Her body had swollen up quite huge, and she had difficulty in walking, or getting up from a chair without aid. She had received rather a bad turn late in the eighth month by the appearance on their doorstep of a breezy lady from the Ministry of Labour, uniformed, arm-banded, wanting to see Christina. Christina lumbered downstairs.

'Hello dear, I won't trouble you for long. I just have to fill in these forms. Yes, that's right, you sit down. Now, you're a skilled worker, we don't want to lose valuable women like you, so I'd just like to know what your plans are for after Baby's born?'

Christina blushed, fiery red. Her voice came out little and mumbling. 'To look after the baby.' She looked down and aside

12

from the conscription officer's jolly and official face.

'Don't queue with the shirkers, join the women workers, that's what they say, don't they? Perhaps your mum would consider looking after Baby while you go out to do your patriotic work – locally, mind, you wouldn't be called upon to move out of the immediate vicinity.'

Christina pursed her lips tight, and sat immobile, her arms guarding the bulge of her pregnancy, which in turn guarded her from these battleaxes who wanted to put you in a prison of raging noise away from your people, filing, riveting and drilling, turning out tanks and planes and shells and lorries. She wouldn't go back there.

'Or alternatively, you could put Baby in a nursery. He'll be very happy there, you know. Away from the claustrophobic atmosphere of home, with lots of other children to play with; they develop so well together you know, Mrs Llewellyn, there's a lot to be said for it.'

'I'm afraid my husband wouldn't allow me to put my baby in a nursery, he has strong conscientious objections to mothers going out to work.'

'Come come. In this day and age?'

'He would *never* allow it, I'm afraid.' Christina dared to look up, and even to smile sweetly, regretfully, at the bureaucratic lady with the fruity voice. She had heard it all before, this stubborn resistance to doing one's patriotic duty, phrased in terms of an appeal to a higher authority: my husband would never allow, my father wouldn't consider. Mr Bevin and Mr Churchill had foreseen it all from very early on. They had liked to approach the question of women's conscription rather as an 'invitation' than as a legal requirement, meeting evasion with evasion, screwing out compliance by the application of a vicious moral pressure. When women failed to show a sense of gentlemanly honour by shrugging at the pressure, ignoring the call to arms or drifting out of work when they'd had enough, they issued the compulsory call-up order on young women; but the young mothers they couldn't force. Still, one could but try. She noted the pulse throbbing at this one's neck, and how hard she breathed. She was definitely rattled. They'd get her yet.

'But there's the matter of patriotic duty, Mrs Llewellyn, to take into account: I'm sure you're most sensible of it, would wish to do your duty to your country now that we're so well on the way to winning?'

'Yes, but my husband . . .'

'I feel sure your husband would see the justice of what we're asking you to do. He's a member of the armed forces, isn't he?'

'Yes.'

'Well then. You can argue him round to your point of view. A clever woman can always find means of persuasion. It will be your way of bringing him home all the quicker.'

Christina could feel the net descending on her; she struggled for breath under its fine mesh. The baby beat and threshed about angrily inside her agitated body. It punched upwards into her diaphragm, aiming at her heart. It slithered across her bladder, causing piercing pain.

'What shall I put down then, Mrs Llewellyn?' She held her fountain pen over the form, expectantly. Her expression was blandly jovial. Her face was caked in powder, clogging the pores, chalky, like a mask, Christina thought as she glanced up.

'I can't do anything my husband wouldn't approve of, I'm sorry but I can't.'

Is he your God? the woman seemed to ask.

Yes, thought Christina, yes he is. It was illogical but although he was himself a man, he seemed to have saved her from the men's world; a fighter, but he held off the brutal fighting machine from her.

'Do think it over,' said the recruiting official, marching out. 'I'm sure you'll change your mind.'

She was badly shaken. Lilian helped: she was categorical about it. 'They can't make you do anything,' she said. 'Just tell the swine to eff off if they come round here bothering you. Look at me, Chrissie, I'm a law unto myself, aren't I? I like work, but on my terms not theirs. Sod them all. Have an Ovaltine tablet. Cheer up. I'll see her off next time, trust your old Lily.'

Christina had awful dreams of being put back in the munitions factory, where the overseer had slipped his fingers into the bodice of her petticoat, so that she had felt grubby afterwards and washed every item of underclothing. In her dreams she was labouring again with the killing machines, shut in to the vault of the windowless factory, never seeing daylight, echoes of hammering in her skull, traumatic noise of riveting, heavy stench of oil, nauseous work of war, weeping weeping she stood at the capstan eleven hours, twelve, coming in the dark and leaving in the dark, one in the army of eight million women fuelling the war. They were the ghosts

14

buried underground, they were the deafened, muted, blinded shades set to toil in hell. Occasionally they mouthed things to one another but nothing could be heard above the clamour of the machines. Their hands were pitted with sharp metal splinters and covered with oil sores, as if they suffered some communal poxy disease.

She awoke in a sweat, and cried out for Lily who was a hairnetted hump in the next bed.

'What's up Chrissie?' Bleary but willing, Lilian hoisted herself up on one elbow.

Christina could still hear the cacophony of the dream. It was pounding and grinding inside her head, ear-splitting.

'Got a pain, my love?'

'No.'

'What is it then? Had a dream?'

'No.' The noise was still reverberating inside her, eliminating thought. Lilian switched on the lamp. She smoothed Christina's forehead, rubbing the temples.

'It was that woman wasn't it, the old bag from the Labour? You don't want to let these nosy-parkers worry you, girl. They can't touch you. All blab they are. I told you that.'

The noise was still there, but it seemed to be rumbling gradually lower, like a storm passing over. 'Lily, Jim doesn't seem to be getting my letters at all. He doesn't know about the baby. It feels so dangerous, that he doesn't know – can't keep his mind on me, defending me, if he doesn't know, can he. I feel they might get me – send me back to the factory – I'd die, Lily, I would.'

'Yes but they *can't* send you back, there's no law to force mothers of small children, forget about it.'

The noise had abated, finally; she could hear herself think. But now the baby had taken it into its head to perform a series of extravagant gyrations in her stomach. She lay on her back, stranded, while it toiled in its prison, like a titan, and the bedclothes rose and fell above the place where it fought. It felt like rival gangs rather than one baby, engaged in mortal combat.

'Believe me?'

'Yes all right Lily, if you're sure.'

'Do you want to sit up a bit?' Lily heftily lugged Christina up higher on the pillows. She goggled at the display of force going on in her sister's revealed abdomen, which the tussling child was heaving from side to side.

15

'A proper little prize-fighter you've got in there. Knock it off you ruffian, go to sleep.' Lilian placed her hands on Christina's tummy, and the baby swiped at them with vigour. 'You're a real size now, Chrissie. What do you weigh?'

'Thirteen stone,' muttered Christina, ashamed.

'What a whopper! And so energetic. Bet you'll be glad when he's out, won't you?'

'Yes. But I *don't* want it to be a boy, Lily. I really don't. I couldn't cope with a boy.'

Lilian didn't know what to say. Christina was so queer these days, full of whims and frights, and you were supposed to humour people who were expecting, for they did unlikely things such as eating coal.

'You'll love it whatever it is, Chrissie. Course you will.'

'Yes, but it's a girl. I'm positively sure of it.'

Thank God you're a girl and aren't going to terrorise me, Christina thought, going back to sleep; and when Jim gets back and the war's over we'll get a house of our own, and we'll be safe in there with him.

Henry steered down the glacier of the embankment from the station in his ancient leather boots, which I've had, he thought, at least twenty-five years, since the Great War in fact, and they're still holding the water out. They made things to last in those days; the cobblers were craftsmen, not like now. Through a combination of accident of age and tubercular lungs he had missed being called up in either war. Wish I had been sometimes though, he thought to himself, and got in the way of a spare bullet at Wipers or some other foreign field, pushing up poppies by now nice and quiet, I'd have missed all these winters coming off the nightshift like tonight perishing with cold, still in the dark. The accursed stars refuse to set. How many more Decembers am I going to have to wade through?

Any day now for our Chrissie, he thought, turning up the deserted main road toward home. My God, what a size she'd spread to – a slender little body she always was too: thin when a small baby even, with narrow shoulders and tapering fingers, hands open from the outset, not clutched in tight like other babies with their fat little fists. She was a dextrous little creature from the word go. You'd have thought her umbilical cord was hitched to me rather than Mother, she tweaked a string between us and I danced like a puppet from her very first day. She made a real fool of me.

Henry thought of her coming baby. The nights would be filled with hullabaloo again, the house wouldn't be their own; no paper barricade would be able to repel the foreign occupation. Anschluss all over again. The house had always been too small to contain them all, jammed up against one another like pilchards in a tin. Henry could not summon the slightest enthusiasm at the thought of the advent of a grandchild. He had a plentiful collection already, and grandchildren are not slim like stamps to be kept in an album. They have to be fattened at cost to the family, and they take up space, of which there is so little. Henry's experience of grand-children was so compendious that he even had one dead. Small Albert, Minnie's eldest child, who lay in his grave in Devizes Cemetery in Salisbury, poorly bedded there for they had no money to afford a gravestone despite being offered special terms by the monumental mason; his grave marked only by Minnie's love-letters which she placed there for the infant ghost's inspection on a weekly basis. 'My dead darling, I do love you so. Albert from Mum.' Better off there, most probably, safer than live up here to disappoint or to be disappointed. He thought again of the inviting wheels of the locomotive, hypnotic black slicing edges for un-desired lives. And what would they all do then without him, these dependents and descendants?

Yet when Christina had been born, a late, unplanned addition to his family, he had been caught night after night rocking his baby in his arms, kissing the warm, cleanly forehead. They laughed at his unmanliness, great vulgar gusts of laughter. Female hands plucked the baby from him and thrust it, thumb-sucking, fontanelle beating, back in the wicker crib, out of harm's way – for men, they said, do not understand babies. They are liable to drop babies from great heights, thus fracturing their skulls, or else through unidenti-fiable means they are likely to impart wind into the infant's lower abdomen, causing it to raise its legs toward its chest and bellow. But night after night, braving the mockery, Henry would tiptoe from the matrimonial bed, and catch up Christina. Once by moonlight, he was standing by the open window holding her, not thinking about anything in particular, in a kind of reverie, sniffing in her smell, so milky-sweet, when he saw her open her eyes and stare at him, and recognise him. His heart distended as if love unsqueezed its fist in there and thrust its fingers out, open-handed, against the walls of his body. He wanted to cry out in pain; to expel

17

with a rough gesture the alien sensations of need and tenderness. It was the lack of freedom the little blighter entailed that bothered him, the being called out of himself; the being called upon to protect every hair of her head. Which can't, in the nature of things, be done. Thus his passion for Christina increased his desolation, and made him come to look upon her from time to time with an expression aghast, outraged, as if he wanted to smack her off and banish her. But his passion, together with his unfitness to love, increased as she grew; and his nocturnal visits were carried on past her babyhood until she grew to expect him in the funeral hours of the night, and would be waiting for him to come, kneeling up holding the bars of her cot, her eyes gleaming in the darkened room, mute, secretive.

But this was prehistoric. It was all done before time equipped Christina with a memory.

She woke with the dawn, from a sleep composed of shallow troughs of oblivion rising to shallow dreams, of Jim and the trouble of obtaining visas to visit him, interminable waits at customs, negotiations for a passport, boat journeys from Southampton Dock. In her dreams she was not pregnant, but slender and willowy, a head-turning beauty so that people in armchairs commented, 'What an adorable girl, so fetching, such classic high cheek-bones, you ought to be a model, Christina.' And she was malleable in the dream world, too, as she had been for Jim those few precious nights, and bent for him, and melted out: and then had been surprised, so shy a girl, so shy a man, and lay with her head on his breast disbelieving until it happened again; and she was bathed in his adoration of her, and the night before he embarked he wept, but she could not, and all the pillow sodden with his unmanly tears; and herself as dry and fragile as a wild flower pressed in the pages of the family Bible, at Ezekiel, or Job.

But waking now was into a world in which you had fattened into something monstrous and ugly. The mountain of Christina's flesh lay like a stranded whale resting on the pillow her mother had said would support her tummy; and she had been cross then and said 'Oh don't nag me, Ma,' but tried it anyway, and found it eased the weight. Even the midwife thought Christina's pregnancy was hefty, and felt called upon to make quips to that effect. Now Christina's opening eyes took in the poky room. The rocking horse and the rocking duck were grey-faced at the window, immobile and

18

expressionless as if, after all, they were only the wood out of which they were made. The tasteless and frayed curtains carried on hanging. All was as before, but something unimaginable and new had taken over the room, she found. It was in the nature of an earthquake, or a volcano. The whole room was moving. Its walls were contracting inwards on her, then distending outwards until it seemed the room must burst and expel her. Time in the form of the clock face loomed into a mighty O and shrunk to an evil speck, its beating hand thundered each second out like doom, like the black metal machinery that works the clock in Salisbury Cathedral – which is where the ghosts live, and they pulse in this manner, they dilate like the immense pupil of an eye and then they worm away into invisibility, under the slabs. And there too the light resembles the light within this terrible room, where dawn sheds thick layers of ash upon the optic nerve, ash which Mother clears from the grate downstairs each morning, and the cinders scrape like the sides of the brick walls creaking out, clamouring in. Then the room began to lie down, it went still. Christina, reopening her eyes, looked again, and the familiar objects were not forcefields any more but just things: things in themselves, for touching, hard or soft.

'Mother!' shrieked Christina, deafening herself, 'Mother! I'm dying!'

Mother came in, very smartly, as if she had not been asleep at all, but shamming all night, with her ear alert.

'What's up then Chrissie? You had a dream or what?'

Christina, meditating in the safety of this lull, now divined what was up.

'I think it's starting,' she whispered. 'What are we going to do?' She squeezed Mother's rough, scrubbed hands with both of her own. Mother's thumbs stroked the back of her hands.

'Best get you off to the nursing home,' she said, as if this were an idea that had just occurred to her on the spur of the moment. Christina clung on mutely. 'You'll be well looked after there Chrissie: you know that. You seen the matron and you know her's a kind soul.' Christina tightened her hold. Mother put her face down beside Christina's on the pillow, and Christina always remembered the touch of her mother then, and the noticing of how abnormally soft her mother's round cheek seemed, like silky petals, unageing. Mother said, 'You be back home in no time, the both of you. Up you come.'

Christina wailed out, 'But I'll be all on my own, Mum!' as she came up on the leverage of her small and sturdy mother's determination.

Lumbering downstairs went Christina, out of the house where she had been born, and married Jim, and conceived his child. They went on foot, processing down the snowbound road and round a couple of terraces to the Maternity Home. Lilian on one side hoisted her bodily along, and she leant on her mother for balance. Mrs Smith and her aged mother from next door accompanied them, emitting good advice.

'Keep going, old girl. You all right, my love?' Thank God there was Lilian, so large and reassuring. Christina did not think she would ever be able to manage without her. The baby trying to be born pressed down, forcing her legs apart so that walking seemed impossible. She voyaged slowly through the snow, her pelvis ready to crack with the pressure. She said nothing. Every step was an act of concentration. In her odyssey she seemed to view each quartzy flashy crystal of snow before it cracked beneath her boot, each shining like an individual gem. The miraculous beauty of the world bombarded her eye, demanding entry. Why hadn't she noticed anything of this before? Concentration of pain brought out its savage beauty. After a lifetime they reached the bottom of the road.

Here they paused. Rounding the bend was going to require navigation, for the snow had drifted deeply. Pain was a belt being lashed in tight around her abdomen. Again and again it wrung her body like hoops of steel, fiery, driving out breath. Sunrise burnt sulphurous on the eastern horizon, but above it the skies were a ripening grey blue where the planes used to come, but surely they must come no longer, she thought, looking up, and she recorded in her mind the dim presences of the departing stars, and saw it all: the beauty and peace of it all, though her body beneath like a seething cauldron came up and up to the boil of pain.

Lilian dragged her up round the snow-covered embankment garden, and up the drive to the Home; she clamoured at the doorbell. Christina clung to her sister.

'Don't leave me, Lily,' she whispered. 'Don't leave me on my own in here, I'm scared.'

'Ah, Mrs Llewellyn,' said the matron upon opening the door, having the craft of maintaining a morale-boosting jollity despite having been up all night for weeks and months. 'Come in, dear –

though how we are going to *spell* you with that lovely Welsh name of yours I just don't know. No, not you, dear, just the patient. Well done.'

She drew Christina into the Home, politely excluding family and friends. They veered uncertainly away from the sealed entrance and plunged back down the terrace. The sky was entirely clear, the sun showing bloody at the rim of the town.

Two

Minnie, having left the two children and the baby with a neighbour, was making her weekly pilgrimage to Devizes Cemetery, carrying in her pocket the letter she had composed for Albert the previous evening. It was a long walk, and in the drifted waves of uncleared snow, a business of slow wading alternating with skidding. She carried a small shovel for clearing the grave, and occasionally used it as a walking-stick. Minnie contemplated her aged boots and wondered how long they would hold out through the winter. The threadbare coat had patches that could no longer be rendered invisible by crafty mending, but they advertised themselves triumphantly as providing the major structure of the garment. She thought as she plodded, 'I am a patched woman, a patched woman,' and thought how it still offended against her self-respect to be seen thus; and she was glad no eyes were upon her in the silent convexities of the snowbound world. Christina would never have appeared in public demeaned in this way, wearing her poverty as an outer garment. Christina, with her spine straight and head held characteristically high, seemed to wear her destitution in decent secrecy beneath an outer layer, so that you might almost take her for an officer's wife. It was children, children, who brought you low, thought Minnie ruefully, and being only a cook-private's wife with an allowance that was a pittance; and even now that had gone up to sixty shillings you could not pay off the debts. It was half what a munitions worker in a cushy job got, it was a

21

national disgrace. But it will be said of me, Minnie thought, her small stocky figure pausing in its walk, breath smoking out, that in having given children to the nation, I have been patriotic. That meant something. Even if you were patched, and not well in yourself, and always as it were grieving after something fatally lost, and your underwear in a hopeless condition, and your husband given to the bottle and not above thrashing you if you annoyed him by looking too mild, which he called 'milk-and-bloody-water', and inclined him to one of his rages. But even so, there was something in it for her: patriotism, which Chrissie sneered at (but never in), the giving of something. And besides, the elder Albert was hardly ever at home. She was forgetting what it felt like to have your eye punched or to see a kitchen chair sailing through the air at you. She was almost beginning to discredit her memory that these things ever happened. And life was hard for everybody, even so. Minnie now reflected more gently as she turned into the pathway bordering the cemetery, luxuriously freed from the presence of childhood grizzling and coughing and clamouring with its eternally runny nose, pulling at her skirts. She thought of the fierce love she had given to the first boy, the little Albert, and never had rescinded, nor could do so. She remembered Christina as a twelve-year old aunt holding Albert on her lap to be photographed in his christening robes; and how gravely Chrissie sat, holding the little white lacy form with the curling fingers, with the same neat care with which she did everything; in her gymslip holding the baby, she looked the camera straight in the eye, her face so clean and candid. Beautiful candour of Chrissie with her lit, still face. She had handed Albert back to her sister saying, 'I'm very close to Bert, Min. He's my most special nephew.' Granted, that might not have been saying much, seeing as Chrissie only had the one nephew at that stage, but still it's the way things are said that counts. And he did not last long, being settled in his grave by his first birthday. That was all before the war, before death became normal and everyday, so that one became almost ashamed of having just the one dead son.

As Minnie passed in through the entrance that was always open now because the black wrought-iron gates had long ago been requisitioned for scrap, a small blizzard whirled up and, lifting the top layers of snow, drove them hurriedly before her like a sandstorm. She followed the driving snow across the great white garden, and all the dead were equally anonymous, both those who

22

could afford a headstone and those whose means had not quite run to it. Snow piled up steeply against the slate-grey stones and reached a covert hand up over the names. Minnie's compass-memory located the place by the west wall where Albert was, and she started digging him out. It was like after an air raid, she thought, where the women and old men and the ARP wardens come haring out with spades to free the survivors; and later the postman with unique fidelity comes climbing over the heaps of rubble to deliver the mail into the vanished doors of demolished houses.

Albert was nearly a foot deep in snow. We have all been raided in fact, she thought: we have all been hit. She shovelled with energy, eyes running with the rheumy tears the blizzard forced out of them. And we have all been hit from the beginning of time, generations of us. From his first setting-out Albert was a marked boy. Something was aiming at him. Minnie had begun to identify Satan with the Germans, not just the Germans with Satan as was commonplace. She went to church at Christmas only, and Easter, and Remembrance Sunday, but when she did, and mention was made of Satan and his legions, she saw as clear as daylight the Fiend in the sky with his tin hat and his swastika, and hailing their Führer the nasty little devils with identical black moustaches, million upon million, got into their tanks and aimed their guns from across the universe at a certain baby whose name was Albert: and had been aiming since the beginning of time, and there was nothing we could do about it but wait. With their infallible secret weapon, which in Albert's case had been called diphtheria, they could not miss a child so beautiful and empty of guile. God held out Albert in his arms as a first appeasing sacrifice in 1938; and the Fiend laughed and took him with a mere cough and a fever. When Minnie told people of these thoughts they gave her queer looks as if she had a screw working loose. They said things about the Ministry of Health and the success of the mass immunisation campaign since Albert's time, and not to brood, 'no point in it, Min.' So Minnie had stopped speaking about it. She did not brood. She just knew.

She had now dug down to the dark, bruised grass, and released Albert from his coverings. There was an odd moment as she scraped away the last layer of snow when she thought the baby must arise with his fat, toothless face crowing to her and his bald head warm from sleep, which she would raise on her left hand and smile to and call him her Beauty. For he had been such a good baby: not much trouble, not colicky or fretful, but jolly and simple.

23

He never cries. Instead her shovel stabbed through last week's note, refrigerated. She picked it up and exchanged it for her composition of last night, laboriously written. She tried to say a different thing each time. For though Albert had not been noticeably forward for his age, it may be supposed that when children become angels they do not remain illiterate, but branch out in capacity, and would like to hear fresh news and be encouraged by fresh endearments from their relatives. She read it through: 'Never never shall forget you my pretty dear, though Another is on the way, and ever shall remain Your Own Loving Mother.' She wedged it in with the stone. The transaction brought comfort and relief, such as comes in the night, when you feed and change a restless infant, bind him tightly in his swaddling sheet, and he drops off to sleep, neat as a pippin; so that you can get back to your own bed, putting him comfortably out of your mind.

Henry saw Minnie's dark, squat figure from a distance; watched it turn and stump back against the wind, coat flapping; saw her singleness and struggle. This insight caused inchoate murmurings of feelings that might if allowed become words, or hugs, the terror of emitting which made him hunch his shoulders, partially turn from her, and stamp his boots crossly in the compacted snow. When she caught up, he was quite himself.

'What you doing here then, Dad? You need your sleep on nights, keep your strength up, you don't want to get all low again.'

'Thought I'd find you here, Min.'

'Something up, Dad?' Minnie was vexed at being interrupted at this important moment of ritual tranquillity. Just as she could be nodding off a treat, in her mind, God and Satan being temporarily at peace with one another, up pops trouble. To be interrupted at visiting time. Still your family's your family.

'Not up girl, no, nothing wrong exactly. Just thought you'd want to know our Chrissie's gone in this morning.'

'Bit early isn't it? She weren't due for three weeks, I thought. Mind you she's as big as a barrel. If it wasn't that Jim and she only had the one time together I'd say she miscalculated. Looks at least ten months gone. All right is she?'

She linked arms with Dada, and they sailed before the wind up the path beside the barren hedge, blitzed and scorched by winter. Minnie's face was chapped, and scalded ruby red with cold. She thought, what I could fancy is a cup of tea piping hot and a soft-boiled egg. She could positively scent the aroma of tea (her weekly quarter was almost gone, she was down to using the same tea leaves all day long) and taste the gold of the yolk. But she wasn't due another egg until next Tuesday. Dada was being rather odd this morning, coming out all this way. She pulled at his sleeve in a fractious manner.

'I said, is our Chrissie all right, Dada?'

Henry thought, how odd Minnie is getting these days, coming out all weathers with her bits of letters for the dead child, when she has more than enough live ones waiting for her at home, all in urgent need of scrubbing and sorting out. The thought of Min's tribe of screamers – more horrible children would be hard to find – made Henry sigh into his scarf and shake his head.

'She wasn't so bad, Mother says, only in a bit of a stew. Natural enough. But the thing is, I was in too late to see her off.'

I don't remember you ever bothering about me when I was confined, thought Minnie. I may be mistaken of course, but I don't *think* you all went on panic alert as if an air raid was due when my time came. There's a bloody great queue of women reaching to the world's end, and I'm always shuffling along at the very back. I've always got a cold, I'm always worn out, my old man beats me up, but does Mother save her coupons for me? Can anything happen to me that will count as an emergency to my family? Oh, poor old Minnie, they say, stubby figure, greasy skin, short legs, lank hair, a proper disaster of a woman. I don't count. Now what is there in Chrissie, she thought, that makes Dad mind so much about her, and clump around town bearing news of her in such an unnecessary way? What reposed in Chrissie that had not been available in his existing children which, from the hour of her sister's birth, had softened Dada's melancholy and qualified his alarm; as if he had with firm step approached a cliff edge but, intent on taking the final plunge, had somehow changed his mind and wavered there, now peering over dizzily, now turning back with a faint grin.

Of late, however, he had been showing fresh signs of being tempted to step off. As when he had put away a few pints one night and was found fast asleep and snoring in the river; and looked most baleful at being awoken, when they grabbed him out and scurried him shivering homeward. What if it was only six inches of water, he'd manage it in a teacup if the fit was really on him. The strain for Mother; in fact, for them all. Why would he do it? No one knew.

'Don't you go fretting about our Chrissie, Dad,' she said, scolding. 'She's going to be fine. She's a lucky old girl, you know.

25

She always has been lucky and she always will be. She was born like it. And she has all of you to make a fuss of her.'

She could not help darting a bitter look sideways at him, but all he caught, huddled down into his overcoat, was a glimpse of a red face chapped with cold, plain as pudding, middle-aged before she was out of her twenties. But the thing was, she was off his hands, that was a relief. His heart lightened; he smiled, taking the spade from her, in a rare gesture of affection pressing the hand she'd threaded through his unresponsive arm. She had her husband and her home, and what if Albert was a bit of a rough character, well Minnie was quite a basic sort of woman, not sensitive like Chrissie.

'Come on then, my girl. What we need is a cup of tea.'

They struck out through the snow with new energy. Minnie decided against choosing that moment to give Henry the news of her own impending happy event. She tried to look on the bright side of things. There was a bright side, of course. For instance, there was her darling baby boy counterpaned with snow, her angel, whom nobody could steal from her. And, for instance, her Albert hadn't murdered her yet: the worst damage he'd done was to gash her face under the eye with the milk bottle. And then again, he was good with children when they were very little, teasing and chuckling at them, and blowing raspberries on their bare tummies to make them squeal, which was his most elaborate way of showing affection. Even when he was blind drunk and roaring, Albert never laid into them on any scale until they were older, and that was something to be grateful for. Most important of all, he wasn't actually here to get at them. The Army had him to itself, and would keep him at a safe distance until the war ended, which she hoped wouldn't be for a long time yet. For when he was demobbed her own war would begin. Oh dear God, she prayed passionately, let him be posted to India or Burma, there's still time for that, if it be Thy Will. That would be a blessing indeed.

Weighing up this blessing, Minnie said to her father as they turned into St Christopher's Road, 'Did *you* ever thrash us when we were young, Dad?'

'I can't remember that I did, Min. Can you? I may have given it to George a few times. He deserved a wallop, the little tyke.'

'No, I don't think you did either.'

Back home, a cluster of aunts and cousins was drinking tea and listening to the midday news. Under cover of the fog and foul

26

weather, the German 5th and 6th Panzers had breached the Allied front line on the German border, and were plunging into the Ardennes. The Battle of the Bulge had begun. Minnie sat down with a cup of tea, listening vaguely, ruminating as her numb hands and feet thawed on the potential blessings of the war in relation to her husband. Oh God, she prayed devoutly, let him be posted to the Ardennes to cook for the Yanks: give me a chance.

'Any news of Chrissie?' asked Henry when the wireless had been turned off.

'It'll be hours yet,' said Mother. 'Brace up, Henry, don't brood for God's sake.'

Three

In the ward where the nursing auxiliary put Christina were two other pregnant women, both evacuees. 'The Limes' emergency nursing home had been a Workers Education Centre before the war, but very early on the books and the desks had made an exit, along with the studious quiet of the atmosphere of self-improvement, to be replaced by squadrons of beds, an army of rotund women and the caterwauling of infancy. Christina was in a state of hysterical fright. She was scared of the smell of polish on the dark-brown wooden panels of the hall which made her think of a funeral parlour though she had never visited such a place; she was terrified by the smell of Dettol sterilising the atmosphere. In a rigid anguish of shyness, she saw that she was going to have to share a room with two unknown women. Her labour pains stopped at once and completely. However, as she did not impart her state of mind to anyone, it was believed that she was just a very good and well-behaved girl, no trouble to anyone, and a model patient. The overworked staff smiled into the distress of her wide-eyed, heart-shaped face, and ignored her. The two evacuees, one of whom never stopped knitting except when she laid aside her work to groan or curse her way through the paroxysms of her labour,

27

chatted busily betweenwhiles and did not seem to mind that Christina never replied. Their names were Molly and Cass.

These women seemed to have accumulated an almost infinite horde of children back home in London, about whom they passed parallel anecdotes at speed backwards and forwards, like the shuttle on a loom. Christina tried not to listen to the gruesome accounts of these infants' protracted illnesses, their croup, their ringworm, their bouts of vomiting, and their headlice. She lay with her eyes tightly closed while the horrors of the various labours Molly and Cass had undergone were described, in intimate detail, peppered with medical terminology of a daunting and hair-raising kind. From between the slits in her eyelids, Christina could see that these strangers – almost foreigners, it seemed to her, from their dialect – were actually enjoying the memories of their previous encounters with the monster in the uterus. They were old too, they made her feel like a child, far from home.

'Hello, dearie.' The plump one, named Cass, had caught her sheepishly staring. She had sharp, rat-bright eyes; they delved into Christina from above a buxom bed-jacket of dusky pink tied with a complex of tattered ribbons. Her lustreless hair was flecked with grey, gathered into a net. She seemed to be enjoying the prospect of her confinement, anticipating the worst with militant relish as if re-acquainting herself with an ancient enemy, one who fought foul but all his tricks were known.

'You from round these parts, then?'

Christina nodded. 'We're from London, us two. We get sent out for two weeks lying-in, in the lap of luxury, in these Homes – a real treat. No more of them snivelling brats for a while; my old ma's had to take them, poor old cow, while I put my feet up. Your first, is it?' Christina nodded again. 'My ninth, believe it or not. How about you Molly?'

'Five in five years,' said the other one with pride. 'Done my patriotic duty despite the Blitz and the doodlebugs, and I think I've earned the rest. Each one by a different father, soldier, sailor, airman, *lovely* boys.'

Christina stared at the crimsoned mouth that talked these shocking words. Who were the lovely boys, she wondered, the fathers or the sons? But suddenly there was a terrible shouting, it was Molly bursting out in pain, like an animal she was, nothing human. Christina levered herself up on her elbows, took one look at the purple face unrecognisably distorted in the next bed and joined in the screaming. Staff removed Molly to the adjoining room, large muscular women each with a shoulder under Molly's armpit, lugging her across the lino while she roared like something not of human kind. Outside the room, she suddenly ceased to bawl, and Christina distinctly heard her saying, 'Don't lose my knitting now, will you', in such a matter-of-fact way that the two orderlies laughed out loud, and Cass from her bed of pain gave a snort of amusement through her nose that made Christina think of sties, and troughs, and women who were like sows in litter, fattened up for the kill; and they were not nice people at all, such as she had used to regard herself; but great, fat, bulbous livestock, when it came down to it: hams, meat to be jointed.

Somebody said, 'There, there' to Christina when the commotion had died down, and patted her kindly on the shoulder. That somebody went away; and then another somebody came, and asked if Christina was all right, or had a pain. Just as Christina was saying 'No', a pain came on. But by that time it was too late to say so, for the person had gone, and there was just Cass, lolling on her bed asleep with her mouth hanging open; and there was the squeaking of shoes on linoleum outside, coming and going; and greyish daylight shoving itself rudely in through the window like an unwanted visitor. Long tracts of time now began to pass, in immensely slow sweeps. They occurred between pains, and the spaces between the pains measured them. Christina's labour was incredibly slow. It washed her gradually out of the real world and on to another dimension, coloured grey and filled with shades that flitted with bat-like wings in a cataleptic limbo world. Amongst the shades, she seemed to meet all the hosts of the dead. They were queuing to meet her, patiently one behind the other, like the women in the butcher's queue, and they were anxious to meet her, one at a time. One by one they looked into Christina's countenance with their whey faces, emaciated, and she saw how they twitched and jittered one behind the other; and the queue of the dead reached to the end of the world. It was such an exhausting prospect. She felt tired to death, and old, and every so often fell asleep. Then it seemed as though she had angered and agitated the shades. For the moment her head relaxed against the starched cotton pillow-case, and she nodded off, the infuriated dead began to stir her. They reached their red-hot forks into her entrails and stirred a terrible scalding cauldron there; to wake her up, it was. And when she had gripped at her taut abdomen and jerked awake with the spasms, the appeased dead gradually let her go, and with blank insistent faces they lined up muttering in the butcher's queue once more.

The whole day passed in this manner. But part of Christina's mind hovered above her body on the bed, like that of a clairvoyante. This dissociated part of Christina watched dispassionately as the sun rose to its full height; and Cass' time came, and she was removed from the ward on a trolley, and replaced by a pale-faced, haggard young woman with a Roman nose and a military look about her, who lay in the place Cass had so recently and volubly occupied, mute, dignified and wakeful, as if on guard-duty, bearing her pain with soldierly stoicism. The hovering spirit of Christina observed the sun wane into an orgiastic sunset, flaring and billowing with scarlet and orange waves in the centre of the window frame; and felt the descent of twilight; the pulling of the blackout and the switching on of the naked electric light bulbs. She saw the orderlies and the matron coming and going. When they brought her messages from the family – from Mum and Dada, and Min, and Lilian – she did not believe that they were authentic: but listened to them with sardonic detachment; for no reliable messages can come down from the living into the underworld.

Christina's labour continued throughout the night, and all the following day. By now, the hovering spirit had sunk down into its cup of matter, and joined in a unanimous mobilisation of forces against the queuing shades, which seemed to have gained in power and loquacity. They loomed bigger; and they jabbered and sneered, and they poked at Christina with really vicious fingers, straight in the face. It was clear they were winning. The shades did not bother to stir the cauldron with any vigour: occasionally they just swirled the waters of pain around a bit, idly, as if for form's sake. Christina's life force ebbed down to a tiny, minimal flame.

'Not looking too good, is she?'

'How long is it now, exactly?'

'It's a good forty-eight hours. She came in at dawn on Thursday. I think we'd better give her an injection, to try and speed things up.'

'Mrs Llewellyn! Mrs Llewellyn! Wake up will you dear. Open your eyes. We're going to try to speed things up a bit.'

Christina looked into the doctor's face as if it had been simply the millionth ghost of the day, with boredom and inertia. Her heart was set on going to sleep, and not waking up again. But when they speeded things up a bit, with the jab of ergot, she had to rally; and

30

fight; and expel what was obstructing her power to live, splitting her open like a pea-pod, until it was all over, and the blood-drenched baby's embattled cry was heard, like a siren going off. And she watched them hold the child by its heels, slapping it so that its lungs trumpeted a sound more irate than continents going to war.

'You've got a lovely little girl, Mrs Llewellyn,' said Matron, laying the baby in Christina's arms. 'Worth waiting for, was she?'

Christina's arms trembled with exhaustion almost too powerful to hold the little person, but she put all her effort into clinging on, and she eyed the minute, round, squashed-up face of Jim's daughter, with a sense of absolute familiarity. It was a meeting not so much with someone new as with lost kin once taken for granted, sprung all fresh like the crocus or the snowdrop from between the grasses of some forgotten mound. Within herself, she said, categorically, yes. A girl. Yes.

The girl did not cry at all, nor seem any the worse for her dangerously long passage out. Demobbed into civilian life, she lay in swaddling clothes with eyes of an almost navy blue, wide open and unblinking, making inventory of what was to be found on the far side of her journey. The girl looked at Christina, and Christina looked back. It was complete. It was finished. No more ghosts. We are safe.

'Get Dr Kemp back, there's something funny here.' The midwife's voice was muffled; she turned her head and gestured. A vast squeaking of shoes; plunging of persons in and out of the room; inspections made of Christina; the girl-baby ripped out of Christina's arms and made to sail away across the air, but managing somehow to keep up to the last moment her steadfast perusal of Christina with those decisive eyes, shape of almonds, which seemed bent on extracting a promise: be on your honour, I am Jim's daughter. Christina waved feeble arms to try to get her back but her arms were as heavy as the cartridge cases at the factory, which she could hardly shift at all.

'Mrs Llewellyn, are you paying attention? The job's not quite done. You seem to have another one in there.'

'Another what?'

'Another *baby*, Mrs Llewellyn. You're having twins.'

Christina laughed scornfully at Mother Nature's mirthless joke. She said, 'I can't.'

Matron said, 'You have to. You don't have a choice, Mrs

31

Llewellyn (what's her Christian name?) Just one more effort.'

Christina said 'No'. And she wouldn't. When the huger pains came again, and the demons with the red-hot rakes began ploughing at her insides, she would not respond; and even when they raised their boiling-red lewd faces up to hers and harassed her with grinning intimations of a more catastrophic and final torment, she just smiled and turned her head away. This was in part because she simply could not respond. She had no more strength. But also it seemed to her that she had already had her baby; and that in the distance she heard its tiny cries, which being interpreted, signified 'Keep faith with me.'

'Push on the pain, Christine.'

'No. I've had enough.'

'We all have to do our duty. Many mothers would be grateful to have twins. In time of war, we have to do our duty. For King and Country. Come on now, Mrs – Christine. Make an effort.'

So it was war, was it: so it was shells, and gas masks, and bombs bursting, that called for this endeavour. So she was giving birth to a shining-cased bomb, made of heated metal. So she was contributing to the war effort, was she: labouring for victory. The legions of the dead were massed on the other side of the river of tar. Their black and spiteful faces crowed with triumph; and they were hurrahing and hurling their bayonets high into the air, for the curse on Eve was being fulfilled. Christina made up her mind to drive out the thing that was in her, which was now a drill; now a cylindrical shell; always a weapon of death, for King and Country. Out flopped the second baby, and a river of blood poured warmly with it, and she was evacuated, totally.

'Ooh! how lovely!' an inane, high-pitched voice squeaked. 'It's a boy! Second time lucky!'

The thing that she had driven out was roaring in gales of hectic crying.

'Lucky Mrs Llewellyn,' said the horizon-filling face that loomed toward her. 'A boy and a girl. *What* a good thing you made the effort. *Now* you're pleased, I'll bet.'

They pushed the boy-baby into her arms, but she would not hold it. She turned her face resolutely away, squeezing her eyes shut, and would not look at it. The boy-baby lolled precariously on her chest, unheld. It clamoured and raved. Severely, they took it away, and put her in a tiny room like a death cell to rest. Here, she saw a black net come down upon her face from the ceiling, descending slowly, again and again. Here, she heard voices telling her terrible news in gibberish that only she could understand, beginning, 'Down there in Burma, where the void is . . .' And she thought her own hand was that of a huge baby, seeing which made her scream out in terror; and that the bed rocked from side to side so that she must cling on to its crisply laundered edges to avoid capsize; and that one came in a white coat and declared in brisk tones, 'Psychotic – Disturbance – Postnatal; Not – Fatal; Keep An Eye On.' At which the great single eye which had started as a microscopic dot of dirt on the wall opened beadily, and stared, lidless and inflexible, judging her day and night.

Four

'What does it matter?'

'It matters to me. I'm darned sure it matters to her. She'd want to have me with her at a time like this, and don't you tell me otherwise, Beat.'

'Yes, but look at it like this, Amelia, they know what's best for her in there. They're trained people. They know how to look after her.'

'Packing me off like an interfering busybody, the old so-and-so. Who do they think they are? Her own mum. Telling me she wants peace to get on with it.' Christina's mother fumed, defiant but impotent, red in the face. She glared malevolently at Henry's sister, Aunt Beat, in her green WVS uniform, a representative of the officialdom that barred her from access to her labouring daughter, filtering bland, censored news of her progress through a half-opened door, which it repeatedly shut in her face when she made as if to enter. It was the morning of the third day of Christina's labour, and still no sign of a baby. 'There's no law in the world to keep a mother away from a daughter. You ought to stand up for me and tell them so, Henry.'

Henry peered out from beneath his cap, which he wore indoors whenever there was company. His magnificent height sought to crumple down into itself in the chair. He executed small nervous yawns behind his hand, and drummed his fingers softly on the arm of the chair. The room seemed awash from wall to wall with superfluous family, women carrying china, women digging spoons into the pooled rations in the tea canister, a jabbering, powerless parliament. Aunt Beat sat to attention in the best chair, in portly uniformed splendour. She had come to urge Mother on to further smelly efforts on the salvage front involving collection of chop bones for conversion to cordite, but had stayed on to enjoy the crisis over Christina.

Her strident, monitory voice rasped on Henry's nerves. He chewed the ends of his moustaches, meditating escape. He decided to go and rummage in the dustbin, to exhume for salvage purposes some refuse stinking enough to engage Beat's interest and get her out of the house. He slunk out.

'You see, Amelia, before you go working yourself up into a fit, you've got to think to yourself, "There's a War on".'

'No, go on, Aunt Beat, you don't say! Fancy that, a war on, and I never noticed.' Lilian considered her uniformed aunt to be little better than an imbecile. 'Have you heard anything about this, Minnie?'

'That's enough from you, my girl. What I'm pointing out to your mother is only what Mr Bevin is constantly saying on the wireless, that the pregnant women are on the Front Line just as much as the men. You just have to let them get on with it, doing their bit. After all, you don't go asking to get down in the trench with your George to make sure he's all right, now do you Amelia? "Come on now Georgie, let Mum hold your hand and wipe your nose for you." We're all equal now, men and women, aren't we? You just have to let your Chrissie get on with her bit of the battle in peace.'

'Hadn't you better get on with your bone hunting?' asked Lilian, pleasantly. 'We don't want to hold up your heroic work with our trifling problems.'

'Did I tell you we got a whole horse's skeleton out of Hinds the butcher?' asked Beat. 'Wonderful man, very patriotic.'

'Lily, just run round and find out if anything's happened yet,' whispered Amelia.

'I'm on my way.'

'Is there a law against me insisting on going in to be with her?' She had got to the point where she could contemplate flouting her own absolute quailing before authority. 'I'm going right up there and demand to be let in. I know my rights.' But she spoke the decisive words in the limp tone of an alien in her own land, knowing she would never dare. The language they had grown up with did not contain the imperative voice.

It was just after ten thirty when Lilian returned.

'She's had it! She's had it!'

'Oh thank God. What is it?'

'Little girl, five pound eleven ounces, right as rain.'

'Oh dear, never mind, better luck next time.'

'A girl was what she wanted – wasn't it, Lily? Yes – Henry, it's a girl! Did they say how Chrissie was?'

'No, they just shut the bloody door on me again.'

'Come on, we're going round. They'll let us see her now.'

Amelia's relief was intense. She stamped her boots on to wade through the slush toward her daughter and granddaughter. In the midst of the fuss, Henry thought of the new girl, born of Chrissie, born of all the pain gone through alone, door behind door; and how she could have died overwhelmed him now. In his mind it was as if Chrissie herself had been born all over again. She was a scrap of a child once more, with her thin blond arms and legs, coming to him, laying her head against his waistcoat. She stuck to his heart like a burr, having all over her nature tiny, living hooks, so that he could never pluck off the memory of the weight of that small head, the inconsequent fluff of her downy hair on his mouth. He rubbed at his mouth now, the sensation was so real. He could never be rid of this. And she could have died, he thought, bricked up in her confinement like the bodies in the living tombs of the Anderson shelters where nasturtiums grow over their heads and the flooding damp of the soil seeps into their half-sleeps.

'Smile, Dad, smile, come on. Just a little one. It's all over.'

But it wasn't over. Amelia and Henry were allowed to enter the hall of the Home, where they were told that, though a girl was born, Christina was still in labour; and that things did not look good for her. She was in a bad way. Amelia plucked up courage to ask, could they see their daughter? The matron was out of breath, short staffed, in a tearing hurry. No, it wasn't advisable. She was showing them the door. My granddaughter, then, could I see her? Just for a minute? I wouldn't be any trouble. Amelia pushed back against the hand that was gesturing her off the premises, forcing it to shove her impolitely if it dared. Not yet, no, your granddaughter is asleep, we have a strict regimen here, sleep for four hours, feed for twenty minutes, all babies must comply, we are sure you understand: please, if you don't mind, we are severely under-staffed, pushed to our limits, will let you know of developments in due course.

They came home silent and bewildered through the ooze of slush. Amelia had never known what to say to members of the higher classes with the posh accents who commandeered your life at its deepest sources. As a maidservant in the genteel clerical house in the Cathedral Close, she had seldom spoken to her employers, only curtseyed when they made some request of her. The doctor's surgery was a place of humiliation; she frequently came away with the haziest idea of what he had instructed her to do, having failed to translate his utterances with their nasal twang into the English she knew, and being too shy to ask him to repeat himself. The familiar Cathedral was a place where foreigners came to converse with their own God in their own bizarre language: she thought of it with animus as having nothing to do with the likes of her. Her whole life had been spent menially making ends meet and giving birth to dead babies. Her four children were the survivors of twenty-five years of miscarriages, an innumerable horde of blighted selves that parted from her in fountains of blood four or five months grown. They had been discernibly human, slips of white curled flesh in a garment of blood. She had grown stoically accustomed to their bloody prematurity, taking it as a version of normality, getting on with her jobs round the house while the pains came on, incinerating the product of her pain, wrapped in newspaper. It was not something she bothered to think about, but it had taught her to associate childbirth with ugliness and threat, so that she had feared for Christina throughout her pregnancy. Occasionally in spring, walking in the woods around Grovely near Sarum, seeing the embryo ferns crouch like tight green springs close to the ground, it came over her to think of the miscarriages, budlike fingers clasped, eyelids shut fast. She wondered then who these lost ones might have been, coiled in so secretively upon their own natures. Once she dreamed of them all, bursting through the sac of being, out of which genesis all sorts of suffering sentient forms emerged, and teemed and multiplied. She woke with a violent start, and reached for Henry who was out somewhere on the track between Salisbury and Swindon, for once wanting the sanctuary of his dolorous shadow.

36

'It can't be right to keep me from her at a time like this,' she said to Lilian. 'It just can't. And they call this a free country. There are times I really do wonder what we're fighting for.'

'After the war things will be different,' said Lilian. 'A fairer society for everyone, justice and rights. We'll send these tinpot Hitlers packing.'

'What does that matter now?'

What does it matter in wartime that a young girl of nineteen years is in temporary difficulties of a purely natural kind? What right has she to be attention-seeking when the parachutists are being picked off one by one over Europe; when our boys are meeting their Maker in the jungles of Burma amongst the steaming vegetation, in whose juice their remains liquefy. The trivia of the female's life, her incapacity to grasp the great issues of the grave-diggers' arts: what is her claim when calculated alongside the statistics of her falling sons? They pitch down; they are raped with bayonets, exploded with shrapnel; they are sniped off the cliff face they have scaled to reach the Continent in her name (not just King and Country, but queen and mother, the nest with all its eggs). Shouldn't you be doing your bit and not complaining? Shouldn't you? If a grown girl can't behave herself, shouldn't she be given the evil eye and the cold shoulder? If she were my daughter, I'd give her a good slap, and tell her to buck up, and – so thought Alice Wheeler, Matron of the maternity home, who had been up for 365 nights in a row, accompanying the armies of the fretful, the terrified, the whimpering and the frankly noble, through their travail.

The faces of the women were indistinguishable, unmemorable. They all went the same impersonal way of pain, mindless faces distorted like gargoyles in their extremity. They died to the world of individuality and underwent burial in the common ground of the race, the species. They resembled headless torsos. They endlessly replaced one another in the same set of beds, they cried and writhed, sweated as they clutched the cold metal of the bedrail, called for mother, roared like animals in the last fight to disembowel themselves of the child. But the thing is, the pain is finite, they generally don't expect to die in childbirth these days, given the improved care the war has made available, together with the sulphonamide drugs with which we mop up puerperal fever; and they've got something to show for it, the child, after all. She could remember a few aberrant types which stood out from the general anonymity, the tragedy queens like this Llewellyn girl; the London slum-dwellers evacuated for their confinements, who cursed her ripely and could not be put in their place; and that tribe of experienced mothers who took very little notice of you, they came in, the babies slipped out softly after half an hour of labour, dreamily they looked at you, got straight up and walked off with the child. A good third of the babies were unwanted illegitimacies (her stock-in-trade) these days.

When there is such a stream of females all doing the same thing, demanding the same thing, reproducing the same thing, supine, open-legged, so that you are more fully acquainted with their private parts than with their personal faces, it is both essential and inevitable that your behaviour should be businesslike, clinical and efficient. There is no surplus of energy for dispensing sympathetic words to individuals; waste of time. Staple cheering formulae ought to be enough. All that is asked of them is that they should behave themselves reasonably and accept the necessary regulations. Most do. Most show a proper sense of the insignificance of their particular sensations in a time of national crisis. It's the ones who think they're something special who really get my goat, she thought. This Mrs Llewellyn rejecting the second twin is one thing; but sitting bolt upright quite rational all of a sudden, saying, 'Tell my people the second one died. *I know you do things like that.* I've heard', that's quite another. Who put the knowingness and threat in the voice of a docile, biddable girl like that? It rattled her. She sluiced her face with cold water at the tap; in the mirror the face was blanched, albino, like that of a creature adapted to living underground without the use of daylight; her eyes were crimson-rimmed and parched from want of sleep. When the mother is a local girl, getting rid of the unwanted baby is too tricky, she wouldn't normally consider it: the families can so easily get to know. On the other hand, it might be risky not to, if the local girl goes saying *I know you do things like that*, with pointed stare.

She entered the nursery, a raving bedlam of hunger. The babies were ranked around three walls in alphabetical order, more than ready for the ten o'clock feed. Staff were very short, and another load of preggies had arrived at no notice on the London train that morning, many in a somewhat advanced state. The babies were being shelled out like podded peas. *I know you do things like that.* There has to be some recompense for this treadmill of nightwork filling the world with human nature, which immediately teems like shoals of fry back to its spawning ground, to begin the cycle afresh. After the war, Alice intended to retire and live comfortably on her fat little nestegg, and never again be subject to a baby's bellicose squawl or wipe the muck from its backside. She picked up the loudest shrieker from the nearest row of cribs and stabbed a bottle in its mouth. The mouth sucked furiously. It was the son of the unmarried WRAC girl. She had shown unusual stoicism in the face of the forceps, not a peep out of her. But then, the WRAC girls could take it, didn't want anaesthetising, didn't want anything. Whether it was just a matter-of-fact sense of a job to be done that impelled this fortitude, or a case of despair, a despair almost off the map of the emotions, it wasn't possible to know. The Army wouldn't have them back, of course. This baby was for adoption. Even since the Adoption Regulation Act had prohibited the selling of illegitimate babies, a booming industry, it was still laughably easy, with precautions and a reliable network, to arrange it in a satisfactory way. The Ministry of Health knew perfectly well she traded in babies, that many of her staff were unmarried mothers working off their fee, they watched her like hawks but they wouldn't get her in a million years. She was used to taking the children on long winter train journeys down to Cornwall or up to the lush farmlands of Shropshire, only hours after birth, handing them over to the new parents, cash on delivery, no questions asked. Only the faintest shadow of a sneer had marked the soldier-girl's mouth as she handed over the baby into the common stock.

'I'm making a patriotic gesture. I'm bequeathing it to the State. As food for powder.'

The sweat was hardly dry on her face; the afterbirth still coming.
'Pardon?'

'Nothing. Just get rid of it for me, will you.'

'Him, not it.'

'Whatever.'

An hour later, Mrs Wheeler had looked in and seen the girl asleep, her hand shading her eyes from the light in a childish gesture. She marched over and shook her awake, on the spur of the moment, gratuitously, and in a rough voice commanded her to sit up and have her temperature taken. She started awake all of a sudden, she did not know where she was, she fell back trembling and appalled.

Now why did I do that, wondered Mrs Wheeler: behave so unprofessionally? It was as if the army girl were a standing

39

accusation, her cool impenitence, her aloofness as she rejected her child. Let her go back to sleep. As for myself, I think it's a moral position I try to hold. We are only doing our duty in these abnormal times and circumstances, by extending welfare to the casualties, spreading the unwanted babies around a bit. We tolerate and ought to tolerate the unmarried mothers as we would not in peacetime, being no better than they should be; but now, perhaps, as good as they can be. The Yanks stuff the little girls full of doughnuts and ice-creams, fit them out with nylon stockings, they are cut loose from home ties, what do we expect? *I know you do things like that.* Yes, but it is only an extension of duty, the way I see it, not a violation of anyone's rights, to get money for the transactions I undertake: a favour to the natural mother, a kindness to the adoptive family. Boys, of course, are particularly easy to dispose of (though most families will take anything that's going), for every woman in her heart wants a man-child, doesn't she? A real Christmas present you'll be for someone, my lad. She laid the replete infant against her shoulder, rubbing its back round and round, to get the wind up. The milk upon its bud-like mouth bubbled. Night and day had long ago merged for her. There must in all justice be some remuneration for 365 nights devoid of sleep.

As if the earth were a great mouth wide open and bellowing in its agony, the howl of mortar and rocket ascended without any let-up. The fluid in the labyrinth of his ear roared like the sea in the continuous blast of sound. He crouched in a bunker, the only intact structure in a crater a quarter of a mile wide which had been scooped out by bombing, mainly the accidental jettisoning of their loads by Allied planes upon their own men. The German retreat from Italy was marked by such savage counter-attacks and ambushes as to seem a spectacularly victorious manner of losing a war. The skull-splitting noise they put up was unbearable; the deafened brain ceased to work in any consistent way, his thoughts came in occasional fits of intense anxiety, or in wistful halluci-nations, brief, gauzy, as if on the other side of the blank wall of sound. Everything around Jim seemed problematic. There was someone who used to be his friend spreadeagled in the far corner shooting a blood-forged smile at him. He avoided his eyes. There was an eye-socket in the bunker from which he occasionally peered into the near-darkness of smoke and curdled mud. The only patch of something like light was implied by the wheat-pale hair of a young soldier whose body was one of half a dozen partially incinerated toward the mouth of the bunker. From the charnel landscape black smoke poured into his shelter, along with the violent blare of sound, so that his mouth seemed filled with ash, his eyes wept black tears. He cowered against a wall, covering his ears with his hands and closing his eyes against the charred, acrid air. His brain seemed to have boxed the noise within itself, it howled and crashed within him, his mind was beaten to jelly, to foul water slapping around the interior of the skull. There were no thoughts, no language, no presences discernible, not even his own. But then he heard it, the music. Phrases of 'Bryn Calvaria', or 'David of the White Rock' came frailly into the bunker in the occasional lapses in the orchestration of gun and mortar. The sound presented itself as being so nearly real that it seemed inconceivable that, should he look out of the spyhole, he would not see the whole of Morriston Orpheus perched on the rim of the inferno and singing vehemently. He had sung with them once when a very small boy in a production of *Trial by Jury*, so proudly, his mam still kept the photograph in a prominent place in the front room. But to imagine they sang here in this hellhole, that touched him back to life again, that brought all sorts of things to mind. He listened intently to see if he could catch it again. But in his mind's eye Christina came to life instead, like a God he could honestly pray to: oh Chrissie come down to me now, come down.

He looked at his dead friend again. He had known Alastair for five months, he had his twenty-fifth birthday last week. He hoped to be alive to bury him when this lot died down. He had known Alastair far longer and more intimately than Christina, though he must deduct the wedding night from his measure, for that was not in this world at all, but sacred, and strange, and safe beyond the reach of any known enemy. But we too have lain together, Alastair and I, he thought, glancing over to where the hole in his friend's forehead stared like a third eye. We lay together for two weeks in the slit-trench near Camino, sodden to the skin, in six inches of water, bailing out at night. It rained for thirteen days and nights into our grave-shaped place of salvation seven foot long and two foot deep, and shivered and cursed and our teeth clacked when we tried to talk, behind the wall of roaring sound. So wet we were we had to lie in one another's arms for warmth. I dug my face into your throat within your sodden greatcoat, and we were constantly whispering things to one another, I can't recall what we found to

41

say. That sour putrescence of the mud caking our noses, ears, mouths, hair, eyes, lining stomach and gut: we tasted it, tasted of it, were being swallowed in it. The earth was a moist mouth sucking us down. The Italian mud, it has a foulness all its own, you never get used to the stuff. The mud was the enemy, and the cold and wet; some condition larger and more engulfing than the merely human Germans. Pressed together in the burial pit, we tasted each other's squalid mortality, literally. One night you kissed me, it was more than love. You knew the Italian language, and Dante; you speculated which circle of hell we were in.

He listened again intently, during a lull in the barrage. He could have sworn that echoes of tenor and bass filtered in: 'When I tread the verge of Jordan/Bid my anxious fears subside'. How come, he wondered, that if I think of Christina these fears do subside, though Jordan's waters are filthy with blood; how can something as tenuous as the dream of a girl I hardly know matter at all when I wade up to my chin in death? But the fear melts off. For she is with me. Her body and her soul they comfort me. Even though I never liked it when Mam was preparing kidney or liver in the kitchen, I hurried away whistling. The sight of raw beef made me retch. I had to drown a litter of kittens once for Mrs Roberts, Mam said I had to, I took them down to the stream in a crate and tried to do it, I got them wet and pulled them out, tears streaming down my face they were, then I took them round half the houses in Swansea trying to give them away. Out here I've seen more than kittens killed. I've helped explode people so that bits of them hang on trees and bits of them shower to the ground like red rain. One day a man's severed hand was washed into our trench. 'Christ, Jimmie chuck that thing out!' you said, Alastair, and you threatened to throw up all over me if I didn't, so I got hold of the thing, it felt like a handshake and I hurled it up in the air, it sailed away waving.

The hellish racket outside had intensified but the smoke was less. The ground beat and pulsated under his feet: it was like perching on the ventricle of a wildly fibrillating heart. The bunker's solid walls seemed to quiver and buckle inwards with the reverberations. It was planes. He tried to peer out into the murk. Was it ours bombing them, or the remnant of their air force having a go at us, or just the Yanks taking pot luck? It was no longer clear who was doing what to whom. He crept back in from the great shout of sound; the earth's seismic convulsions went on and on as if a monstrous birth were endeavouring to take place. The wave of planes had suddenly gone over leaving an eerie silence, with just a faint stuttering of individual gunfire. He thought it must have been ours, on target, after all.

He must take farewell of Alastair, without burial, and try to get back to the line. But the silence bewildered his ears and mind like a totally new kind of noise. Alastair stared at him in outrage through his three eyes. He stood looking back recollecting a medley of what they had seen together, the city of Pompeii whose inhabitants are petrified in lava, the first operas of his life at Rome Opera House, *La Traviata* and *Il Trovatore*. He was a well-spoken man, though Glaswegian. He liked a laugh too. 'We Celts must stick together,' he said to me back there in Naples where we drank off the local vino by the pint, reeling drunk we were, and singing. He called me Taf and I called him Jock. 'Really imaginative that is,' I said; and when they got him the first time he said, 'Plant a daffodil for me when you get home Taf or a leek don't forget now.' Jim rummaged in his friend's battledress to find his ID and the wallet with the pictures of his wife and two small girls, Elspeth and Amy, which he put in with his own for safety. In the silence he took hold of his friend's rigid hands and kissed his filthy, blood-caked face. Then he turned his back on him.

At the mouth of the bunker he got ready to make his break. But it was hard to move, the bunker now seemed to him the safer option, a stone womb over against the abyss. He tried to pluck up courage. That Bible I won for Good Attendance at Morriston Baptist Sunday School, I wonder where Mam has put that? It was a white lie in any case for I largely played truant, down fishing by the river with the lads. When they ask me what my religion is, I say, 'Put down OD.' Other Denomination covers well for my present state of mind: not English, not murderously-inclined, not a believer.

She is my denomination. In the wilderness there rains down the manna of memories, dancing with Chrissie that time when I thought so loudly I must have been audible, 'Will you marry me? Will you? *Will* you *really*?' And so it is possible to dance to the very verge of Jordan and not lose footing; and to go through the roaring waters toward Canaan and not to drown. He levered himself up to get a view. He hoisted himself and his kit over the edge and scurried off bent double through the crematorium of the upper world, like the creeping things with which God infested the planet, in the beginning.

Five

Four and a half million Englishmen were enlisted. One million men were stationed abroad; half a million were now dead; a quarter of a million had been overseas for five years with no leave. Nobody now had a man to fall back on, except in the category of the old and toothless, or a sleek-haired phoney in a reserved occupation. Everyone wanted a male. Even a dog or horse of the desired gender could fetch a better price than a bitch or mare. The air was heavy with the synthetic perfumes of womankind, clipping the bus-tickets, servicing the lorries. Rank male sweat was an odour lusted after.

But Christina could not love her boy-baby. She gave a little scream when it was brought to her and shot down into her bed, pulling the blankets over her head like a child in a tantrum. The habitual acquiescence of her demeanour yielded to an access of disorderly willpower. She had no clear idea of what the hostility born in her meant, only an urgent sense that something had been assigned to her to keep through life that did not belong to her. There was a mistake, she had to correct it. Her little girl was brought to be fed at four-hourly intervals, and was dutifully held afterwards for a ration of ten minutes before being replaced in the communal pool. Its imperious square face was resolute. It reminded her to recall the original bond and abide by it. She held its head in the palm of one hand and carefully inventoried its features. Wisps of pale down fringed the dome of its head, through which the fontanelle beat out its silent tune of life still vulnerable, not yet closed over in self-defence; but the slanted, blue-black eyes were clear in their moral claim. They seemed to Christina to threaten and challenge, while the mouth battened on finger or cheek, frantically seeking the breast.

She was still hearing and seeing things, though she denied this when they questioned her. Most of the time she was normal. Then a remark floated down from the air, as if there lay a hidden wireless up toward the ceiling: it was a thin male voice, sinister but (if one's sense of humour had been in operative condition) ludicrous, like that of Lord Haw-Haw. The voice claimed to be speaking for High Command. Its message was that the only way the killing could stop was for Christina to jettison the secret weapon, and do it secretly, and do it at once. The accent was distinct, clipped, aristocratic; the mood the imperative.

Beads of sweat stood out on her forehead, clammy and cold upon the burning skin. The breast that the little girl seized was sore with engorgement, hairline pains shooting round the nipple. The baby closed her eyes at last, releasing Christina from the despotism of her meaningful stare. Like a healing leech she fell away. Christina lay back against the crackling laundered pillow. She dozed, still holding the child for comfort.

The cell-like room was originally a store cupboard, which came into use when difficult cases needed to be closeted alone for the sake of patient morale. Christina could have felt quite peaceful in her solitary confinement if it were not for the hired intimidators licensed to swoop in at her to deliver hearty harangues or veiled threats. Their speciality was to wait until she had dropped off, and then to barge into her sleep with words of hectoring and reproach.

'Matron do say he's such a good little chap too. But he do want his mum real bad.'

There was an orderly wedged between bed and wall, carrying the white parcelled form of what Christina, waking with a start, realised must be the boy. The woman sat down with a bounce.

'Come on then Chrissie, give en a suck. Don't be stingy. You'll take to him that much better if you give him a cuddle. Now you come to Polly then, greedy girl, and let your brother have his turn. Come to Polly then, my pet.'

The girl-baby fastening her mouth on the nipple at once began to suck hard.

'Who's a lovely boy den?' Crowing and babbling with fleshy, pursed lips at the boy, she sought to arouse Christina's maternal guilt. 'What'll your ma say then Chrissie, when she knows you won't have none of him?' The sudden sharp tone lunged and swiped. 'She'll tell you off right and proper.' Christina had known the woman by sight for many years, but she wasn't the type of person she condescended to speak to. She came into the category of common. Her voice was heavy and flat, full of long burring

45

Wiltshire 'r's. Christina recoiled, but the shock was to her fastidious sense of niceness rather than to her moral sense. She saw a fat face, with piggy bloated cheeks, looming into intimacy with her own. She had a crisp recollection of walking along behind the same woman in the street, the image of sow-legs waddling, with holes in her stockings and the white flesh bulging through. She was coarse, she was not nice.

'Your ma won't half give you what for, my girl, with all your airs and graces when she knows what you're up to. I know your ma, she's all right. And what about Hubbie? What's Hubbie going to say when he finds out you're rejecting his son and heir while he's doing his bit against Hitler?'

'Shut up, you cow, and mind your own bloody business!' Christina's descent into the low-class language of the tribe amazed her, it was so easy, she so fluent. 'Go on, bugger off, get out of it.' She had never spoken so before. It was like being sick, it was disgusting.

'Oh *that's* your level is it, Miss High and Mighty. Right. Now that I've bleeding well gone to all this trouble to bring him to you, I'm darned if you aren't going to hold him and see to him and bloody well like him.'

The carrying-blanket was whipped away and the boy was thrust in the direction of his mother's right breast, as much as to say, 'Be a man. Get a suck of her or die in the attempt!' The threshing infant combatants in Christina's loaded arms seemed to fight with the ferocity of an absolute terror, like fledgelings too numerous for a nest, of whom the feebler must necessarily be sacrificed. Their toppling forms shrieked volumes of terror, arms flailing out, attacked by inundations of sheets, rain of air, the incomprehensible elements to which they had each been committed in company with a hostile enemy. From the square mouth of the girl-child came a mounting wail like the air-raid siren's call to panic-stations. The larger boy-baby's wobbling head flipped crazily sideways until it hung purple and roaring in mid-air.

With the clumping of thick shoe-soles up the stairs, and the squealing of linoleum, came the forces of law and order. The orderly was packed off to attend to a new consignment of inmates just off the London train, completely unannounced. Matron sat on the bed holding the little boy against her shoulder, soothing his hot terror and circling her hand upon his back.

'What a carry-on. Poor little soldier. Poor little chap. What's it all about, Mrs Llewellyn? You're causing complete chaos in here. We simply haven't got the time for this kind of thing, we're short-staffed, and you must realise that you're not the only mother in here with problems. Come on now.'

'I'm ever so sorry. I don't mean to be a nuisance.' By her docility and downcast eyes, Christina knew herself again.

'I know you don't; of course you don't. The thing is, you haven't taken to your little son, have you dear? Why do you think that is? You seem to like the little girl all right. You had a bad time in your labour of course, and you weren't too well afterwards, but the memory soon fades . . .' She spoke with businesslike kindliness, as if permitting the whole beneficent Ministry of Health to make ventriloquial use of her throat.

In the ensuing pause, the Haw-Haw Voice spoke to Christina. It told her the time had come, the hour of action, and how she must act. A trance of elation came over her: she liked obeying; hated resisting. The girl-baby's steady blue-eyed gaze mirrored her own and confirmed her in her obedience, one peaceable soft hand possessively lying upon the blue-veined breast that her lips gently milked.

'I want you to do something for me, if you would, Matron.'

'That's what I'm here for.'

'I can't keep that other baby. I'd like you to find a home for it. Far away. I know there are any number of families wanting boy-children, who would give it a good home.'

Matron had personally sold to good families just under 250 babies, of both genders.

'Him, not it,' she said automatically. Her mind was already preparing the details of the transaction. She had a good network of contacts across the country, and could mobilise at any moment. Adoptions had for years been arranged in pubs and meat queues. She could take the two boys together, the WRAC bastard and the Llewellyn twin.

With shocked countenance, she replied, 'You do realise that what you're asking me to do is against the law nowadays. Strictly against the law. You could land me in prison.'

'But will you do it? Can you?'

'I don't know, Mrs Llewellyn, I don't know at all. You would have to convince me you are serious – your reasons – the consequences. I don't go handing babies around like sacks of beetroot. They're human lives. And if I helped you (and it's only *if*,

47

mind) you would forfeit all rights to the baby for the rest of your life: you'd have to understand that you'd never see him again. Never, in this world. You can't come running back tomorrow whining that you didn't mean it, you want him back. If you sign him over, he no longer exists as far as you are concerned, he has no name, he is wiped away, dead and gone. *I* shan't acknowledge anything, you can be sure: we have very efficient ways of shutting mothers up who come back to break the bargain.'

'I'll do everything you say.' The nasty woman was relieving Christina of all responsibility. 'Tell me what to do.'

'A little test, to make sure you know what you're doing.'

She exchanged the twins, looking curiously into the face of the now sleeping daughter to see what special characteristics might privilege her over the more normally preferred son. There was nothing exceptional that she could see.

'I want you to look at him carefully and tell me how you feel.'

How do I feel? Here is a fat round head the size of a fist, rooting restlessly with its pink mouth. It is ugly, with pearly white spots over its nose and cheeks, and gum sticking the corners of its left eyelid together. The top of its head is swollen to a bruise through its back-to-front delivery, and the sides of the head are wounded with forceps. Its mouth trembles and it has nervous arms that bat and flail – I see it as mortal and capable of causing mortality and its piteous exposure terrifies me, and its bleeding stump of umbilicus that no art can ever heal, and its genitals worn outside the body, unsafe, unsafe, I see millions of it at war, like insects they swarmed over Anzio beach and when they kill each other they cry for their mothers in pools of blood, their bowels spill out, and it can fly too, it is a flying insect this casualty of nature, it cannot breed but it discharges capsules of death over London and Dresden, and at Monte Cassino in thousands it has called out with pain from its unhealing bleeding stump for the cord not to be cut, and what it cries out is *Mutter Mutter ich sterbe, Mutter.*

'I can't know the language to tell you. Just, it isn't mine. Something tells me that; a voice tells me, it's extra, it's animal.'

Boiling tears, volcanic as the flooding matter of birth itself, poured down Christina's cheeks. The other, level woman tested further.

'Will you put the baby to your breast and nurse it?'

Only the farrowing sow with her great litter, the poor bitch on a bit of blanket dropping them one by one, voids these multiple births and calls them each her own, licking them with baptismal juices, supine in the dirt while they all crowd in squealing to suck. Mother Nature with her many heavy udders is not human. Christina's sensitive individualism, the highest value she knew, said, 'No, I've fed my baby already,' and thrust the unthinkable claimant from the sore, tired nipples that wanted cool and rest. Once the creature had her milk on its mouth, she would have had to keep it.

'Your husband – your family?'

'Not to know.'

'All this is going to be expensive, I'm not sure you can afford it. People are such filthy racketeers, I'll have to buy them off for you.'

'I saved a nestegg from the factory. Have it all, if you'll just help me.'

'Yes, all right then, dear, I think I can help you out. As a special favour to you.'

When finally Christina's family were admitted, they were told that, though she had had a twin birth, the second twin had unfortunately been born dead, having ceased to live at an early stage in the pregnancy. But never mind, look on the bright side, Christina had recovered well and they had a bonny bouncing granddaughter. While Matron was imparting this half-joyful, half-distressing information to Mother and Dada in her office, beyond the wall partitioning her from the nursery lay a child weighing just under six pounds with a shock of black hair, piping dismally in concert with a dormitory of his peers. A nursing auxiliary who was herself an unmarried mother working off that portion of her own fee for an adoption, which she had been unable to afford in cash, approached the child. Ascertaining that he had spent the statutory four hours of hunger required by the clock between feeds, she picked up their grandson and stifled his grief with a bottle of milk. The child's eyes focused crazily on the dark blob of her bored face, and wandered loosely in response to shafts of light and strands of colour that chanced to fall within his radius.

He pulled lustfully on the teat. Warmth flooded him, well-being bloated him. Buoyed on the lap of the universe, warmed by his own urine, he trusted that the arms would not fail, and the teat be forever available. Rage died, peace swam in his mind as the milk went on entering him with sweet taste spraying on the bud of his tongue, again and again. The recollection of his early and violent bereavement slid away: the evacuation down the tunnel that

49

scalded and gripped him to the bone, and hardened its soft mouth round his naked head, fatally squeezing him out of the original inland sea in whose warm waters he had ranged and tumbled. The rage of indignation died as he filled and overflowed with milk. Dim voices reached him, waves of sound travelling in one behind the other to break upon the shoreline of consciousness in hisses. Lights, aimed at his eyeball obliquely from strange directions, wrote a signature upon his closing eye. Dark forms converged above his head and folded down upon him, shadows fellowing shadows. He forced open one sticky eyelid to peer again, but the eye slid off sideways, or the world slid off sideways, beyond control. Almighty sleep opened her cavernous jaws at him and snapped him shut inside them. Abruptly, he was gone.

Along the swaying, half-lit corridor of the Exeter train, Mrs Wheeler and one trusted helper carried Baby Llewellyn and the army girl's bastard, swathed in crocheted, white holding blankets. They were out of uniform, so as to avoid advertising themselves to any Ministry of Health baby-racket snoopers who might be hanging around. Mrs Wheeler was in high spirits this evening, pleased with herself. She contemplated the small fortune accumulated in significant bank balances held under various names in a number of branches in several south-western towns. She enjoyed a sense of the worth and utility of what she was doing for these young girls. She was socially responsible in an age of crazy irresponsibility, sensibly redistributing babies from where they were not wanted to where they were wanted. It was in Baby's interest, she believed, to be thus redistributed, for Baby left an impoverished, unsound background for a genteel family life. From being an outcast, surplus to requirements, he was translated in one train ride into expensive upper middle-class property. What kind of life could that WRAC girl have given her bastard? Surprisingly, she had insisted on saying goodbye to it. She stood with her case at the office door, ready to leave, dressed in a shabby grey civilian two-piece suit and highly polished lace-ups. Her contemptuously patrician face, with aquiline nose and steely eyes, resembled that of a Roman citizen in a slave market.

'What will you do?' Mrs Wheeler had asked with unusual curiosity.

'I shall go to London to find work.'

'Not back to the Army then?' They won't have you back, she thought.

50

'In Civvie Street, naturally. Army life doesn't suit my tempera-
ment, in any case. I want my freedom and independence, and I
think I'm entitled to them.'

Whistling superior-sounding tunes in the dark, aren't we,
thought Mrs Wheeler. 'What about your family?' she asked
innocuously.

'I have no family.' They've turfed you out and shut the door on
you have they, thought Mrs Wheeler.

'Well, good luck.'

'I don't want it, thanks anyway.' She glanced down dispassionately at the crooked matron who was to dispose of her child. 'Life is
different for women nowadays, if you've got a certain amount of
brain and self-esteem and initiative. If you don't mind, I'll say
goodbye to my child now, I've a train to catch.'

Mrs Wheeler had stood in the doorway with folded arms,
observing the tall, slender figure as it bent over the cradle. She
caught the words, 'God bless you. God keep you.' Then the girl
straightened up, turned and walked out past Mrs Wheeler, picking
up her case, with a curt nod. You'll come a cropper again in no time
at all, my girl, she had thought. I've seen your sort before. There
was a vulnerability in these girls who thought they were a bit better
than the common run. She quite pitied their simplicity; catchwords
being their sole weapons against the sharks cruising out there
hungry for lean meat, the booby trap of drab jobs and squalid
housing that mined the paths of the freedom seekers.

Mrs Wheeler swayed on down the corridor of the train hugging
Baby Llewellyn to her bosom in a maternal manner, and smiling
slightly helplessly, so that the jam-packed mass of soldiery
travelling west on leave pressed back to let the two laden mothers
pass. Two elderly Jewish gentlemen who had lately themselves
experienced radical redistribution, vacated their own hard-won
seats in their favour. Taking up positions amongst the jostling
horde of standing passengers, they spent the journey nodding and
smiling in to them. Fellow passengers within the carriage glanced
in a friendly way at the infants, privately hoping they would remain
asleep as far as Exeter. Mrs Wheeler sighed with relief as she settled
Baby Llewellyn in her arms and laid her own head back to take a
well-earned rest. Just before Yeovil the train halted with a grinding
shudder, jerking her into wakefulness. A prolonged halt followed.
Someone stuck his head out into the sulphurous night air, and
reported that the men were testing the line: the clink of their

hammers was heard approaching nearer and nearer. Everyone grumbled in the usual friendly, resigned manner. After a quarter of an hour the locomotive steamed off again. Baby Llewellyn behind the darkened pane of glass had set up a doleful howling.

Henry Gartery, standing back from the line to watch the train through, passed within a yard of his outgoing grandson.

Six

Radiant in her newly-liberated beauty, Christina pushed the pram before her with pride. It was the New Year, 1945, with victory imminently expected, and for Christina the first ever real excursion with her daughter, a day in a million. The sunlight's unfamiliarity was dazzling after the indoor world of her lying-in and homecoming. She kept blinking off the smart of light. Broken nights imparted a strangeness to the objects of the daylight world, and she had constantly to censor a curious mental sensation as if she had forgotten something and were trying to recall it. Some phrase, or name, was always on the tip of her tongue, but it curled up and vanished back into itself at the last moment. Each successful act of oblivion brought ecstatic relief. Day and night she was unnaturally alert and elated. As soon as she was out of the Home, the sense of freedom fizzed in her veins, like stimulant or alcohol. She never seemed to get tired, or blue, like other mothers. Such bright spirits had seldom been known in Christina's lugubrious family. In anyone else they would have viewed it with disapproval, as a species of delinquency.

'You feeling a bit queer then, girl?' asked her Aunt Beatrice suspiciously, on a visit.

'No, Aunt Beat. I just feel good.'

'Maybe you've got a bit of hysteria, consequent upon the loss of so many red corpuscles in the birth. Better take it easy. All this laughing. It can't be good for you.'

Christina laughed. When she had first got out of bed after the birth, she thought she might float or fly off the ground, she felt so light. She discarded the past with the lumbering bulk which had made her body so alien. She retrieved her slenderness. The darkness surrounding her vision she could ignore, like the frames of black-rimmed spectacles familiar to the user.

Minnie, more bloated with every day, and in complexion more reminiscent of a boiled potato, had thoughts as sallow as her skin about the emergence of her sister's butterfly-self. She dragged through her chores, the children coming down with whooping cough and preventing her from visiting the younger Albert's resting place. She kept to herself the news of her own impending 'happy event'. Christina would not go to see her in case little Florence caught the disease, Florence who was everyone's pet eclipsing her own brood now occupied in whooping and vomiting into basins through the long watches of the night. She smacked the elder boy for bringing the illness home, and then she smacked him again more savagely for forcing her to betray her bond with Albert. She herself suffered daily from morning sickness. When she thought of Chrissie being made much of at home, it made her livid; then she just shrugged and resigned herself.

Christina seemed to wear a nimbus of happiness and triumph as she turned and waved to her mother from the corner. Her coat was composed of an old RAF blanket appropriated from Sarum barracks as a gift. She had cut and sewn it in imitation of the latest fashion to look as non-utility as possible, stitching imitation fur round the collar and giving the insinuation of a flair in the tightly-belted skirt. On Minnie it would have impersonated an old sack, but on Christina, with her straight spine and head held high, the Air Force blanket acquired glamour and caste. Her friend Betty had come round to perm her hair as soon as she was out of the maternity home. She sat in the kitchen half the day with a towel draped round her shoulders having her head stuck full of curling wires and soused in stinking chemicals. When the hair was finally brushed out it was the authentic filmstar look, everyone said so. She spent hours at the mirror pushing at her hair with her fingertips, turning her head this way and that, admiring the full and softly crinkly style, with its high wave at the front, and giving little smiles of welcome to this new and lustrous self. She gave most of the extra Welfare milk she received to her mother, and insisted on sharing round a quartered orange, that unheard-of luxury. It seemed somehow easier than ever before to be kind, and to see the beauty of ordinary things and over-familiar people. Florence flourished and put on weight, for Christina's milk was abundant and given with no respect for the imperatives of the clock.

The first destination of her walk was the postbox. She still wrote to Jim every day, telling him of the baby's development and of her passionate longing to have him back. She had received only two letters from him since Florence's birth. They contained no news at all, and no indication that he knew he had a child. They were written on airgram forms, scaled down by the photocopier into miniatures carrying writing minute and blurred as if it had suffered from transmission down a telescope. They contained no address, and you could see from the fact that passages in the second of the letters were blanked out that the censor had been at it. Only a few sentences of simple, anguished love remained. She seemed to love him down a microscope, it was impossible to speak to him, so tiny on the specimen tray of Italy. She kept the little messages always in her pocket and fingered them unconsciously. They were testimony that he would come back. The war would soon be over. They would settle down in a house of their own, and one day visit Italy together in peacetime to hear the great operas at La Scala and Rome Opera House. She kissed her own letter for luck before posting it.

In the Cathedral Close a look of impending peace seemed built into the sunlit lemon stone of the palatial houses and school. The shadowed half of the road in the crisp early-morning air was deeply cold, like a tunnel. The sunlit part shone wet with melted frost. The reconditioned pre-war pram slid forward silently, its occupant fast asleep, warm in a siren suit cut from the same Air Force blanket as Christina's coat. She steered the pram with care, as if it were a new toy. It was as if, childishly bare of all serious experience, she could only play at mothers and fathers. It will be different when he gets back, she thought, more real. But at least I've got a real pram, not like those pathetic utility prams, mere crates on wheels, pure of unnecessary extras such as springs and brakes. She turned into North Walk and suddenly there was the Cathedral, soaring. It filled her eyesight and forced up the angle of her head; the beauty of it made her shiver. The stone had a bloom of sunlight on it, the spires glowed the colour of copper beech. It was stillness itself, but animate, the building seemed to breathe like a living thing. Christina had never taken much notice of the Cathedral: if you were born and bred here, you didn't, it was just a landmark taken

54

for granted, which visitors came along and stared at.

She perched on a bench so that she too could stare. I've never seen anything like this before, she thought. The world seemed a kindly place, hospitable, forgiving. The war would not go on much longer. Then there would be street parties, bonfires, masses of food, no more rationing, wonderful dresses to wear, Jim could come home and they would have their proper honeymoon then, lasting years and years. The Cathedral was a burning coppery gold, its long early-morning shadow an acre of night. She gently rocked the pram backwards and forwards. The sun's heat was so mild that she could risk throwing open her coat, and she was conceiving the joys of the honeymoon all the while in her imagination, in heart-melting detail. The Bible of her life was open at Genesis. She could go back eternally to the beginning, remake her life from scratch. At home they had a great iron- and leather-bound Bible, rusty with generations of use. It came into her mind now – not that it was read very much nowadays, but as children they had played with it as a kind of sacred toy, clasping and unclasping its two ornate locks, and pasting in scraps of local newspaper cutting relating to events in Gartery history, mainly of a deplorable nature, as in the demise of Jeremiah Gartery by happening to tumble off a cliff blind drunk.

Christina did not actually believe in God: she pretended to, of course, for the sake of good manners. She had chiefly used the family Bible as a flower-press. As a child, she had had a passion for collecting, naming and preserving wild flowers, stocking the pages full of specimens. Now when you opened it, a violet a decade old was to be discovered modestly hiding in that obscure region of Numbers and Deuteronomy to which no one ever turns for its own sake. Sheaves of pages creaked open, the margins brownish with mould, until at the Song of Solomon you came upon the flower head of a giant blood-coloured poppy, gathered at Sarum; at St Matthew's account of the Nativity a snowdrop in white tissue paper. St Paul's exhortations were improved with celandines, and the volcano of the Apocalypse was stuffed full of the flowers which she did not absolutely treasure but could not make up her mind to discard. Now why am I thinking about this, she wondered to herself? That was it. She must enter the birth of Florence there in her own handwriting, adding her contribution to the continuum of her family's past. She would try not to be ashamed of the family in future. There is atonement, there is belonging, there is peace. She remembered sitting at the fireside sorting flowers, on Dad's knee, years ago, at twilight after a day of rambling in the country. The air was full of resinous tobacco smoke from his pipe. As he inhaled he steadily watched her neat fingers separate the stems of different species, grade them for degrees of perfection: these worth saving, these to go. Now there was the same beatific tiredness, in having come through the worst – a third of her whole lifetime spent in wartime, the Ice Age which was ending.

'Pretty as a picture.'

She started from her day-dreaming. A black-haired man had sauntered up and was standing in an attitude of admiration.

'A vision of loveliness. Excuse my cheek but I couldn't help noticing you.'

'Pardon me?'

She was flustered. She got up, drawing her coat together over her chest to button it. It was a spiv, you could tell by the aroma of perfumed oil from his sleeked black hair, and by his pencil-moustache and pinstripes, the air of cheap, gaudy profit surrounding him, the sort of man you have to avoid. She flushed as her foot fumbled with the brake on Florence's pram.

'Don't let me frighten you off now. You looked such a picture, I thought you might actually want to *be* in a picture.'

She had no idea what he meant but she was sure it was nasty. The brake had stuck fast, she had to bend to free it. 'Oh dear, no. I have to get home now. Excuse me.'

She saw that the oleaginous man was holding an open box camera in his left hand, which he now smilingly extended to her.

'My dear young lady, I'll do you a favour, just because it's you. I'll take a photograph of you and your charming baby, guaranteed delivery within the week, money returned if you don't obtain complete satisfaction.'

'Oh yes, I see.' She straightened up, hesitant but tempted. You couldn't get hold of film at all these days, so that she was without any picture of Florence, who was changing every day, her nature seeming to include reflections of countless variant natures, each of which flowed away into the past tense like so many dreams of people who might have been. Christina ached to capture her daughter. She longed to be able to send a picture to Jim. But could she trust the spiv with the black-market film who was loitering round the Cathedral taking pictures of sightseers actually to deliver the film? She looked at him doubtfully.

'If I could pay on delivery?' she suggested. 'And I'll order four copies.'

'You local?'

'Yes.' She told him the address, which he noted.

'Done.' Christina held Florence up to the camera's eye, just outside the dark porch of the Cathedral. Christina smiled in jubilation.

Florence's face appeared hungrily argumentative. The shutter came down. Florence was given a form as permanent as the paper on which she was imprinted. Christina was thrilled. She kissed the angry little face all over and cuddled her hard. 'I've got you! You're real! I'm going to keep you and give you to your Daddy and never let you go!'

But Florence, who could no longer contain her sense of outrage at the milklessness of her condition, had turned into a small hurricane. Christina thrust her into the pram and began to speed home, still laughing inwardly. Florence batted her arms above the quilt in a starving frenzy, her soft skin inflamed by the fibrous rub of the siren suit, each individual hair of which irritated her surfaces. Urgent, urgent, emergency, she cried. Don't you know my need is paramount? I get priority. Not you. Remember that will you? She could not bound her pathological fury.

Christina ran until the pram's jolting rhythms had tumbled the baby back into sleep; then she walked through town at her own pace. Passing the Poultry Cross she saw the familiar figure of a stout young woman chatting under the arches. For a moment she couldn't place her. Then as the girl glanced round and caught her eye, she recognised the orderly from the Home, Polly Cornwell. The dark frame permanently staining the extreme perimeter of Christina's consciousness closed in, the world seemed physically to darken. Somehow she had not imagined the inmates of the maternity home as enjoying substantial objective existence in the outside world. She had bolted from that underworld in a mad dash for freedom and invisibility. How could she have been such a fool? But perhaps Polly hadn't seen her. She quickened pace, head down. She wouldn't go out in future. When Jim came back they would live far away from Salisbury, where no one knew them. They didn't need other people anyway, only each other.

'*Morning*, Chrissie! I thought I recognised you. How're you keeping then, girl?'

'Fine, thank you.' She couldn't afford to show her distaste at this

57

assumption of false intimacy. 'And yourself?'

'Lovely, Chrissie, lovely, thanks for asking. Did you know I'm leaving town? Going down Southampton-way to work with the WRENS, basic nursing work, *very* good money so I'm told. Aren't you going to let me get a look at your little darling then, Chrissie?' She craned into the dimness of the pram hood.

'What have you called her then?'

'Her name is Florence.'

'Oh really?' She appeared to turn the name over in her mind. 'Long name, that.' She paused. 'Long enough for two.' She uttered a little snort of laughter behind her hand; her eyes gleamed. 'Well, you must admit it's a mouthful. Flo-rence. Flo-rence.' She pronounced it in two parts. 'Highly superior name, of course. Reduce it to Flo, I should.' She paused again, sizing Christina up. 'Only teasing, Chrissie,' she loudly whispered, drawing close, face hot with pleasure. 'Don't mind me. Don't worry, dear, your secret's safe with Polly, cross my heart and hope to die. You believe me, don't you?' She smiled cordially, one hand conspiratorially gripping Christina's arm like a metal band.

Christina faltered away, her heartbeats trampling one another down. No, she thought, no. The world was caving and buckling under her feet. It was criss-crossed with tripwires. From each opaque window hidden eyes looked out for her like the barrels of loaded guns.

Christina's mother took the telegram from the postgirl's hand disbelievingly. The horror of the khaki envelope which, as obscenely as bombs, struck whole families down at one blow, from which they emerged white faced and altered, had never touched their house. You saw the families which had received the wafer-thin stigma of death re-emerge from the blitzed remains of their lives, and struggle up the pavement of normality like ghosts, or refugees, or cripples dragging a leg. You knew them at first by their absence – the empty pew at church, the cinema seat they always used to make for, filled by a stranger. Amelia used to dread the sight of the postman at the beginning of the War when George went overseas, and Lilian insisted on going to London to make the first of her war efforts by becoming a fireman, and then when Chrissie was sent off to Bristol and the munitions factory. As the years went by, an uneasy sense of immunity grew. George, and later Jim, seemed to have charmed lives, Chrissie came home, and

Lil seemed noisily indestructible. Amelia had inherited from her mother certain charms and spells to ensure protection, which she ritually told over in odd private moments, and she would sometimes pray, not in a spirit of piety but on the principle of barter, 'If you keep my George safe I'll agree to do such-and-such for you.' But she was tightlipped and parsimonious with God even while making arrangements with him. As in the case of the collaborating Pope Pius, there seemed to be a conniving side to an Almighty who had failed so signally to speak out against the extermination of such masses of his children. She knitted military socks, fed the family as best she could, kept up Dad's spirits and hoped for the best.

Therefore she accepted the telegram into her house with bewilderment. Her hands were wet from washing Flo's nappies, and the telegram was marked with sudsy thumb prints. It was addressed to Chrissie but she opened it automatically. Fighter Command regretted to inform Mrs Llewellyn that her husband Aircraftsman James Llewellyn 980225 was missing in action, in Northern Italy. So it said. She read it through several times, mechanically, feeling nothing at all. She looked round the room, bemused. Here was the thin alloy milk pan with the bottom wearing through, on the hob, and the stale smell of burnt milk. Here were the hoarded pots of blackberry jam, survivors of their autumn forages, crimson-black like old blood. Here was the stained and peeling wall, the meagre window admitting a rectangle of grey light. Soapy water bled down the sink, and dripped into the iron bucket beneath the mangle. All this familiarity had undergone mutation while her head was turned. The contents of the kitchen were betrayed into alien existence foreign to human purposes. Here was the thin khaki telegram, damp and limp in the tropically humid air condensing from the wash. As Amelia read it through again, she heard Christina's key in the lock and the clanking of the pram being dragged up the step into the narrow hall.

Christina came in quietly and took the wafer of paper from her mother's hand. It was purely a matter of form to scan it over. She had read it countless times before, in dreams, at bus stops, standing before the capstan measuring to the thousandth of an inch the component of a tank that would bereave a thousand women. Missing in action presumed dead, killed in action, wounded in the course of duties, lost a leg an arm a hand a life: these phrases were all rehearsed so thoroughly that now that His Majesty's

Government was dealing direct with Mrs Llewellyn on paper, it did not seem strange at all. It's the judgment on me, she saw. It's the answer to my prayer, when I said, *Take it away. I don't want it. It isn't mine.*

Her mother was crying now, seizing her in her arms, saying, 'Oh Chrissie, my poor Chrissie, oh my poor girl.'

'Don't *do* that,' said Christina. She sounded exasperated. 'Leave me alone can't you, Mum. Don't touch me.' She was folding the telegram and putting it back tidily in the envelope.

Her heart was closing in upon itself, its muscles contracted, too far, could not expand. Vacuum squeezed the heart's sides in together till the membranes met, their wet surfaces pressed together, the aorta seized up excluding the blood, there was no blood going round but it was left roaring in her skull, and the lungs clamoured for breath. Stifling she strove for breath, grabbing her throat with both hands, knees giving way.

Then she was being sat down and her head forced between her legs. The blood came bubbling and pulsing back into her brain, the black-out cleared. With a red and clammy face she rested back in the chair, the saccharined tea scalding her tongue.

'How are you now, my beauty? Coming round a bit?'

'Yes.' But don't kneel to me.

'It don't mean he's dead, Chrissie. Look, it only says Missing in Action. You don't want to go inferring.'

'No.' But don't speak to me, I'm no one.

'We have every reason to hope he'll be found, my love. You know that. For instance there was Mrs Smith's Charlie wasn't there, back in forty three, given up for dead and it was fourteen months before they found out he's been in the POW camp all that time. It happens every day. We have to hope.'

'Yes, Mum, all right.' If only you knew.

'But you are still inferring, Chrissie, aren't you. I can see it written all over your face, you can't fool me. It's the shock, my love, the terrible, terrible shock. But you have to think, what would Jim want me to feel now?'

'It's a judgment on me.'

'Come on now, Chrissie. Don't get all queer now.'

'No, I mean it.' Her face wore a cruelly knowing smile, frozen like a mask. Amelia knelt back on her heels as if physically pushed. 'You say I can't fool you and you think you know me, but you don't. You shouldn't by rights come anywhere near me, I should be

60

a pariah, people should cross the street rather than meet me on the same pavement. Oh I'm so good as gold aren't I? I'm such a good girl, such a mealy-mouthed pretty precious little better-than-thou Good Girl – butter wouldn't melt, would it? But I'm not like you think. You'd better cast me off because I'm a stranger, you don't know anything about me. I've done something wicked and evil that can't be forgiven, and God is angry with me. Don't tell me *once more* that there's any hope, I don't want to hear it. Jamie is dead, he's dead forever, and even in the next world – if there is a next world, which I personally doubt – I'll never see him again. I should never be allowed anywhere near him.'

But why in God's name did I do it, she wondered, frowning, propping her forehead on her hand? Why? She had no idea. It seemed incomprehensible. Surely Jim's son was what she wanted more than anything else in the world.

'What is it you think you've done, Chrissie? You've never said boo to a goose until today. I don't think you know what you're saying, poor girl.'

'No, you're quite right, I'm mad, I'm deranged, I've gone round the bend. But I've murdered Jim in my sleep and they ought to hang me for it, for my own sake, put me out of my misery. Will you give Florence a bottle of milk, Mum, I'm going out: no, don't worry, I won't do anything to myself, that's Dad's little trick, I mean the cross he bears. Just don't worry about me, don't think about me at all. I don't want to be in anyone's mind, okay?'

Turning to go, she pressed her thumbs into her temples. What was different inside her head all of a sudden? That was it, the noise had gone, the interference. The wireless message that had been broadcasting inside her brain on some foreign wavelength had been switched off. It was quiet as the grave in here. The air waves were no longer carrying instructions. She had been told what to do, in code only she understood; she had done it; now she was free. But in this evacuated space her own mind insisted on its own perplexity, for why did I do it? Why did I disown Jim's little boy, how could I? She passed Florence's pram without looking in at the sleeper cradled there. I don't want to blame you, I don't want to hate you, innocent one. She dashed out into the high sunlight. As she ran, an image of the interior of the Home where she had borne the babies came to mind. It was a memory of defilement, declaring the issue of life from a black maelstrom of blood. Sensations of pain, unbelievable crucifying pain, reached her, from far away, as if she had been involved in some struggle for survival, fighting foul and blind where one could not identify the enemy, for he was reproduced within her like a vile taste in the mouth which had to be spat out. But even so, why did I do it? She sped toward the Cathedral.

In the great and beautiful vaulted mortuary where the stony warriors sleep, awaiting Judgment Day, Christina paced the aisles. She read the inscriptions and scrutinised their features. Laid out upon his tomb, the mailed and skirted William Longespee Earl of Salisbury, witness of Magna Carta, layer of the foundation stone, carried his pointed shield into death, in case he should find need of armaments there. His toes were neatly pointed. His long thin, equally pointed face rested on a small rectangular pillow. Likewise Robert Lord Hungerford, two centuries the younger warrior, lay at rest, his footstool the back of a little dog couchant. Two small and barefoot angels sat by Robert's ears, either side of his tonsured head, their outstretched fingers nearly meeting in an attitude of protection. At intervals between the effigies of the men of war rested the battalions of the bishops, their faces crumbling in a grisly manner. Some wore their skeletons in place of cassocks to show how their recumbent piety repudiated the flesh and the things of the flesh.

Toward the altar before the window whose stained glass burns the light ice blue stood two priestly men in green and two in black cassocks, conducting the choirboys in rehearsal. A psalm of devastating length was being transmitted through the unripe, unknowing beauty of emotionless boy-voices. As she stood watching and listening, she became aware of other, vagrant noises. Prelatical gentlemen with clicking feet and nervously sidelong-glancing eyes scurried past her; an unseen person in the choir stalls coughed intermittently in the bass register. With the completion of the psalm a sudden Oxbridge voice began to boom a reading into the body of the Cathedral. She sat and listened to the elegant, elderly voice as it read from the book of Joel, prophesying the end of the world: 'Like the crackling of a flame of fire devouring the stubble ... like warriors they come ... climb up into the houses ... heavens tremble ... Lord's Army ... for his host is exceedingly great. For the day of the Lord is great and very terrible. Who can endure it?' During the recital of these cheerful words a tramp began to pace the main aisle, up and down, faster and faster, as if to draw the Almighty's attention: Me! Come on, look at me! Christina watched the wild energy with which the tramp tore up and down God's house; his gaberdine flapped and swished as he hurried on his errand. The reader and the singers took a studied lack of notice. She began to think, how strange it was, and foreign, not the tramp so much as the whole entrancing cosmos of the place, the utter beauty of soaring stone, the stone-cold beauty of it all. The thin tenor of a priest now led off with 'My soul doth magnify' and the choirboys all replied as one nest of fledgelings to their eunuch-mother: that it was, is now, ever more shall be. All this has been going on for seven hundred years, she thought, the flame-throwing God and his warriors together with the flailing tramp who did not want to be the stubble, and was now led protesting out of a side door by a courteous attendant.

No, God is not angry with me at all, she thought. God is too busy with the hosts of his Armies, training up his men for bayoneting and bombing and slaughtering, as if all the children we bring into the world were going to have to play one of two roles, the butcher or the meat in one great Abattoir. God doesn't notice me and my brief errors. I needn't even duck. I can walk out of here bolt upright and he won't notice me at all. The milk coming in for Florence throbbed in her breasts. But God has nothing to do with these petty concerns, my night of confusion, my milk coming in. I shan't lay before him my state of need and my wish for expiation. I shan't flap up and down at him like the tramp, his overcoat a badge of surrender. God must atone to me for his world, he must have a change of heart before I'll step back in here and ask his blessing. Christina got up and, carefully brushing her skirt down, walked to the doors, beneath the ragged and stained Great War banners of the Wiltshire Regiment, hanging high on the wall. God's not angry with me, I'm angry with him, she thought.

The light, refracted through a gauzy film of cloud, poured round her milky and thick as she moved into the unpeopled silence of the Cathedral Walk. Christina looked southwards toward Old Sarum where the radiance seemed most dense, like liquid metal, like mercury rolling and gathering. Jamie, come home, she prayed to him into the liquid light, oh Jamie do come back to me try your best to come.

'What's up then, Mum? You look as though you'd seen a ghost.' Lilian stood at the door in her boiler suit covered in muck and oil. She had just had a row with her employer and told him where he could stick his ruddy spanner. She ended by dropping her tool bag on his feet with a clank and stamping out of the Gents Public Lavatories where they had been working on a leak. All the way home she had savoured the recollection of her reply to his 'And don't you come back you girt useless loud-mouthed pig-faced lump of lard!' He could plainly not have expected her return volley of lush swearwords learned from her workmates in the course of the various manly professions she had pursued during the war, treasuring them up in a mental lexicon of abuse to be called on for special occasions. Now she had that consummated feeling she always experienced after quitting on a job. She meditated on a pub crawl and the choosing of a new profession.

'A telegram came,' said Amelia.

'Oh *no*. Who is it?'

'Chrissie's Jim. Missing in action, it said.'

'Not killed though, it didn't say killed?'

'No, Lil, it didn't say so.'

'Does she know?'

'Yes. She went quite queer – started shouting things about it being her fault, then she went charging out and left me with Flo, told me to feed her but she don't take to the bottle.'

'Want me to go out and look for her, Mum?' Lilian started tying her cumbersome straight hair up in a knotted scarf. 'Did she say where she was going? You don't have any idea? Don't worry, I'll find her.'

Losing Jim will kill her, she can't survive it, Lilian thought. Generally Lilian had little respect for the tender passions. Though once in happier times she had fallen for her employer, a farmer, he had valued her solely for her labour. He never guessed her passion. The bovine eyes with which she fondly followed him made him estimate her as a stupid beast of burden, and he overworked her more than he would have dreamed of taxing the strength of the common run of land girls. The more he asked of her, the harder she laboured. Finally, with the gathering of the last sheaves of the barley harvest, he gave all his girls notice to quit, to save money over the winter: hearing which, Lilian flew into the first of her rages with the employing classes, and left him with a flea in his ear, reeling with bewilderment. She joined forces with the Amazonian hell-raisers with oxyacetylene torches who burned down gateposts in their zeal to acquire wrought-iron gates for government salvage. Her gang was amongst those which ran amok and roamed the countryside leaving a trail of burning fences and hedges, in the name of patriotism. 'Those were the days,' she always said with a nostalgic sigh, after this licensed violence to property had been brought under control. She remembered whole neighbourhoods running indoors when they heard the singing of the salvage girls, and screaming at the sight of the burners, and offering to pay to be let alone. But it was our principle, she remembered, to be democratic about our work, and we burnt the lot, regardless.

Her youngest sister's vulnerability horrified Lilian, it made her wince. 'For God's sake stand up for yourself, girl,' she would say to Christina as a child, when she came home bruised and trembling-lipped from some bully's casual push. 'You fall down before they hit you.' She tried to teach the little girl to box and wrestle. But Christina would always prefer falling to fighting. Christina's nature seemed to call to her for protection and yet always to lie (because of Christina's faint scorn of what she saw as her mannishness) outside the scope of her care. Lilian was jack of all trades, which seemed to her a safe profession though a pirateering one, compared to Christina's lack of resource. She saw Christina shrink from the violence of the most trivial confrontation, seeming to belong to another and more delicate world, one which had not been invented yet. Chrissie was weaker even than poor old Min, with her crazy letters to her dead baby, delivered into the one-way mouth of the postbox of the grave. She saw them both as incapacitated females, crippled partially, like birds dragging a wing.

Lilian, turning a corner at a fast trot, saw, not a pathetic, maimed creature, but an alert and upright figure walking toward her through the sunlight, the waves of her hair all bronzed and burnished, radiating energy.

'Are you the search party, Lily?'

'Oh Chrissie. Mum said you had the telegram. I came out to see if I could find you.'

'Darling Lily. "Consider the Lilies of the field, how they grow".' Christina put out both arms smilingly to her sister, dungarees, oil and all, and compelled their bodies together. Lilian yielded, gathered in.

'I thought you'd be in a terrible state. I'd have to pick you up and carry you home.' They began to walk home, hand in hand.

'Mum told you I flew off the handle, did she? I did go a bit beyond. It was the shock. But it only says he's missing, I won't believe he's dead, Lily, I simply won't believe it. Here, see the telegram.'

'Where did you go?'

'To the Cathedral.'

'That's good then.' Lilian marvelled at Christina's equanimity. She must have had a religious experience in there or something, quite out of character for her but then war wasn't exactly in character for Chrissie. There was a feeling of energy coming from her, you could feel it as they walked, a resistance, an about turn of the will.

'You're going to fight it then?'

'Right. I'm going to fight. I'm going to do everything to get him back.' The first thing being, to get the baby back. 'Are you with me?'

'With you. Right or wrong.'

Christina gave her a quick look.

When they were home, she was suddenly tired, she could have slept, but the determination didn't leave her. Sitting demurely by a log fire whose fuel had been illicitly gathered from Storton Wood, she appeared to her mother to be quite her old self. She sipped tea, seeming very normal, and did not allude other than hopefully to the subject of the telegram. That night Florence woke her repeatedly with her ranting. In those funereal hours before dawn, then she knew Jim was a corpse, days old on some hillside in Northern Italy, with the rain piercing his sodden battledress, and his pale blue eyes washing away into the gangrenous verdure of the countryside. In the night she saw that face, piteous as a child's, that had wept in farewell on this pillow ten months before, and kissed her mouth all softly salted with his tears, and been so warm, and gone away. She saw his skull emerge from the bloated residue of flesh night by night, on the imagined hillside, and creatures eating him, rats and maggots, outside and inside. She heard the death of his rich, humorous, priceless laughter; the Welsh cadence of his dark tenor silenced.

When morning came, her decision to retrieve the baby boy was still strong. But when she tried to get up, she found herself sick with griping stomach pains that bent her double. She could hardly eat at all and immediately her milk dried up. She could no longer feed Florence and, despite prolonged and painful attempts, they had to wean her on to National Dried Milk. The baby resisted this with bellowing indignation, retching on the teat of the bottle and spitting out the rose hip syrup they also offered, as an offence to her palate. The household was in turmoil. Christina was bedridden and Florence losing weight drastically, terrifying her mother by thus pointedly threatening to die unless the status quo were restored. Christina became listless and weepy. The inclination to live and make a fight of it left her under the pressure of physical illness, and in these circumstances Lilian's strictly non-maternal talents were of no use at all. She didn't know one end of a baby from the other, and was not thought likely to learn. The lacklustre look which characterised their father, pulling his long face as he sagged over his tea, Lilian seemed to read on Christina's countenance. She had no idea how to help her.

But the severity of the pains wore off within a week. And Aunt Beatrice invaded, as usual making a crusade of it in her self-important uniform. She sat Christina forward in bed and thumped the pillows into shape.

'Don't wilt now, our Chrissie. This is the time for showing the stiff upper lip if ever there was one. Don't droop at me. Shoulders back, chest out. Get her out of bed, Lilian. What she wants is a change. Don't you, my girl? Pardon? Not speaking again? Come on, Lilian, don't shamble round there like a superannuated cart horse, help your sister out of bed.'

'Old bag,' muttered Christina.

'Beg your pardon? Didn't quite catch it. That's the ticket, up you get. Any pains? No? Well, there you are then, jolly good.' She drew the curtains back as far as they would go. 'We'll open a window and thoroughly aerate the room. The ventilation here is quite shocking. Put a vest on her, Lilian, and give her hair one hundred strokes of the brush.'

'One, two, three, four,' Lilian began a solemn countdown. Christina gave a feeble giggle. 'All right now, Chrissie?' asked Lilian. 'Do you want to go back to bed?'

'No. I'll get up. I do feel more myself.' Her immobile image in the mirror reflected back to her the breasts which seemed shrivelled without their milk, the thin face fined down to the bone.

'We're bringing the invalid downstairs now, Amelia,' Aunt Beat was declaring from the top of the stairs. 'Buck up, Lilian – brace up our Chrissie, we'll soon have your batteries recharged.'

'Can't you get rid of her, Lily?' whispered Christina.

Lilian thought about it. 'No,' she concluded. They put their heads together and snorted with laughter.

67

The following evening, Christina was persuaded to go out to the cinema with her mother, leaving the temporarily peaceful baby to the care of her forcible aunt. They returned purged and uplifted, having healthily wept their way through the full three hours and fifty minutes of their fourth viewing of *Gone With the Wind*. Lilian was slouched fast asleep in an armchair. Florence was seated in the crook of Henry's arm delicately lapping National Dried Milk off a small teaspoon. She had been doing so for an hour on and off, settled, composed, and gazing interestedly at her grandfather's moustaches and his cap brim, and pausing every now and again to execute a broad toothless smile around the perimeter of the spoon.

'There's Grandad's little ducky darling,' they heard him babble. He smiled and nodded, encouraging her to sip again. 'There's my best girl, there's my wren, my sparrow, there you are my joy.'

Hearing them come in, he turned his head sharply, as if detected in some illicit pleasure. His face prepared to adopt its hangdog look.

'What's been going on?'

'Nothing much. Lilian dropped off so we thought we'd do a spot of weaning, didn't we Floss?'

'Better let him get on with it,' said Amelia doubtfully. 'Anything to cheer him up. And he does seem to have got the milk into her. He was like that with you, you know, Chrissie, ducky darling and all.'

'Really?' said Christina. She didn't remember any such closeness. She stared into the magic circle of elderly man and baby girl, eyeing and greeting one another.

'Oh yes, he was quite besotted,' said her mother, with scorn, putting the kettle on. 'A real embarrassment, not like a man at all. He even used to whip you out in the pram while we weren't looking. No man would be seen dead pushing a pram in those days. But Henry *would* do it.'

Florence was replete. Her closing eyelids weighed heavily against her intentions. She graciously permitted her grandfather to hoist her against his slow-breathing chest. Fist in her mouth, she toppled into sleep there, without grumbling. From these origins grew a relationship for which he had longed. In the accommodation of his life to her imperious needs and affections, he clean forgot for months, then years, to follow the gravewards drift of his melancholy.

Seven

Minnie's husband Albert was a cook-private in the Army. When he came home on leave he made a point of emphasising that he did not intend to do so much as to look in the kitchen. The most culinary thing he proposed was to sit at the head of the table with his plate piled high, stuffing himself full of hot succulent roast and knocking back the hooch. This was in itself a worry, since meat was scarcer than ever, and Minnie's swede pie and carrot cake were, as he had pointed out, disgusting: fit for pigs not men. It was a distinction she had sometimes privately thought over-subtle. He was a small, rough-mannered man who might have had a career marked out for him as a boxer if the Army had not claimed him and turned his fists into wielders of ladles and potato peelers. Cook-privates were not highly valued in the Army, despite the indispensable function they fulfilled. Pugnacious as a terrier, quarrelsome and irrational even when he had not had a few drinks, Albert was constantly spoiling for a fight when on duty. His aggression built and built behind the dam of military discipline: only on leave could he let his foul and seething temper erupt in words and blows, so that he could return to the cookhouse purged and jokey. Albert was Mars in person, tragically kept from enacting the business he knew and liked best, wasting his energies among potato peelings and cuts of meats when he could have been carving up the enemy on the front line. Minnie knew with a peculiar intimacy one construction that might be placed on Lord Woolton's popular phrase 'the kitchen front'.

In many ways, however, the war altered Minnie's position for the better, in that, in removing her from proximity to Albert's brutal posture, it enabled her through ensuring his absence to think kindly and sentimentally of him, to blur his faults, and reformulate his character. She could not realistically hope that he might be removed from her altogether, since cook-privates were not

69

conspicuously in the front line of fire, but she liked sometimes to think of a nice, well-aimed bomb as having dropped on him, taking him off painlessly and patriotically, and releasing her into the bliss of widowhood. As a war widow Minnie thought she would make an interesting and touching figure. She would be able to talk of Albert as he had never been in real life (bar the year when Little Albert was alive, when truly he had been something like an affectionate husband and father). To be a widow would mean she could shed a gentle glow on the memory of Albert, remembering the high hopes of their courting days and forgetting absolutely what the mature Albert had done to her face with the broken milk bottle on the occasion of his last leave.

It was on that forty-eight hour leave, plastered and roaring drunk throughout, that Albert had engendered the baby Minnie was now carrying. During the rubber shortage which had made contraceptives hard to come by a couple of years ago, Albert had discovered in himself a moral antipathy to the use of the condom, which had survived into the period when they again became plentiful. Thus Minnie was liable to be breeding from now until the change of life (or, preferably, the miracle of widowhood) returned her used-up body to its original owner, free from intruders. Albert came charging into her perhaps three or four times that first night, and as his buttocks furiously worked he grunted obscenities, and reviled her for her dry cunt and her tears, and ground away at her until his seed poured in like germs of hate. Finally he sank into a malodorous drunken stupor, and the next morning claimed not to recall anything of his nocturnal activity; claimed indeed that she had refused him outright, the frigid bitch; stretched across the bed to grab her, saying, 'Come here, you stupid ugly cow,' and made as if to do it again, save that she escaped and ran out into the kitchen crying, which was when he came at her with the milk bottle. Then Sam came out and found her face streaming blood, and went for his father butting with his head, small fists ramming at Albert's pyjamaed thighs: at which, oddly, the father laughed and seemed comically proud of the lad, and bore him off to bed still pummelling and shouting for revenge. Then together Minnie and Albert picked the splinters of glass out of the wound, and bandaged it, not speaking, and though Albert went off boozing with his mates for the rest of the afternoon and evening, and Minnie sat huddled in a blanket with the children, shivering with shock, when he came in drunk he did not molest her. He helped her up to bed, laid his arm round her in a forgiving way, and went out like a light.

Now that Albert had telegraphed to say he was coming home on sick leave, the dream of widowhood was annulled. Minnie's heart had not been high, what with the children's coughs volleying through her nights, and the black sink of her stomach discharging its contents at all hours, as if her body were trying to throw out the irrelevance of her pregnancy. Now her heart sank speechlessly low. To receive Albert on his last leave Minnie had made quite strenuous efforts to make the best of herself for him, borrowing a lipstick from Chrissie, washing her hair and painting her legs with dye so as to feign the unobtainable silk stockings. Sam, her eldest boy, helped her to paint a line up the back of her legs to resemble a seam: not wholly satisfactorily, for his earnest efforts produced a line voluptuously waving over her calves rather than the uniform straightness required by fashion. The finished effect had been appraised by Albert with candour. He named her 'Yellow Legs', and said, 'You've made a right bleeding ass of yourself, caked up to the eyeballs.'

'I wanted to look good for you,' she whined. 'You can't get hold of real cosmetics these days, Bert. We have to make do.'

'Oh well, you can't make a silk purse out of a sow's ear. Poor old Min. You don't look so bad from a distance. With one eye closed. Seen from behind. On a dark night.'

His jokes forgave her obligingly for being who she was: that had been the first evening.

Now she had ceased fighting, tired out. She had lost weight so that the flesh of her face was slack and middle aged, oily in texture; her hair lay grubby and flat to her head. That morning, she dragged herself out of bed, was sick for half an hour, and then sat in the kitchen in her dressing gown beside yesterday's cinders, meaning to rebuild the fire, and unequal to doing so. She thought she could probably drink a cup of tea but could not stir to make it. If only Mum would come over now, she thought, and set me to rights. If only there was someone to see me through these times, I'd get young again. But Mother clung to Chrissie and the baby, whom Minnie was not allowed to see in case she brought her contamination near it. There was a pounding on the staircase, Sam hared in.

'Shush up, Sam. If they're sleeping for a change, for God's sake let them sleep on as long as they can, my love.'

Sam coughed loudly, hand on breast, at the centre of the room. It was not a real spasm of whooping, as they both knew, but a staged reminder.

'Shut up, Sam. You're putting it on.'

'What's for breakfast? I'm bleeding starving.'

'You shouldn't swear. God don't like to hear boys swearing.'

'God should close his bleeding lugholes and then he won't hear it. I am bleeding starving anyway. Bleeding bleeding bleeding *bleeding*.'

Sam was one of the most unwholesome boys some people had ever met, in complexion dough-faced, built squat like Minnie, with a shock of fuzzy dark hair and a tendency to move in uncoordinated jerks which got on people's nerves. Even when he had just been scrubbed, Sam appeared permanently scrofulous and dirty; his hair was a tangled mass that seemed to advertise itself as a bed for lice. In Minnie's eyes, Sam had from the start compared unfavourably with Little Albert in all his tender-skinned perfection, and the pale of his eyes like wet bluebells, kindred to Dad's and Chrissie's. Sam's eyes were brown as prunes and squinty, his face resentful as though he had always been missing something. She looked with distaste at the angry crimson rashes into which his hectic skin was constantly irrupting. He was certainly, Minnie felt, a flawed boy, a mistake. The deep and passionately protective love Sam felt for his mother, she wholly failed to recognise. She looked beyond him to a love pre-dating his history, of which he could know nothing. Sam was tuned to his mother most delicately. He heard if her pulse should quicken, he comprehended her injuries with grief and outraged pity, he would have put himself as a wall between Minnie and anyone who hurt her, he would have died for her. But the proclamation of his love, many times attempted, came out twisted into indignant calls for attention, rude and exasperating. He ended up shadow boxing in the lamplight, or surreptitiously fisting his brother and sister, being rebuked and threatened with a tanning, inarticulate, remorseful love pouring from his eyes unread. He was four years and a half.

'You'll have to get your own breakfast. I feel too ill. I feel too weak. Cut yourself a slice of bread. Get the milk in.'

'God don't like to see boys getting their own breakfast especially ill boys like what I am.'

'Please. Please, Sam.'

Sam stopped drumming his heels against the chair. He did not

72

know whether he was equal to the task of getting breakfast, he seriously doubted it. He felt he would drop the milk bottles; he sensed he would take a slice out of his hand with the bread knife. He felt the drastic limitations of his three-foot height. As he discerned the white-faced desolation of his mother, sagging motionless in the chair, the scent of stale vomit still about her, terror seized him. Sam saw the frailty of his position, how the walls of home could tear down in a moment, the roof cave in so that rain would come pouring through to the living room down the hole that used to be a bedroom. Seeing his shelterless condition, the terms of his tenancy, the sharp tears gathered behind his eyes.

'Oh Mum. Oh Mum. Come on.'

She said nothing, eyes closed, head lolling on the soiled embroidery of the cloth that protected the chairback.

'Mum, if you don't get my breakfast I'll do terrible things. I'll run away and never come back, I'll go upstairs and twist Rosie's arm behind her back I'll . . .'

It was his last throw. She opened her eyes and they looked through him. She seemed to retch. She said, 'Your Dad's coming home today on leave. We'd better behave ourselves.'

Sam, huge-hearted, squeezed both hands round the neck of the first milk bottle, lugged it up balancing it on his out-thrust tummy, and dashed in through two doors, frowning, biting his lip with concentration. He heaved it on to the table. Three more times he made this dash: the free milk, their life's blood, was secured. Climbing on a chair, he sawed hunks off the loaf, stuffing some into his mouth as he worked. The bread skidded, a little blood seeped into it. Sam sucked the wound, his courage high with success. Motionless in the chair, his mother lay with half-closed eyes. If she was dead, it was best not to know, not to ask. If he did not look at her, she could not be dead. He turned his attention to the fire, his idea being to make her a cup of tea. With the poker in both hands he furiously riddled it until the soft wood-ash was all sifted through. He heaped newspaper and twigs in the grate, and felt round in a drawer for the matches, muttering anxiously, 'Where's them bleeders gone?'

'No, Sam.'

She crawled over, hand on her stomach, moaning faintly, and set a light to the fire. Sam staggered across to place the great weight of the filled kettle over the flame. Together they brewed the tea. She sat and drank, warmed through, resting the cup against her breast, her feet on the fender. Sam sat at her feet, experiencing all he could know of earthly bliss. He toasted himself till his face was glowing and scalded.

'Say "Good Sam!" '

'Well you are a good boy, my love. A real good boy.'

Sam began to cough, whooping and barking, purple in the face, clawing at the air, eyes popping as he fought for breath. Above, the choir awoke and joined in the anthem, the house echoing with the clamour of coughing. When his fit had passed, Sam lay on his side on the motheaten hearth rug exhausted, executing a doleful foghorning wail of misery. He had had his finest hour. Nothing was altered, for all that his herculean love had laboured to achieve a work beyond his years. The four precious milk bottles stood in a row on the table, testimony of love. His mother came downstairs, pulled him to his feet.

'He's coming home. Better get up to bed. Take something up there to have.'

He trailed upstairs, followed by Minnie holding a tray on which three jamjars filled with milk accompanied three wooden plates of bread, cut in strange shapes and very slightly bloodstained.

Albert came home not with thunderous knocking but with a swift turn of his latchkey. All was silent in his house, a glow of embers not quite extinct in the kitchen grate, which he fed and poked at, until a single flame curved out to lick round a log. He clumped upstairs. He glanced into the children's bedroom at the three silent forms huddled down in the double bed, feigning sleep. The khaki warrior stood in the doorway of his own bedroom and surveyed his prone wife lying in her dressing gown on the candlewick cover, a grey twilit woman.

'I stopped by at your mum's. She told me you were all bad. Poor old girl.'

'I'm sorry, Bert.' She struggled to sit up. 'I'm ever so sorry my love, they got whooping cough, see. You're not angry are you?'

'Silly cow! Why should I be angry?'

'Well, you know. You could well be. Spoiling your leave and not being up to giving you a proper welcome.'

'Can I get you anything, Min? Say the word if there's something I can do. I brought chocolate for the children.'

'Where did you manage to get hold of all that, for God's sake? We haven't seen sweets like that for donkey's years.'

He smiled a lop-sided grin, crookedly self-satisfied. 'Been working in the Officers' Mess a bit lately – they don't go short of much, I can tell you.'

He emptied his pockets of the democratically redistributed chocolate, pleased at Minnie's genuine astonishment. Then he sat down on the far corner of the bed in a friendly enough way, but made no effort to come closer. Minnie assessed the smile on his weasel-sharp features. It was equally sly and fugitive. That's it, he thinks I've got whooping cough, realised Minnie; hasn't had it himself; doesn't want to catch it: he won't bother me this time. Relief swept over her whole body in a great warm flush of pleasure, almost sensual.

'Where's your kit then, Bert? You haven't brought anything with you?'

'Can't stop this time, Min: just looking in to see if you need anything.'

The visiting hero let himself out. Minnie lay on the bed like a half-drowned swimmer recuperating on a raft, and heard the click of the latch, the quick march of boots purposefully making for the pub, the booze-soaked evenings, the smutty songs, and (with any luck, he thought, accelerating) a succulent bought girl in a hotel bedroom. As the fact of her reprieve dawned, the perishing cold of the room seemed to abate before a flow of warmth and vitality within herself. The smell of damp in the squalid little bedroom, which offended her highly-wrought senses in her pregnancy, dissolved away. She chuckled out into the darkening emptiness of the room. It all seemed a great joke. Her heart came up from the silted misery of months and years, floated to the surface like a salvaged wreck.

Sam heard the laugh. He felt like that too, released, off the hook: yet sad too, sad to the marrow of his being that his father could just clear off like that.

Minnie got up and dressed. She felt more herself, the seething stomach quelled, and her spirit full of purpose. 'My own darling Albert,' she wrote, in careful script mingling capitals and lower case letters indiscriminately, while the melting, cleansing tears fell on to the paper so many times recycled that it was grey and brittle, 'This comes to let you know my Beauty that your father has Let Me Be and am Forever thinking of you above all on Earth and in heaven my Angel, from Mother.' Weeping with delicious joy she read and re-read the letter, folded it into the envelope, and went up to say to Sam:

'I'm going out for an hour, I'll lock you in. You look after the others, Sam, I shan't be long.'

The door seemed to him to clang shut like iron gates. From the window, he watched her figure half running down the street in the direction of Devizes Cemetery, in the gloom, with the white rectangle of the envelope pale in her hand. She looked gleeful, sprightly. He opened the window and began to cough out of it after her, imperatively, but she was already rounding the corner, out of earshot. When Rosie awoke, he and Billie took turns competing as to who could moan out the loudest, to drown her lonely sobbing; and Sam scratched the flaking skin of his wrists and calves so raw that the eczema bled.

Eight

Thirty pieces of silver she had given the woman for making this bargain. Once she went and implored the woman to tell her the address to which the baby boy had been taken. With tears streaming down her face she clasped her upper arms, she could keep the money, she would pay more to get her son back, all she had or could borrow. Name any sum you like, I'll find it, mortgage my life to yourself, I don't mind, only I must have him back. She told her about Jim being missing, the need to undo the bargain.

'It's true, you did have a little boy, dear, of course,' said the woman gently. 'But don't you remember, the little thing was stillborn. Remember? You've got the death certificate. The poor little chap never suffered anything, he'd been dead in utero a long, long time. Think of it like that. He never saw the light of day, never grew into anything fully human, and now he's at peace. You'll feel so much better if you can see it like that.'

'No, no, we had it adopted. It didn't die. You know it didn't die. You took it away.'

The woman was very tender. She put her arm around Christina's shoulders, protecting her weakness, forgiving the slander.

'You've not told anyone about this, have you, dear?' Her benign tone menaced Christina, she shivered.

'Of course not. I couldn't.'

'That's all right then. The thing is, you see, you've been very unwell. You have, you know. After the birth you experienced what is called a psychotic reaction, it's not unusual in a mild form. You saw and heard things that weren't actually there. The doctor came and saw you. Don't you remember that? And now you've had another terrible shock, it's making you imagine things. You want a good rest.'

Christina paused. She wondered if she was going off her head. 'If he's dead, then, where's the grave?'

'My dear child. Don't ask about things that are only going to upset you, quite needlessly.'

'But where is his grave?'

'A stillborn child hasn't the status of a grown one if it has died at a very early stage in the pregnancy. We incinerate them. It's done quickly and privately, to spare the feelings of the parents. Now dear, can I advise you,' moving her toward the door, a busy official who has to return to work, '*not* to pursue this line of questioning. I'm not cross with you – your nerves are all shot to pieces, which is only natural, and I do understand, believe me I do – but I could actually get quite irritated. You're a nice, decent girl, and I'm sure you value your good name in the neighbourhood. *I* know, of course, that you're not one of these low, good-time girls. You want to be well thought of, you want to enjoy a superior type of future. So don't make me lose my temper. Be sensible. Look forward. Not back.'

They passed the filing cabinet as Christina was being marched out. She thought, there might be papers in there. She thought, I might be going mad. Perhaps there was no boy. But there was. She felt frightened, cowed. Habitually submissive, she caught the threatening tones of authority. She knew from experience, you couldn't win against these people; girls couldn't. But she noted the filing cabinet, even so.

'Is Polly still here, the orderly?'

'Left for a service life, I believe, a while ago. We have quite a turnover of staff here as you might expect, what with one thing and another. Goodbye now.'

Later that evening Christina, very agitated, imagined Jim

77

coming home and being told she had been going with other men, Negros from the US base, over-sexed Yankees whose appetite and uninhibited potency were legendary amongst British troops; how it might be suggested to him that Florence was not his child; and how, in his pain, so shy and passionate a man, he might go off forever and leave them both. And how, even if he didn't come back and was already dead, his Florence would be called a bastard in the town. She minded absolutely what people thought and said about her.

Lilian watched her sister grappling with some internal enemy, sitting with furrowed forehead, hunched, wringing a handkerchief in her fingers. She took her in her arms.

'What is it, my love? Please tell Lily. Tell me anything. We're as close as two people can possibly be.'

'I'm working something out, Lily.' She looked carefully at her sister, as if stretching up on tiptoe to peer over a wall of darkness.

'Let me work it out with you, Chrissie. Let me share it. Whatever hurts you hurts me as well. Whatever you mind about is my trouble too.'

Christina cupped the big, plain face so close to hers, blurred with tenderness, between her two palms. 'Consider Lily,' she said. ' "Even Solomon in all his glory was not arrayed like one of these." ' The love growing between them surprised her constantly. Lilian was a necessity now, a requirement for life, like bread, like water. But she would never tell her.

The following morning, the agony had grown so acute that it surged like electricity through Christina's veins, pain charged her like a current of power. No, I won't accept this, she thought, I'll get Jim's baby back. If I lose this chance, I lose him for the rest of time.

She rapped on the door of the maternity home. 'Let me in. I have to see the matron.'

She marched straight into the office. The woman looked up from her paperwork. She had been up most of the night. Her face was brutal with tiredness.

'Shut the door behind you,' she said. 'What do you want?' She remained seated behind the desk, arms folded, all blue uniform and starched white cuffs, leaving Christina to stand.

'I want my baby back. I want him and I will have him. You get him back for me or I'll go to the police.'

'I will say this to you once and once only. You are making yourself a nuisance by refusing to accept reality. Your behaviour leads me to feel that you have not recovered fully from the mental trouble you suffered after the birth of your child. Don't worry, it's quite common – hallucination, hearing voices, lack of grasp on reality. We have hospitals for people suffering from postnatal psychosis. There are powerful drugs available to treat it these days. You would only need to be kept in for a matter of months – it's not a life sentence as it used to be in the bad old days. To do you and your family a good turn, I could get in touch with a specialist right away, and have you admitted within hours.' She placed her fingers lightly on the telephone receiver. Its brown cord snaked down into the blank wall. 'Is this what you would like me to do?'

Christina shook her head. She covered her mouth with the back of her hand; the choking sobs crammed the well of her throat, unuttered. The woman took her hand off the telephone.

'Good morning then, Mrs Llewellyn. I don't expect we shall meet again.'

She turned for home. As she walked, the world swung away from her, so that she moved suspended in vertiginous space. The flat road dipped and tilted. Familiar faces assumed a ghastly and alien perspective: the world was a hall of mirrors. She walked amongst its flocking shadows like a ghost. They stood back to let her pass. The children pointed. She groped along the walls and hedges for balance and direction. But I did try, at least I honestly tried, she pleaded.

Unable to swallow her food, Christina lost a stone and a half in ten days. The food stuck in her throat, it was so dry. They fed her cups of tea like a little girl, for when she raised the cup herself, her hands trembled convulsively. At night she could not fall into a proper, healing sleep, but when she did doze woke again screaming, until the doctor prescribed the Neurinase sleeping tablets which put her out like a light, blessedly. Letters came. The War Office deeply regretted that, though no body had been found, her husband must be presumed dead. The thunderbolt of shock at this epitaph on official paper felled her physically to the ground. The RAF benevolent fund wished to know if material help was needed. A cheque arrived for the last month of Jim's wages. Each message dealt a further mortal blow.

One evening a deviant V2 rocket, sailing over one presumed target, London, failed to reach another in Bristol or Southampton, and exploded in the middle of nowhere. For miles around they saw the bright flash and heard the supersonic bang. A ton of explosive left a deep crater in the allotments at the edge of town, exciting the interest of small clambering boys, and causing tremendous casualties amongst the Brussels sprouts. Though 'The Limes' Maternity Home was not in the immediate vicinity, the blast wrecked enough of its structure for the authorities to take the long-sought opportunity of closing it down, and moving its dubious matron from the area. The filing cabinet still fixed on as a means of extenuation by Christina's mind was no more. It was spirited away to the land of vanishing into which so much of their world poured. She could obtain no visa to that land where the lost lie. She had done her best to get there, and failed. She would have to put the little boy to sleep in her mind, and let him rest. She understood this.

In glittering morning light Christina sat looking from her bedroom window. Florence slept on in her crib, and would continue to sleep for at least two hours longer, till eight o'clock. She was ten weeks old, thriving and full, it seemed, of private inward jokes, which had her gurgling with what seemed to be laughter through most of the day. Florence was understood to be very forward and precocious. Everyone said so. Christina's whole attention was now focused on her daughter. In her devastated, cloven life, Florence now represented the embodiment of futurity. There was no future tense save in the book of the baby's life, scarcely yet opened at the first page of the first chapter.

Spring was invading the bitter winter of 1944-45. From her window, Christina's eyes lingered on the silk-stemmed crocuses, their delicate softness shouldering aside the trampled crust of winter. The daffodils struck their green bayonets up through the cold. They stood so tall and proud, facing outwards to the road, she thought of them as vigilantes, defensive of the lives within the terrace. It was impossible not to respond to the power of beneficence surging up from the war-weary earth. Even in her present crisis Christina responded to this prelude to spring, in which all Europe would inevitably participate. Victory Day was visibly coming near. Allied troops had liberated Brussels, Antwerp, Athens; the British and Canadian armies had reached the Rhine. Soon, on the second day of April, Christina would attain her twentieth birthday. Unlikely hopes, huge and fantastic, sometimes took possession of her being; she shook with the killing intensity of hope. Here was the rocking duck, she sat with her hand on its agreeable, smooth-worn head, she could see Florence seated there before another year was through; she could see Jim holding her on, sailing her across the wooden boards, keeping her buoyed on the still, idyllic pool of childhood. Feeling absent-mindedly in the pockets of a pinafore she had not worn for months, Christina's fingers had come upon the wishbone of a long-eaten chicken. She could not help taking this as a good omen. The world seemed a system of signs and clues at such times, alleviating her heart-shattered condition. He would be found, he would find his way home. The War Office, the Air Ministry, His Majesty's Government, God and all his Legions had killed him in their minds but in hers he was imperishable. She pored over the remaining beloved baby, reinvesting her hope in the healthy, growing child. While Florence was so tangibly there, she could not undertake the belief that Jim could fail to return to see her. The ancient chestnut trees at the far end of the terrace were pushing forth great gummy buds like cones.

Under her bed she kept a case containing her favourite, private things. She pulled it out now and unlocked it. Here were letters from Jim, tied round with a red ribbon, and the picture of Florence and herself taken outside the Cathedral. There was a set of pink silk underwear she had been given before the war, and kept for best, and trophies from her childhood, rag dolls and a bag of marbles stolen from her brother. At the bottom lay the family Bible which she had long ago requisitioned as an object of special character. She heaved it out on to the bed, ran her fingertips over the rusty leather binding and unclasped the iron locks. Its immense weight impressed her, and its age. Turning to the family tree, she read through the Jeremiahs and Jacobs, the Abigails and Susannahs of the last century; then she read solemnly through her own generation, George, Minnie, Lilian, herself, and their issue.

'Florence Sarah Amelia,' she wrote, 'beloved daughter of James and Christina, born 10.27 a.m., 18th December, 1944.'

Underneath she wrote:

'James, beloved son of James and Christina, also born on the evening of 18th December, 1944.'

She wrote slowly and painstakingly, in her best handwriting. Her hand paused. She could not fabricate the death of the younger James. She left the inscription to stand as testimonial to her final acceptance of the lost child. Christina had a fearful respect for the written word. If something was written down, it assumed a truth

81

and finality which it could never achieve by hanging in the air unverified. She felt the dignity of what she had written, its legitimation of a simple version of the past. Repeatedly, she closed and opened the book, to familiarise her vision with the authorised facts. In the depths of the book, the pressed violets, cowslips, poppies shifted the positions of their frail, papery forms.

Outside the window shoots from buried corms and bulbs had cut their passage through the chalky soil; their new buds lit the ground like thousands of candles. It was the turning point, the crossroads of the old year. She clasped the locks round the creaking book. Then she wrapped the Bible in layers of cloth and tied it with a length of cotton, in a complicated knot so that she would know at once if it had been tampered with. She replaced it at the base of the suitcase, which she stowed under the bed. When she got up, she found that the baby was already awake, and studying her with critical eyes from the crib.

Minnie had arrived when Christina came downstairs with Florence, ready to heat her bottle. She was nattering dolefully about how sad she had been when Albert wasn't able to stay at home for his leave for fear of catching the whooping cough. But something jaunty in her voice and eye would keep declaring itself. Christina recognised the tones of suppression. She looked at Minnie suspiciously, from the doorway.

'You are officially out of quarantine now then, Minnie?'

'Oh yes, don't you worry Chrissie, I wouldn't have brought our germs round for your little Flossie to catch now would I?'

'You look healthy enough. Don't come too near though, perhaps. Could you boil up Florence's water for her bottle, Mum?'

'Oh yes, I'm lovely. Can't complain at all,' said Minnie, managing not to look insulted.

'You even look happy.'

'Shouldn't do really, should I? Our Albert came home on leave and couldn't enjoy his nuptial bliss because of the contamination. Real sad isn't it?'

Minnie forced the joyous grin down from the corners of her mouth. Liberation was hard to feign. She'd won a war. She'd escaped. She wasn't destroyed. Oh God, the good God; he'd seen her plight and let her off. The angel of Death hadn't visited her. She sat and reviewed her situation. Now she could eat. Her pregnancy had stabilised; her hair was lustrous. She took cod liver oil and orange juice and rose hip syrup; and her body had softened and bloomed like the golden flesh of peaches in Italian sunlight. She hadn't felt so young, even when she was young. She thought of how she kept wanting to burst into giggles, bend double with laughter. It was good to feel free to visit Devizes Cemetery more than just the rationed once a week without worrying that people thought her mad. She could indulge herself. The little Albert was near her heart. He was a breath away; around every corner. Behind shut doors the essence of him had just whisked in and vanished. She felt most surely she would find him. As her body firmed outwards and she experienced the quickening of the baby within her, its winged spirit-body's moth-like fluttering, she had allowed herself to think: 'This is him again: being born of me: because I wanted him so: it's a sign: he's coming again.' She felt slightly ashamed of her own elation as, remembering poor old Chrissie's predicament, she watched Florence being sat up for her feed. Obviously Jim was dead, but Chrissie wouldn't admit it.

'No news then, my love?' she asked Christina in a hushed, respectful tone.

'No news.'

With that ravaged look of tension, Chrissie's beauty was definitely on the wane, Minnie noted. You could see how she'd look when she was fifty: bony, taut. And quite honestly with the best will in the world Minnie couldn't see that this Florence they all idolised was anything to write home about. An ugly little thing, baldish, bow-legged, certainly not a patch on the first Albert for beauty and good temper.

'Diddums den,' she remarked to Florence, in compensation. 'Who's Auntie's ickle girl?' Florence glared balefully from her mother's lap.

'We knew someone whose dad was missing presumed dead ten months,' said Lilian. 'One day back he comes whistling down the road with his kitbag over his shoulder, and all the kids ran off screaming they'd seen a ghost. We don't despair, do us Chrissie?'

Lilian, clumping around in the flapping bags of her workman's trousers, towered above Minnie. What a sight. Albert mocks her something wicked behind her back when he's in a good mood. She looked with distaste at Lilian's fingernails grimy with coaldust, fingerprinting everything from humping the coal, her latest trade.

'You want to stand up to that husband of yours, Minnie.' Lilian was always free with this advice. 'He only knocks you about because you won't resist him. Get the kitchen knife to him next time and see how he likes that.'

'Shush, Lil, don't speak like that. What a thing to say.'

'Well, it's true, Mum. Min's always whining at him, I've heard her voice when he's around, creeping and grovelling, it's a standing invitation: I'd quite like to kick her myself when I hear it.'

'Lilian!'

'Well, not really. But I'd like to sock *him* one in the eye, I'd see him off I can tell you.'

'That's what his mum tells me,' said Minnie plaintively. 'She says I make him worse by lying down and taking it. I know I am too weak. But I'm made weak. Some people are just like that, Lil. You can't see that because you're made on a different scale – and besides, not being married, you don't really know what it feels like. He's all right really, he's not too bad. He just wants understanding.'

'It won't be a black eye next time, it'll be a broken neck. That's my understanding of poor dear Albert.'

'Don't keep on, Lily,' said Mother, her back turned. 'Minnie's life is her life. Let her be.'

'And Minnie's death is her death,' muttered Lilian.

To Minnie the whole conversation seemed spurious. Albert was irrelevant; he and his foul temper were far away. He was incarcerated in some steaming kitchen boiling spuds for soldiers, and he could not get at her. Her life, her precious life, was contained and safe within a globe of glass in which she enjoyed invisibility and freedom.

'How's your Sam?' asked Christina, taking her attention for a moment from Florence.

'Oh he's all right.' Minnie shrugged. Sam was a drag on her, a prosaic matter which somehow could not hold her interest.

'He's a real good boy, your Sam,' said Lilian. 'He may look like something the dog brought in, but he's got no harm in him, and he'd die to please you, Min.'

'Yes, well, at least he don't rack the house with coughing any more. But his eczema is something shocking. Still, he can act tractable from time to time: he'll look after the little ones for hours together and make sure they don't burn themselves.'

Mother switched her attention from Christina to Minnie, and swiftly brought it back again. The trouble was, there was nothing you could do for poor old Min. She needed too much, on every

hand. She was useless and helpless. She had been an accidental
child from the time she first took her tottering steps, launching
herself from Mother to Dad (a source of pride at the time of course,
despite being six months late), fell heavily and dislocated her collar
bone. When it was mended, she ran into a door and did it again.
Nothing could be achieved for Minnie. It really was best to leave
her to her own devices. Although a four-year-old boy left in charge
of a household did shock her. Minnie was getting a little touched in
the head.

'Anyway, Mother and everyone, I've got something to tell you.'
Brightness and bliss livened her voice.

'What's that then?'

'I'm expecting a happy event.'

'You can't mean it. You can't mean you're expecting again? Oh
Min.'

'Well you're a proper let-down – you don't sound very excited
about it, Mum. I'm happy.'

'It was the shock. You've got so many already, and not enough
money coming in to feed and clothe them.'

'I don't neglect them, Ma, if that's what you're inferring. They're
all right. Anyway, this one is different.'

Pausing, Minnie looked round for fellow feeling. No one seemed
to want to credit her with any importance. They did not see that
this child was the gift of God. She filled the vacancy of their
response with her anger.

'Oh it's all right for Christina, isn't it. She can do anything. I
have a baby and it's a shame for the world that scum like me ever
bothered to bring anything into it. Christina has a baby and it's a
bleeding miracle – a sodding Nativity Play – Three Wise Men from
the bleeding East expected at any moment – Dad up all night and
making faces at it, Mum boiling up the milk for its bottle. Is it
teething then, poor little thing? Does it want its nappy changing?
It's an honour for us to do it for you. Don't let poor old Minnie get
anywhere near it though, she'll give it nasty germs. Don't let
Minnie's filthy brats in, they'll make noises and wake the little
darling up. Fancy that ratbag Minnie thinking of adding to the
population though, what a bloody cheek what a nerve, doesn't she
know who she is? That's right Chrissie, you run off snivelling. Go
on, lie on the bed and have a real good cry . . .' She followed
Christina into the hall and ranted up the stairs after her. 'Don't
shed too many tears though, you might spoil your pretty face and

85

make your eyes all puffy. All right, turn the tap down, they're all coming up to comfort you.'

Lilian shoved her aside as she leapt up the stairs.

'How *could* you!' Their mother followed Lilian. 'Don't you have any idea of what Chrissie's going through? I'm ashamed of you my girl.'

The righteous vision faded, and Minnie sat down and wept, disgraced. Later Christina was helped downstairs, eyes still brimming with pearly tears, to confront her sister, who had cried herself into a state of red disfigurement. Minnie felt so grieved for Christina in her beauty and pathos. She felt so sorry. All the generous love in her welled up in response to the wrong she had done her sister. And after all, Christina had been young Albert's teenage aunt, and had loved the little fellow most truly, and this should be an eternal bond between them.

'I'm ever so sorry, my love. I don't know what came over me.'

'It's perfectly all right, Minnie. Think nothing of it. We'll forget it now. It never happened.'

Nine

The young mothers of the village of Santa Hermione, ten miles north-east of Naples, had been sitting lined up with their backs to the church wall. In their emaciated faces, the eyes were huge and black. Their thin arms hung limp at their sides as if waiting for a puppeteer to jerk the strings. Their countenances were without expression, blank as the faces of the dead. Beside each mother was a small pile of tins, containing Yankee rations of corned beef or mutton. A growing crowd, mainly of American soldiers but also containing British and Canadian servicemen, gathered in the square confronting the mothers. The crowd shifted and murmured. Sometimes it emitted a great belly-laugh, which it rapidly stifled. Those at the back pushed those at the front forward, but the front row was troubled, stood its ground, showed reluctance to be launched forward. Jim had strolled into the square from his billet to buy a bottle of the local vino when he saw the gathering. He entered it and elbowed his way forward, to see what was going on. At first he could not understand what he saw. He had liked to smile at the Italian girls and be kissed by them too, touched by the sensual grace with which they clothed their ravening search for food to sustain them through the famine, drawn by their ink-black hair and gypsy faces and their availability. It wouldn't matter, once or twice. Everyone was doing it. But then he had pictured Christina. The Hiraeth rose in him as a habitual moral code might have risen in another man. There was no desire dissociated from her. To take her back a dose of VD; to impart the seeds of the death and destruction he had witnessed would be to have endured for nothing at all. Long-term yearning had for him a passionate, accumulated force, which overlaid the flickerings of present desire.

He was at the front of the queue, staring at the line of Italian mothers with their dead faces, perched on wooden seats at intervals of a yard or so, each with her small trove of tins. It might have been market day. The women were respectably dressed, in black. They sat with straight backs against the luminous white wall of the ancient village church. The church bell tolled. It ceased. He still stupidly failed to grasp the significance of the occasion. What were they all waiting for? A hint of death was in the air, a fume, as if they all awaited the dropping of nerve gas, the lighting of an overdue fuse. A drunken GI was being shoved forwards, his comrades hooting and joking (but subdued, uneasy, now that reality was in view). Here, Jim grasped it, of course. The mothers were on sale for tins of food. The GI put down two cans on his woman's pile. She placed her hands upon them, closing her eyes, opening her legs. The GI fumbled to unbutton his flies; bent his legs. Rapidly his haunches worked. It was over. The soldier returned, head down, angrily butted past the throng, loped off. An atmosphere of shame hung over the crowd of men, like the smell of disease, though these were men who had seen and done most of what there is available to see and do in the way of human atrocity. Only the blank eyes of the women registered no shame, but looked straight ahead, or at the food they had earned for their children.

He turned to face the crowd, he plunged back through its eddying ranks, his stomach a well of bile. Beyond lay the circle of the village, planes of dimpled light on whitewash, green sprays of

87

boughs splashed with golden light. Line upon line of washing at miscellaneous angles to the houses hung motionless white flags out in the radiant air. Beyond again, in a foreshortened vista which seemed straining to enter between the houses rose the ancient vineyards, avenues of shadow-dark olives, and then the mountains to the left, the curve of the great Bay to the right. They had swum in the astringent, saline balm of the sea and he had thought of home, the bays, Bracelet, Brandy Cove, Pwyll Du. Dominating the whole scene Vesuvius towered, waiting for his time to come round.

When, in March, Vesuvius erupted, he remembered the mothers at the church of Santa Hermione. He had now visited Pompeii. He knew the everyday attitudes in which the ancient dead impersonated eternal life. A solid-seeming tree of smoke formed and swelled in the air above Vesuvius, several miles in diameter. The ash began to sift down from its graceful, larch-like branches. The lava flow rolled crackling downhill toward San Sebastiano. As the volcanic flares like Roman candles fountained from the crater at night, fizzing into the Bay, he remembered the line of mothers. The whole world the following morning was an inch deep in grey ash. He imagined the women sitting there throughout the apocalyptic catastrophe, like funerary monuments awaiting the end of time. The ash accrued on their patient heads, greying the black. It sifted down on to thin garments and shrouded their hoarded treasure of American meat. He had visited the underworld and met the shades, silent, inturned, the violated women turned to stone by the war. The dead do not feel the fall of ash, gathering around them eternally. He thought of Christina, of her family, of his own mam. He imagined them starving thus, mouths flaking with thirst, reduced to final exposure. He would shelter, he would protect, he would defend. But Vesuvius' vile temper poured out its inchoate vomit all the while.

The memory was over half a year old already, yet entirely vivid. He had walked down the avenues of golden light for a brief month, he had viewed the temple at Paestum, its columns pink in the sunset. Then, moving on to Rome, he had received the blessing of Pope Pius, twice for good measure, and been photographed with Alastair in front of St Peter's. At the Opera House, the tempestuous warblings of Verdi's music had made him think of home and the steelmen's singing, but loaded with grandeur and glamour beyond anything he had been born to know. His heart melted and rained down hot as lava at the sound. At the core of destruction had been discerned this amoral glory. They sang for the Germans, then they sang for him. When he got back home life would be expanded by these horizons that had been opened for him: the classic light glowing on the white marble that was sculpted to sinuous flesh. Around the monuments poured the silent, sallow people ready to die for a chicken's gizzard or a bit of intestine to sustain them and their families; under the statuary waited the syphilitic children thrusting their flat childish chests at you. It would not be possible to take back a censored memory. The voluptuousness of beauty could not be purged of squalor.

Then he was posted out to join the partisans pushing the Germans back up to the Gothic Line. He came down with a third bout of malaria. The family which constituted the entire population of the mountain village in which he lay in hiding was wiped out in reprisals by the retreating Germans, save for one old woman, all skin and bone, who habitually lay in a filthy corner and was easily mistaken for a pile of rags by the German troops, while he lay beneath the floorboards in a feverish underworld. Two months later he was declared officially dead by His Majesty's Government.

He had viewed the landscape of Wiltshire many times over in the malarial dream world of the mountain village, netted down under raving fever, sweat pouring out of his forehead, his skull one globed migrainous ache. The woman had wetted his mouth with red wine. When he focused his eyes on the bottle he thought he was drinking blood. Logic of war leads inevitably to the drinking of blood, his malarial mind thought. I must be able to do this: adjust, dehumanise, until I can temper my thirst on the blood of fellow men. Given for me, the Christ of them. So he did drink. Like a communion he received the dark vintage upon his cracked lips and into his bloodstream reverently.

'Vino?' The priestess was offering more blood. Vino though, it is red wine not blood she offers. He had escaped: a narrow escape. In the malarial haze he laughed out loud. When he raised his left hand he saw that the back was covered with carbuncles. He laughed again. The old ash between the aerodrome and the hillfort at Sarum was gnarled with growths like this, he saw it most clearly. His temperature rose steeply. His body was one scalding ache, very heavy. His mind was light and airborne. It sailed up, buoyed on fever, till it found itself above the great Salisbury Plain and saw the early morning mists swirl like tides below him in every direction. It saw the little mounds of the round barrows, like grassy breasts. The silent circle of the Henge with the fallen monoliths came within his aerial view, and when he looked back his dreaming eye took in the spire of the Cathedral like a fine needle pricking a cloud layer of ashen grey. His clairvoyant eye cast about; it stared and searched. It seemed to be hunting out someone lost in the immensity of the aerial map: someone lost both in space and time.

Now wedged in a corridor of the London to Salisbury train, Jim sees the landscape in reality but to him it seems dreamlike compared with the actuality of his visions. The train has passed through Andover. It is on its last lap, but creeping so slowly, lamely, halting with a clank, running back a few yards, having another go, never picking up steam. American troops combing the mountain villages rescued him and sent him to Rome where he got involved in a lottery to send a few men home on leave: and, incredibly, won a place on the plane. He is still sick. Through his body's weakness, hardly able to stand but that the press of soldiers wedges him upright, his charged heart keeps up a hurtful hammering. It pounds out Chrissie's name as his destination, too urgently, and he thinks, Chrissie be there for me Chrissie by all that we hold sacred don't have altered, don't have turned away. There is fear in meeting her, in case, just in case. The only rest is when his eye settles on the soft swell and dip of the countryside outside the rocking windowpane. He leans in relief to its gentle curvature, the gradual tilt of descending contour toward its rising sister, the huge simplicities of light-reflecting green surfaces. Blessedness of sanctuary quietens his eye.

He half sleeps, jerks awake. He glimpses blue overalls, steely light on tools as the gang of elderly, arthritic railwaymen moves cumbrously off the track. The illness gives his arrival an alarming discontinuity. For hours he was carried, almost off his feet (he is not a tall man) by the jam-packed soldiers in the train corridor; the next minute he is voided, with his kitbag, unbalanced on the platform of Salisbury station, weakly single. He staggers into a mass of yellow, primroses and daffodils in tubs; the lemon-yellow light of late afternoon, dancing with motes. Spring is far advanced. The jostle of the ordinary and everyday encompasses him. The echo of a woman's laughter in the vaulted gloom where he must somehow find a ticket to surrender rings round. Porters hurling mail sacks utter broad dialect. It is all a shock, this familiarity. Life has gone on without me. There has been no war here.

He toils up the hill from the station, homewards, breathing hard, past the steep tulip-filled gardens, dark pink against the soot-caked embankment, round the corner toward St Christopher's Road. They begin to greet him and exclaim; they clap him on the back; they pump his hands, the momentary beaming faces, caught in late light. Their names he cannot recollect. His mouth smiles, his heart stampedes, his long shadow journeys before him like a giant's, coming home. Yet how slow it seems, the lifetime spent labouring upward here where the air becomes almost too thin and rarefied for human breathing: the final homecoming.

The house is surely far smaller than when he left it, a doll's house boxed between its fellows. Womenfolk gather him in to it, their screams of excitement rising like news cawed from a disturbed rookery. Tears pour down his mother-in-law's face. A vast girl embraces him hugely, gruffly. There is a mêlée of children. 'And are you Sam, you little rascal?' The boy claps bony arms round his uncle's neck and bursts into tears, since this seems the right thing for the occasion.

'Where's my Chrissie?'

'Upstairs. Sleeping. Not had a wink for nights –'

He crashes up the stairs, four at a time. Sam sits still deliciously weeping, clasping the kitbag in lieu of the man. Mother wipes her eyes and starts to fill the kettle.

The room is filled with gentle breathing. Closed curtains filter a little dusky light articulating the shape of a woman in the bed, lying on her front with dark hair dishevelled, one bare arm crooked round her sleeping head. Time ends here. The drumroll of heartbeats goes silent. He is over the threshold where earth falls away, yields to truce and armistice, a new heaven and a new earth. Softly he starts to move round the bed to meet her from the direction toward which her face is turned. He passes the shadowy forms of the familiar toys, the rocking horse and the rocking duck, a wooden chair piled with clothes neatly folded, a dark rectangular box draped with a tasseled shawl. Glancing into the box he sees the face of a child.

He kneels at the head of Florence's crib in an attitude of worship. The stiff skirts of the air force greatcoat fan out over the floorboards around him; his cap is pushed to the back of his head. He does not try to touch the baby, but his hand draws back the curtain a few inches so that he can see the face more clearly.

Florence studies and analyses the sudden face that is presented to her. At nearly four months she has compendious knowledge of the universe. She has scanned a full range of possible human experiences, from bliss to boredom, through humour to agony; she has been cast out and gathered back in; she has loved with the fullness of a milk-filled belly and responded with murderous fury to a sense of deprivation. Florence knows the mysteries of hard and soft, dark and light. She can join her hands together to unify the contraries of the world, and pass a rattle dextrously from one to another. She knows reality by its smell and by its taste; burning green of foliage scalds her eye in the park amongst the rinsing flute music of the birds. Now a new face is shown, a pale planet from skies beyond my world lodges here, and fixedly stares. Like me it smiles; like me it weeps. Yes, thought Florence, yes, yes I will be pleased to accept you as my vassal, you are permitted to assume the likeness of reality, and be conveyed in my orbit, and be framed by my knowledge of you.

The baby crows and puts up a hand to the cheek of her father. She kicks her feet up energetically and waves her arms in wild circles to express gratification. She catches his offered index finger in a firm grip and takes it to her mouth. The new face comes nearer, smiling not with his mouth (she saw that) but with pale blue eyes crinkling up with laughter.

Like Lazarus still entombed, her mouth gagged as if with grave wrappings, Christina struggles up from her sleep. She kneels on the bed staring. Daylight through the partially drawn curtain throws a ribbon of white light all down her cotton nightgown, irradiating the blue of one eye as she panics there, wordless, racing-hearted.

The slate-blue figure stretches out one arm for her, as if to rescue her from drowning, the baby having tethered the other hand in its tenacious grip.

'Oh, Chrissie, who's this?' he bursts out.

'That's Florence. That's your daughter, Jamie.'

'Come here Chrissie, oh come *here* can't you.'

Their tears well and spill, they are awash, they cry healing salt all over one another's cheeks, shaking with sobs, they are washed and blessed by the sharing of tears, and they kiss each other's wet mouths again and again.

He is fainting with weakness. She sees his face drawn thin, and it is lined, so that he appears less twenty-seven than thirty-seven; and his skin has an unhealthy yellowish tinge. His hands are pitted with pockmarks, and they tremble on her face.

'Are you ill, Jamie?'

'Malaria. Just ridiculously weak. Can I hold her?'

Florence's first sensual memory is of her forehead fallen inward against the fibrous material of an Air Force greatcoat, scratching her silken skin, discomfort more delicious than fleece or down. But he feels he ought to have washed his hands before he took up her perfection in his red-stained hold.

'My blessed lovely Chrissie.' The miracle has come about, they are together whole and entire. The comprehensive intentions of Death which have included samples from every family in Europe in its reckoning has let them go scot-free; almost.

'How am I going to be able to kiss you properly for God's sake with this baby between us? How do I put it down?'

He opens his greatcoat wide and wraps Christina away inside it with him. The white wraith of Christina buried there becomes warm flesh. His ghosts and her ghosts file off to the extreme perimeter of their universe. She incarnates herself in his hold. Yet the softness and warmth of her body under the light cotton is that of a foreigner. He aches with reticence as he takes her unfamiliarity to himself. The brass buttons and buckle of the tunic of his battledress dig into her. The purple-faced baby on its parents' bed rants and flails indignant fists at its exclusion. They laugh.

'She's in a right old temper now,' says Christina. 'She's got a will of her own, your daughter. She won't be left out of anything.'

'I've got something here for her to play with, if I can find it. Here, will it hurt her?'

'Well, I don't know. Whatever is it?'

'A bit of pumice from Vesuvius. I bought it in Pompeii as a souvenir – you know, the city that was caught in the eruption centuries ago, and preserved intact by lava. Can she have it?'

Christina fingers the triangular wedge of cool grey matter, its satin-smooth surfaces.

'It can't do her much harm.'

She goes back into the greatcoat while Florence transiently distracts herself by analysing the fragmentary relic of the stoppage of time in the city of the dead.

Ten

They were being conceived, Florence's father and mother, as one flesh, in Christina's narrow bed with the baby's crib at the foot. In a sea of sheets and blankets they were wordlessly swimming like the original egg and her incoming partner, the fused dual cell that journeys down the channel of being, eyeless and self-involved. Together, their eyelids tight-shut upon the one pillow, they multiplied and divided; they teemed with one another. They were implanted in the curving wall of the containing universe, that is safe and nourishes its conceptions. They were growing in strength and beauty, like the embryo that turns and tumbles and plays in its own ocean. They lay with the palms of their hands covering each other's foreheads, prior to birth, knowing no language, recollecting no evil. Fronds of underwater shadow, the last strands of time, wavered upon their minds' eye before it was finished. Perfected, they were being born, Christina and James. They were being discharged altogether from the wounding, wounded universe of time and space. They lay bathed in sweat like the amniotic fluids, beyond the ruptured membrane, selves coalesced into self. They opened their eyes. 'My baby,' said Jim, meaning Christina.

'Shall I just see how she is?' whispered Jim, hours later.

'She's fine, darling. She's nicely asleep,' murmured Christina, nestling up to her husband drowsily, with one arm staying him, encircling his naked torso.

'Well, I'll just have a look.'

'Don't. She's fine, really. Stay in the warm with me. Don't go.' She kissed the side of his breast. He reached down for his cigarettes and matchbox beside the bed, extracted one and put it back unlit, and, kissing Christina soothingly, surreptitiously slid out his legs.

'Think I ought to just make sure, though, Chrissie.'

94

'Sure of what?'

'Well, that she's still alive.'

'Of course she's alive,' said Christina, sitting up in bed with tender exasperation. 'Babies are supposed to sleep, Jim. And she's sleeping. We ought to count our blessings.'

'Yes, but the thing is, Chrissie, I can't hear her breathing.'

On tiptoe he manoeuvred round the bed and listened carefully at the cradle hood.

'I can't hear anything.' He put his ear to within six inches of her gentle open mouth. 'Oh my God, what are we going to do? I'm sure she's not breathing. Had I better pick her up and pat her back or something?'

'Jim.'

'What?'

'If you're going to give Florence artificial respiration every time she goes to sleep, we're going to be absolute wrecks within a fortnight. She's demanding enough as it is. A real little tartar. Strong as a horse. Really. Come on back to bed.'

He came back under the covers, drawing her nakedness against his, calling her whole body with his own, cradling her head in both his hands. He entered her softly now, his palms enclosed her breasts, his lips stroked her lips with tiny movements, they lay still and becalmed.

'I love you both so much, it is pain to love you so much. I can't bear for anything to hurt either of you, not so much as a hair of your heads, for the rest of your lives.'

He moved inside her body, one deep soft slide of his flesh into her private inwardness, toward the centre. The sea of sensation rippled outward in pleated waves following each other to the remotest edges of her infinity. Slowly the waves of pleasure sought the shoreline and never found it; and were succeeded by new waves swirling out after them yet more slow and glistening with light.

'You don't wish I'd given you a son?' Her voice spoke of its own accord in an urgent whisper, from some dark place of burial beneath the sea of pleasure. 'You aren't disappointed?'

'How can you ask me that, Chrissie? I love my little girl absolutely. What a question to ask me!'

'Oh good. I thought you might mind. Some men do, I know. They prefer sons. I didn't somehow want a boy, Jamie. I had some funny thoughts when I was pregnant.' She spoke so low, he could hardly catch the words. 'I don't know exactly, now. It all seems so

95

long ago. But whenever I thought of a boy I saw the war, the war was going on inside me – a newsreel was running in my mind of men rushing up to each other bristling with bayonets and things like that and they were going to stab each other, it went on and on like some dream you can't control. I saw my baby ending up covered in blood, killing and being killed, and it would have been for nothing, all my labour. I can't remember exactly though. Does it sound really silly to you, does it seem unforgivable?'

'That friend I had in Italy, Alastair – I told you about him – he would have known what you meant. He used to say the same sort of thing to me Chrissie. There was some line of poetry he used to be fond of quoting: "Was it for this the clay grew tall?" He used to ask it when things had been particularly bad, and there was a lull, very quietly, as if it genuinely puzzled him and there might be an answer if only he could hit on it. But Chrissie, you went through a hell of a time having the baby all on your own – but we've got the child we want now – and peace, very soon.'

'What happened to Alastair, Jamie?'

'He died at Camino. I'll have to get a travel permit to go up to Elgin and see his widow. A lovely man he was, Chrissie, father of two little girls. And he was gentle too, sensitive, well-spoken, not the sort of bloke you normally expect to meet with in the Other Ranks. We had some good laughs. And we went round Rome together – the Opera House. He knew all about opera, he told me a lot. I appreciated it all a hell of a lot more through him. You won't mind my going to see his wife? He would have come to you if it had been the other way round.'

'Oh thank God, thank God it isn't.'

Immorally thanking God for the benefit accruing to herself from the chance substitution of one mortal for another in the grand equation, she gratefully seized him back to herself; lay over him and quite roughly made him enter her, struggled there blindly weeping, and thrust her body hard between her one beloved and the other unredeemed terms in the algebra of the war, who had to be dead so that she could retain his life. I do not care, her body said, fierce, hard, as it rose and fell, her stomach taut, her breasts that had been milkless and wasted tense and firm, I do not care who suffers as long as I have possession of you; they do not matter, they are the sacrifice, let them lie. Beneath her ruthless appropriation of him, he was passive; and he hardly knew her in this iron sensuality for the shy creature he had married, but remembered suddenly the

96

other intimacy of the friend in the slit trench lying body to body, whom also he had kissed, with some such passion, final, murderous, holy, as lovers sharing a grave might kiss. Mud he tasted on his companion's cheek, the friction of the army greatcoat grazing his face, the flaring yellow of the promise of daffodils he gave him. Christina's spent body fainted down upon his, trembling and soft as rain.

Dawn light was coming up, and sprays of birdsong pierced the silence. Florence began to fidget in her sleep, and then to babble musically, finally to make distinct claims for attention. Christina dragged herself up from bed, pulling on a dressing gown.

'Couldn't you manage to feed her yourself, Chrissie?'

She swung round, holding the baby, scalded, defensive. 'At first I could. Then I stopped being able to.'

'That's good then. I'll be able to do it.'

He sat up holding Florence and singing softly to her while Christina went to heat the bottle. Then he insisted on giving the feed, the baby's head close up to his naked shoulder and her eyes scrutinising his features item by item. As Christina slept, and morning brightened, he felt that the quality of the happiness was so pure, it was almost unbearable. *I was a visitor at Genesis and witnessed God's Creation. Then I entered the wilderness, crossed the Jordan, and lived to see the land that overflows with milk and honey. Finally I came here to Bethlehem, to be a guest at the Nativity.*

'Jamie, when you were in Italy, did you have much to do with the – civilians?'

'Not a lot. How do you mean exactly though?'

'Nothing really. Just wondering generally.'

'Come on, Chrissie, what's on your mind?'

'Well, for instance, did you get the chance to meet any Italian – women?'

'Plenty.' He laughed. 'You couldn't move for them, pro-positioning the troops, for food, you see, and even for water. When we got to Naples, the water supply had been blown up. The people were trying to distil sea water to drink, they were that desperate. The women would sell themselves for a bottle of water.'

Christina turned over in bed, facing away from him.

'I hope you didn't buy one, Jamie.'

'Of course I didn't. Are you jealous, Chrissie?'

'Certainly not.'

'Turn round then.'

'Were they really beautiful, Jamie?'

'Who?'

'The Italian girls. Like in the pictures. Torrid and bosomy and dark and passionate.'

'They weren't bad. Not bad at all. A bit emaciated perhaps, for normal tastes, a bit skeletal, a bit puffy round the eyes from the effects of famishing. Oh for goodness' sake, Chrissie. You know you're the only one for me.'

'You needn't be sarcastic. I only wanted to know.'

She wants to know. The swaddled baby wants to know. Mother's spoilt darling is jealous of what he might have enjoyed seeing and doing in that foreign country where the clouds rain blood and the ground we tread is solid bone and gristle. She wants to know but she can't know.

He cast her a vicious look. It was his third night back, and he was feeling the effects of his illness and the shock, in weariness as her family pecked and fluttered round him, raucous in its excitement, and in jadedness and a tendency to bitter utterance. Now let's see, what shall I tell her that she can relish hearing? The ash sifts down from Vesuvius like cindery snowflakes. The air stinks of carbon.

'I saw a gorgeous full-breasted girl at Herculaneum.'

'Oh.'

'Yes Chrissie she'd been stifled by volcanic ash two thousand years or so ago. Most of the female flesh I've been lucky enough to see on my travels has been in the form of casts of corpses.'

Christina made no reply, her face buried in the pillow.

'Or on the other hand I could tell you about the prostitutes I've seen in Pompeii? Like to hear about them? Some were in the brothel, Chrissie, and others were busy at their profession in the gladiators' barracks.'

And the gladiators themselves were polishing the tools of their trade when Vesuvius went up, swaggering round under the sign of Priapus. He remembered how succulent and fertile the countryside was in those volcanic areas, cropping at least three times a year. The unseasonable beauty I have seen; the beauty of it all, inexpressible. I'll never forget it, never in a million years. Ash drifts down night after night, preserving all that I have seen, intact, exactly in its original form, but dead. A line of mothers up for sale by the church at Santa Hermione: black dresses up against a white

98

wall, blank faces, pumice grey. Christina lying here in a sulk wanting to know about the Italian women.

'Sorry, Jim. I didn't mean anything.'

'Yes, all right. Go to sleep now.'

'I don't feel at all sleepy. Tell me about Naples – and Rome. I want to know everything you've seen, I want to imagine it.'

'Some other time Chrissie. Sleep now.'

'Please tell me, darling – tell me about the opera.' She pestered him with kisses.

'I said "Some other time", and "Some other time" was what I bloody well meant. Look here, I'm ill, I'm sick, I've come home for a rest not to be nagged and badgered by some bloody ignorant female who knows nothing of real life. There's a storm in your teacup, all right Chrissie but I've seen slaughter, I've seen things you women in your cotton-wool world can never guess at. Nurse me, I'm sick. Feed me, I'm hungry. Warm me, I'm cold. You owe me. And when I speak, woman, try to understand plain English.'

Who is this stranger, this foreigner in my bed, thought Christina, shrinking back to her own side. Who has bruised me all over with experience, so that my lips are tender and swell and my arms are sorely fingerprinted where he has grasped them. Who now disclaims me. So that I am an exile, a cast-off, widowed here in our shared single bed. And it's so cruel since I have loosened all ties save this to him, from the moment he came back. I have cut adrift from my family and am distant with them. I have given Lilian to understand that I can no longer need her in the same way. I observe her wandering round the demarcation I've drawn round my private life, glad for my happiness but baffled for herself. I've a husband home, I'm a married woman: all other ties are counterfeit, I've cast off the stitches like wool in a finished garment.

But who is this hard-breathing stranger, after all? I scarcely know him. And his language of contempt. Words could lash you, sharply, without warning; a man's words. He could turn them against you, brutal and crude. He could bring them home from the barracks into the inmost chamber of self. He could make you flinch and cower back to the extreme edge of the bed, just by cracking this whip of words at you. 'Woman' he called you, 'woman' in a voice not his own. It is only our third night. Probably one day he will hit me, as Albert does Minnie. Probably he won't like me now that he's come home. He'll compare me adversely with the Italian women. He'll see through me. I'll be punished.

Jim lay looking at Christina's sleeping face by lamplight, still wet with tears he had not tried to assuage. He was leaning up on one elbow, inhaling the cigarette smoke deeply. He watched her with callous eyes as he smoked. I'm sick, he thought, that's what makes me such a vicious bastard; the sweats, the belt of pain round the skull, the heart that chimes and tolls, oscillating in my breast out of all control. A wonky ticker. My hand holding the fag, yellow and gnarled. Ash all over the sheets. Chrissie won't like that. He hastily brushed it off on to the floor. Golden light fell on her sleeping face, touchingly beautiful in its dejection. She is my denomination. If my faith to her goes, my nameless sacrilege had better be buried with Alastair in the ruins. He put his head down against her cheek, with ruth and remorse. Her breath came with small, faltering sobs as she woke.

'It was nothing. It was my own fault. Please forgive me, I asked for it. Jamie, don't take it so seriously. I've forgotten it already.'

'Chrissie, I'll never never say an unkind word to you again. Never. Never in my whole life.'

The following morning he was better rested. He stayed in bed late, and came downstairs in his shirtsleeves wondering about eggs and bacon, to find his sister-in-law Minnie installed. He listened from the kitchen while she held forth.

'My old man's coming back at the end of July,' she said. 'He's posted to Bidworth to cook for the officers.'

She was growing corpulent, thick in the ankles and plump in the wrists and fingers. The flesh bulged around her wedding ring. But her skin was hale and glowing, her hair shone and her mood was one of relentless complacency. It grated on Lilian's nerves so violently that she sometimes found herself screwing her hands into fists and digging her nails into her own skin. Lilian was in favour at home now since her trade of heaving coal enabled her to bring home pocketfuls of coal from the yard, as a bonus from an appreciative employer. Mother was storing it for next winter, counting the pieces individually and keeping a tally.

'Bad luck, Min,' Lilian sympathised. 'I thought the old bugger might be posted to the Pacific, but it was not to be.'

'Never mind, Minnie,' said Christina, speaking down from a turret of her own castle in the air. 'He might reform once he's settled at home again. And he doesn't dislike very small children.'

'Oh I'm not worried about him. He won't hurt us now.' The

100

beatific expression on Minnie's face was difficult to explain. She seemed to have achieved a plane of existence where things which had previously registered as sore trials, nearly crushing the life and hope out of her, were perceived as the merest flecks on the surface of creation. The normal world appeared most remote and insignificant to her in this novel state of fresh discernment. She had even ceased to fall back on the cheering dream of widowhood. Christina's bliss was no thorn in her side. She smiled upon the bashful young couple holding hands in the corner, as upon a pair of children to be indulged and tolerated. She rather took to Jim, anyway: she liked the humorous smile his eyes could transiently wear, as if he saw a great joke which he was desperate, but too shy, to share. She had to keep from laughing at his barbarous Welsh accent, so antithetical to the rhythms of the correct English spoken in Wiltshire. But frequently Minnie gave the impression that she was not paying more than cursory attention to the doings and sayings of those around her. She sat with her head tilted slightly to one side and seemed to be listening. Mother had heard gales of laughter coming from the kitchen one day, looked in expecting to find a crowd, but found to her surprise Minnie alone, sheepishly wiping the smile off her face. She had also been heard talking to herself when making her departure for her own home, glancing constantly sideways at what seemed to be an exceedingly small imaginary companion. When Sam answered the door to them nowadays, he was always in a filthy sulk of truculence and suppressed wrath.

'The gormless old bat's up the bleeding stairs writing her bleeding letters if you want her, Gran. I'm off out.'

Mother would sometimes collar him as he slipped past her and insist on scrubbing the dirt off his neck. Sam and his smaller brother and sister were becoming increasingly unkempt, grubby and uncontrollable. Christina flinched at the foul-mouthed little guttersnipes and tried to pretend they were not related to her. She could not conceive of them as belonging to the same species as her Florence. She kept the baby fastidiously clean and neat, changing and washing its clothes several times a day.

Now Minnie sat by the stolen fire in their mother's house, toasting her feet and wearing an expression of ineffable smugness, even when the return of her husband was being countenanced.

'You'd better start standing up to that husband of yours, Minnie, before it's too late,' said Lilian. 'Knee him in his private parts. That's the way to put them out of action, so I'm told. Sorry, Jim,' – she raised her voice to reach him in the kitchen – 'but he does knock her about. She ought to stand up for herself.'

'Don't you worry about my hubby. There won't be a problem soon.'

'Why, Min, what are you going to do? Poison his tea with paraquat, or has the old devil undergone a religious conversion?'

'It's the baby, you see. The One That Is To Be. He'll change everything.'

Lilian tapped her right temple, drew in her chin and cast a meaningful expression round at the family.

'How's that then, Min?'

'I told you, he's special.'

'What does your Albert say about that then?'

'I wrote and told him I was expecting, a couple of weeks ago. He wrote back by return and said he didn't believe the baby was his.'

'What?'

'Well, you see, Lily,' said Minnie in a perfectly placid tone. 'That night he gave me this baby, my Albert was so plastered he didn't remember anything about it the next morning – and then I ran away from him and he ran after me with a broken bottle and slashed me one in the eye – you can see the scars can't you. So anyway my Albert refuses paternity; says the little bastard must be another man's.'

'Christ. He'll murder you.'

'What are you going to do? Mum, what's Minnie going to do?'

Amelia came and sat down beside her, white faced, taking her hand. Jim stood in the doorway watching.

'No,' said Minnie. 'No, don't worry, Mum. He won't murder me. The baby won't let him.'

'You're going completely loopy, Min. Round the twist. Up the creek. No paddle. How in God's name can a newborn baby stop a grown man from doing anything whatever?'

'Lilian, you just don't understand the situation,' explained Minnie with great patience. 'You can't be expected to. I've had a Sign, you see. This is no ordinary baby. This is God's chosen one. This is my first baby, Little Albert, who died and is buried in Devizes Cemetery; he's coming back again, a second time. He won't let any harm come to me.'

'We'll never let any harm come to one another,' said Jim to Christina.

102

'No. Never. Nothing can harm us because we are utterly safe in one another.'

'Nothing can ever separate us.'

'And Peace so near.'

On his last evening before he had to fly back to Rome, night had deluged the blotting-paper plain with its blue-black Quink. They walked out the two miles to Old Sarum hillfort, leaving Florence at home with her grandparents. Christina wore a pale creamy coat refurbished from another old-fashioned coat that had once been a spare blanket in the airing cupboard, dating from the First World War. She wore a matching knitted beret at an angle. She looked like a beautiful ghost. Around her the black of hedgerows shone like coal in the night dews; invisible blossoming trees dispensed tart fragrances, bitter as lemon.

They kept on walking past Sarum, alongside the aerodrome where Jim had first been stationed, following the lane to the open countryside. They saw the lights of the camp and heard the booming of the hangar doors being dragged open. Bedlam was delivered from the gaping orifice. The brood of planes, once evacuated, set up a mounting whine and roar. Jeep doors slammed, men's voices carried miles out over the acoustic plain. Christina covered her ears as she walked. That kind of noise rattled her, it throbbed in her temples. The control tower kept dark vigil beside the twin domes of the hangars.

'This will all be over soon, my love.'

'And then you'll come out of the RAF. We'll be free.'

'Well, I don't know about that. My mam and dad say there's going to be no work for the boys when they come out – it'll be the Depression all over again. We'd best wait and see.'

No. I don't want to be an Air Force wife, trailing round the world while you drill and turn out at all hours of the night and get posted to killing places, and I've no roof or bed of my own, not even cups, no. I won't let you. The Ministry of War must return you to me as borrowed raw material, belonging only to myself. How dare they requisition, allocate, redistribute one so precious, from whom they have had plenty of use already? Why are you so willing, Jim? She took hold of his arm, stopped him in his tracks.

'I don't want you to stay in.'

'We'll see, love. I've got a good trade, you see, and the money's not so bad. And somehow it's a safer world than Civvy Street.'

'Safe! Look at you! Your skin's still all yellow from the

mepacrine tablets for the malaria – and you're all sick and thin. Surely you aren't even well enough to go back, Jim, you can report sick, stay with me. It's so near the end, they don't need you, you can't be lost now that the war's so nearly over.'

'But look here, girlie, I'll be in Rome or thereabouts, just servicing engines from now on, tame work, no danger at all, and home soon. Then we'll travel, get away from it all. You'll love it.'

'Yes, I want to travel, to get away.' Perhaps it wouldn't be so bad, after all. We can totally erase the war, as if it never happened; start again, with a clean sheet.

'Nothing can harm us, Chrissie, till the end of time.'

'Take care then.'

A plane ascended at a little distance, a bird of prey from its metal nest. A chaffinch in her nest of twigs and grasses unwove her sleep, sang part of a scale, drowsily, and bound herself down in sleep again.

Moonlight like a tracer beam cast Christina's face and coat into phosphoric light. White blossoms of briar in the hedge behind her head clustered in a pale garland. There was a gathering of power and sadness in her beside which he found himself exposed as a stateless, languageless beggar. He kissed her repeatedly. His mouth found her face the texture of chill petals. Between the airfield with its clamour and the silent breast of Old Sarum, they turned for home, and their last night.

Eleven

These first three years composed the perfect period of Florence's life, inscribing upon it the classic curve of beauty. The tiny terraced house in St Christopher's Road, carpetless and dingy, was her Golden World. For her benefit it thronged with fascinating and vivid faces, faces she learned to name with attitudes she learned to expect, like the vivacious painted people who crowd into the stable in Gentile's *Adoration of the Magi*, to be blessed by the omnipotent hand of the amused infant Prince. Her hand spun the world like a top, and the peopled globe obeyed her, fast or slow, according to her desire. She rewarded its obedience magically, royally, with huge and toothless smiles, with crowing and babbling, with pats from dimpled hands. Florence's world fed and warmed her; it admired her most vagrant fancy and put a favourable gloss on her most prosaic action. According to her mother, Florence's first words were feats of prodigious brilliance, miraculous in one so young. The baby obliged by producing whole sprays and fountains of these self-blown bubbles, and could speak at least fifty by the time she was fifteen months old. Christina kept a scrupulous tally. She pointed out to everyone the infallible evidences of her daughter's genius. Adorers queued to hear the prodigy speak, and Florence produced another fifty words, reeling them off with fantastic exuberance, as if she were cracking strings of jokes. Christina wrote proudly telling the father that his daughter was a genius. The war was months over, but he continued to be bottled up in Rome awaiting his turn for demobilisation. It was a source of special exasperation to them that the servicemen who had taken Italian brides were given priority in homecoming.

Meanwhile in his stead, Florence had a rich gallery of faces to christen with her love. She was not clear as to where the gentleman with the great grey whiskers and the pipes that blew smoke rings up to the roof of the world had come from; but he seemed to have been a presence since the beginning of the Creation. His long, grey-trousered legs were held out straight from his chair as a standing invitation to small mountaineers to scale them. In his inner folds where privileged hands might burrow were yellow ticking globes held to him on chains. She believed these old fobs, heirlooms from his father's father, to be actual parts of his body, peculiar to himself and not pertaining to the species in general. It was their mutual and occult secret when he detached a watch and held it to her ear, or let her wind the serrated knob on top, and cup the timepiece in both her hands, warm from his chest. She felt he nurtured it like an egg, next to his heart. Or, later, feeling her own heart tick, she considered that perhaps he had hatched his own heart, to be worn outside his anatomy: a round golden heart, free of all the messy blood that she had noted with alarm seemed to fill the sealed recesses of the human body, and seemed to want to well out at the least scratch of the surface. Later again, she discerned a more profound truth about Grandad, which set him apart from the legions of her other admirers. She saw that though she made him laugh, till he was crimson in the face, it really dismayed him to laugh. It was as if this was for him a new skill, learnt uncomfortably late, long after the muscles of his face had set in an attitude of woe, so that the joy she gave twisted his features in the manner of pain. His dear-costing joy seemed in some way double the value. He had loved this way before, twenty years back. Now its renewed brief life span took in both the baby Florence and her own mother, recollected from the babyhood which had alike afforded him reason to live.

Grandmother stood in the kitchen. She was kneading dough, leaning forwards, leaning back, turning the edges of the dough inwards, making the outside become the inside, endlessly returning the rim of the world to its nucleus. Florence watched standing on a chair at the same table, with her own little piece of dough upon which she inflicted terrible injuries. Grandmother kneaded, Florence kneaded. Florence's dough became grubby and grey, from its tendency to fly out of her hands on to the floor.

'We'll never make a housewife out of you, Flo,' said Grandmother.

Florence smiled broadly. She understood everything that was said to her as being complimentary in intention. Beyond this, she understood that Grandmother represented a centre of power. She admired the silver of her hair as the epitome of what was beautiful. She comprehended a substantial security in her, and emanating from her, which was somehow absent in her grandfather. She imagined Grandmother as being surrounded by wisps of energy, curling up into the air like the fragrances of baking. Grandmother was warmth whose surplus constantly turned to vapour, for the advantage of those who needed a bit extra. The vapours rose and curled like invisible flowers upon the air. Such flowers matched the faded rose patterns which distinguished her grandmother's dresses and overalls, dating from long before the war. But the vaporised flower patterns which signed their curlicues upon the air of the kitchen were not faded, like those she had examined at close quarters on Grandmother's bosom, sitting on her knee before the fire on winter evenings. They were young and fresh, in the very prime of life. They had the delicious vehemence of the steam arising from the batches of jam tarts and cheese straws straight from the oven, when she was invited to pick one and eat it piping hot – 'Just one, mind!' – and her hand roved in the air above the squadrons of cakes, seeking out the biggest and the best.

Despite the adulation, Florence was considered for all her gifts to be rather fey. She betrayed a certain oddity, provoking amused puzzlement even amongst admirers. 'Up to her tricks,' her mother said. 'She has funny little ways,' they explained to visiting aunts. One of Florence's tricks was the invention of an imaginary companion, with whom she began at the age of two to hold long and complicated conversations. At times she seemed to prefer this friend to merely human company, though they frequently quarrelled violently, on which occasions the child would be seen to punch the air wildly with demented fists. At other times, the imaginary friend put her up to acts of disobedience. Christina was proud of her daughter's flaxen-haired prettiness, and spent quantities of coupons on buying, and hours of time in sewing, outfits to complement her appearance. From her earliest days Florence took a fierce dislike to being dressed up. She sat down in puddles to soil her frilly knickers. She would drag the red bow from her hair while her mother's back was turned, and stamp on it with detestation.

'You little *fiend*, Florence. All the trouble I take to make you look nice. What do you keep doing this for? You naughty girl.'

'Flossie not do it.'

'Well of course you did it. Bad girl to tell lies. Who else *was* there to do it?'

'Hally done it.'

'What do you mean, Hally did it. There *is* no Hally. Hally is not real, Florence. You make him up. Hally does not exist.'

'Hally do exist, Mummy, because I can see him now. She's standing just by your arm but don't turn round otherwise he goes away. Hally don't like me wearing bows and ribbons, she makes me rip 'em off. And that's the truth.'

'Is Hally a he or a she, Florence?'

'Yes.'

'Well which?'

'He *and* a she.'

'What does Hally look like?'

Florence took time to think it over, but seemed to remain in the dark. 'Not like anything at all. Just like Hally.'

'What colour is Hally's hair, for instance?'

'Black. With bits of fair.'

'And is he big or small?'

107

'Quite big and quite small.'

'You don't seem very sure. Now, you see, Florence, Hally doesn't really exist at all, and you know that perfectly well, don't you. *I* think Florence has made him up when Florence feels like being naughty to Mummy and doesn't want to take the blame. Don't you?' Christina took the child on her knee conspiratorially, pulling her cardigan down neatly at the back.

'Hally do be real but she don't like being talked about, and she gets really *cross* and furiated if you do.' Her eyes were icy pale and unblinking as she studied her mother's face up close. 'All right, Mummy, Hally gone now, goodbye.'

Christina's sense of threat from the weirdness of this invented friend, conjured in and out of being on the spur of Florence's will, was increased by the birth and development of Minnie's Mongol child, Alison, and the mental deterioration of Minnie to the point where she seemed to inhabit an adjacent dimension of reality, connecting only by a dim and narrow corridor of language.

When the elder Albert had come home on leave from the cookhouse, he had ceremoniously beaten his wife up for 'going with other men' as he put it, for he could neither remember nor credit that the child she was carrying was his own. Minnie accepted the beating stoically, without her usual crying and cringing. This surprised and disconcerted Albert, as did the appearance of his sister-in-law, Lilian, the following morning; who stuck her boot in the door and threatened that if he so much as touched their Minnie again she would personally knock the cowardly little creep into kingdom come.

Albert naturally jeered at this, and lunged at her in a derisory fashion, to shove her off his doorstep. Lilian, who was a full head the taller, with biceps and shoulders stout and tough from years of manual labour, grasped the little creep by the tops of his arms, lifted him a few inches off the ground and kneed him in the groin. As he doubled up, she pulled him bodily from his house and kicked him several times in the ribs. The event became apocryphal in Avebury Road, where for years afterwards small boys would hoot and bait Albert, who slunk in and out of his house as seldom as possible, head down, commonly drunk. On occasions he still lambasted Minnie, but most of the relish had gone out of it; the sense of manly conquest was lacking. More obscurely, he seemed to have lost the knack of reaching his wife through his habitual violence. She had entered another world, cow-heavy in her pregnancy. A thick veil like cheesecloth descended between herself and the outer world. When he hit her, she did not really react. She looked straight back at him after the first blow had been dealt, as if he was not really there at all. She spoke abstractedly about the baby as if it were God Almighty she was housing in that ugly bulging belly. She told him with a zealot's tears in her eyes that this was no ordinary birth. Her face wore an expression of divine contentment. Albert was coming back, she said, home to her.

'I *am* home, you stupid cow,' he said ferociously.

'No, I mean the *first* Albert, our firstborn. It's him I'm carrying again. The time has come round for him. The lamb that was lost is coming again from the slaughter.'

'You're cracked. You'll end up in the loony bin.'

'You'll see, Bert. There's a new heaven and a new earth. It's signalled by the end of the war. Have faith. You'll see.'

Albert did see. Their daughter was born with immaculate ease, in a labour lasting two hours. She simply slid out softly into the world like a child on a slide in the playground. He saw her wide, flat face, her telltale slanty eyes. He realised at once.

'The bastard's a bleeding imbecile. A cretin. A moron. Right, you can look after it. I'm having no part in it. It's nothing to do with me.'

He departed for the pub, cursing righteously. Minnie's faith was not distracted by variation of gender, of mentality. She knew perfectly well that Albert could not return as a duplicate of himself, but unpredictably and marvellously transformed. She named the girl Alison, bestowing upon her a passionately tender and utterly reciprocated love. For Alison was all affection, nothing else. Her lolling head wore a look of smiling infatuation; her tongue, too large for her mouth cavity, syllabled a language of pure devotion. It was all that Minnie had ever wanted.

'Disgusting slobbering,' said Albert of his immaculate conception. 'Gobbling away like a bleeding turkey. Gobble, gobble, gobble. Don't even speak no sodding King's English.'

Alison smiled at her father with her imperturbable grin, chuckling to him, liking to hear the sounds of the words which were funny and captivating to her senses. She dribbled slightly out of the corner of her mouth. Her thin hair stuck out very straight and dry in texture. Sometimes she hummed to herself, strange circular little tunes of her own devising. She did so now, broadly beaming into her father's face.

109

'Gobble, gobble, gobble,' said Albert sarcastically, again, wagging his face up at hers. 'Over two years old and all it can do is gobble. My God, what did I do to deserve you?'

'Gobble, gobble,' said Alison, and she laughed cordially, signifying the boundlessness of Grace beyond all imaginable deserts.

'Anyway it won't live beyond thirty,' said Albert. 'That's something to be grateful for.'

'My treasure,' said Minnie, cradling Alison's head. 'Mother's own true love. Come back to take care of Mother.'

Albert slammed out.

'Mully, oh Mully,' said the child, and putting both arms around her mother's neck she squeezed her tight, warming her mind and body, feeding her mother's famine with manna. Minnie was entirely happy with her miracle.

Christina worried when she saw her own adored Florence developing eccentricities. She was extra sensitive to any hint of peculiarity in her daughter, desiring a perfect outcome to the perfect union between herself and Jim. She wanted it to be beyond criticism. For Florence too was a chosen child, representing their joint investment in the future tense. She was relieved when the fictitious Hally absconded from Florence's inner landscape, a disengagement which seemed to happen all at once. Jim was home and the child was nearly three years old when Hally vanished. It was September of 1947 when the whole family got the chance of a trip out to the Henge in a van 'borrowed' by an Air Force friend and filled up with petrol equally 'borrowed' from the fuel dump at Sarum. In brilliant weather they unloaded their picnic and laid it out on blankets just outside the circular bank which is the outermost boundary of the stone ring. Food was still rationed but Mother had been saving coupons, and there were plenty of good things to eat, chipolata sausages on sticks, ham sandwiches, lemonade, sweets and biscuits for the children. Florence, with Minnie's Sam, Rosie, Billie and Alison, kept stuffing their mouths and pockets with food and dashing in to the ring, where they climbed on to the fallen blue-stones, which had soaked in the morning's sunshine and gave back their warmth into the full length bodies of the reclining children. Florence believed the place to be a giant's toy, erected for the amusement of their young by a race of Titans living at the time of the dinosaurs. She explained to the other children, in her lofty way, that it had originally been intended as a game of skittles for the giant children, who, having bowled rocks at the upright stones, had succeeded in scoring hits on those which were now fallen. She sat hugging her knees. She chewed and talked at the same time, showing off her customary proprietorial bond with the place to the cousins. The cousins were inferior (as her mother had made known) but they were hers. Florence never doubted that they would and should accept her version of things; for she had the gift of language, the easy key to precedence, whereas the Salisbury relatives had to grub around for words, she had noticed, as if they were in short supply. They did not seem to share her pleasant licence to make things up if they did not know the answer to a question. But she liked them cordially, and expected them to like her in return.

'This is *my* Henge,' she said firmly. 'I know its stories, and I will tell you them if you want to hear them.'

'Taint your Henge at all!' Sam was over twice her age, and though quite fond of Florence, thought her very much above herself. 'It's everybody's Henge. It was here before you was born, Flo, and that makes it more mine than yours because I'm older.'

'Ah, but not as old as the dinosaurs.'

'Well, no, but – '

'So there you are then, you weren't here Samuel, and you haven't the 'magination to find out; whereas I do have the 'magination.'

'Anyway, your knickers show.' He swiped at the fallen bluestone with his boot. His riposte seemed a bit weak even to himself. He meant to say, you're only a girl, what do you know about anything?

'And what does Hally say about this, Miss Know-All?' Florence jumped from her perch, pulling her skirt down at the back. Her father had wandered into the ring, hands in the pockets of his baggy trousers. He crouched down beside her on his haunches, warm and indulgent, as she liked him to be. He wore an open-necked shirt, and his hair was sleeked back from his forehead with Brylcreem.

'Is this little madam bossing you about again, Sam?'

'She's only small. I don't take notice.'

'Sensible lad. She's a tyke and a tyrant. Aren't you?'

He put his arm round her waist; she wove hers round his neck. So many invisible little elastic threads fine as hairs tied them the one to the other that it seemed to Florence they lived in a network that was daily spinning itself more intricately, like a cocoon. Say there

111

was a mist one day, and the sun came up, you would be able to see the network of lines between them, lit white in the sunlight, beaded with raindrops, like spiders' webs on autumn mornings stretched over bracken.

'Hally says – Hally says –'

'Yes, my beauty girl, what does the mighty oracle say?' Jim had never minded Florence's imaginary friend. He told Christina it was quite normal in a young, only child; nothing to worry about. He did not understand why Chrissie flinched away and went so tense and wire-drawn when Florence referred to him. 'She'll grow out of it,' he always said, patiently.

'Hally says, Daddy . . . he says, Hally doesn't exist. There is no Hally. In the whole world. There is no him.'

Thus with a transient outburst of tears, the little girl flung away her kindred spirit, crumpling him up like a sheet of paper for waste. She never again sought him out, nor seemed to recollect or wish to resurrect him, although she had a trick of turning sharply in her tracks while she was running or playing, and staring back the way she had come, as if she had heard a voice calling her, or sensed a shadowing, evasive presence. She continued with her halcyon, increasingly tomboyish existence, marching up and down the stairs of their home with Grandad, to the music of paper and comb, singing with him the old Wiltshire songs he dredged up from childhood, while he shaved, and she mimicked his actions, shaving her own soft little chin and throat with an imaginary cut-throat razor: 'Oh Grandad, I've got a bleed!'

'You'll come back in no time,' said the grandparents, seeing them off at Southampton Docks on the ship bound for their posting in Egypt. 'Two and a half years is no time at all. Don't you cry now, our Flo.'

They watched until the ship was a speck on the horizon, then the imagined shadow of a speck. The two old people boarded the train for home. Grandmother wept unrestrainedly the whole way. It was over. Chrissie had gone. And the little one. Grandfather was not at that time seen to weep. He shed his life in the spring of the following year, his cast-off body being found in the Avon between Woodford and Sarum.

Part Two

One

Sorbiodunum, Sorviadun, Searoburh, Serebrig, Seres-
beri, Salisburia, Saresbyri, Sarum, Salisbury. Time's declension of
the name of their home, conjugating its serial tenses, shadowed the
remoulding of the countryside in waves of change that would
throw a military hillfort upon the breast-like mound of the Great
Mother. The pygmy men came there all clad in mail to occupy the
central womb of Sarum; and threw up fortifications; and words to
them were chanted war cries let loose like shafts of arrows
fortifying their utility of place. The ecclesiastics came and built
their palace by the breast of the hill, and sang the glory of their king
in rich and swaggering splendour beneath the stillness of the
breast. A community built there and then went away. Between-
times the fundamentals of the name of Sarum remained the same,
the one music of sibilant and vowel, conducting Old Sarum to New
Sarum, past to present, continuing to reflect the one current of
sound through war or peace. The fort by the slow-flowing river,
occupied in turn by Saxon, Roman and Norman men of war
retained its uterine shape, bank and ditch within bank and ditch; its
concentricities of enclosure and protection, its entrance a birth
passage, its focus the mound of breast or womb. Latterly they built
an aerodrome nestling up close to the hillfort, and men in blue
uniforms would wander casually in and out of the sanctuary, hands
in their pockets and cigarettes dangling from their lips. They would
stand on the rim and squint out at the encompassing plain, its
horizons drowned in mist. The rime creaked beneath their boots as
they ambled down the passage, back to camp. Around the
circumference of the outermost ring, the rose hips like globes of
glowing blood fruited year by year, and behind them the redbreast
perched upon the barbed-wire boughs of the hawthorn.

They rarely returned to Salisbury, save for the occasional duty weekend when they felt bound to stay in the old home perfunctorily, and Florence, fleeing upstairs to mount the rocking duck and ride for dear life over the boards, failed to notice the tight-lipped tension which gripped her mother's face into a mask, until the visit was over. The rocking horse had long departed from its incongruous mate, to be worked to death by her Aunt Minnie's eightfold brood; but Florence had no recollection of the horse, only the yellow beauty of the wonderful duck impressed itself on her mind as a memorial of her childhood. They once went to visit her Aunt Minnie who had a screw loose, and her poor child who was an idiot. She was frightened of the poor idiot, who sat cradled contentedly on her mother's knee sucking her thumb and dribbling, though a great girl of eight years. Furtively Florence cast her eyes round the chaos of their home. It had been wrecked by children's crashing feet. The furniture was covered in dirt, for they scrambled unchecked over sagging settee and stained armchairs. The sitting room was adorned with little piles of socks and underclothes awaiting washing or darning. Florence was surprised rather than shocked at the dirt, for she rather liked mess; though she thought the smell too pungent.

She noticed that when her aunt offered her mother a cup of tea, Christina (sitting with ramrod back on the extreme edge of her chair) hurriedly refused it, shuddering slightly as if she saw in her mind's eye the germ squatting in wait upon the cup's grubby rim. Florence's cousin, Sam, adorned the occasion by bursting in, plucking a cushion off the settee and kicking it round the room in the authentic manner of Stanley Matthews as he pointed out to his Aunt Christina. Florence burst into a giggling fit and would have liked to join in, save for the reproving glance of her mother, which gorgonised her into immobility.

'I can't do a thing with him, to tell you the truth, Chrissie,' sighed her Auntie Minnie, but without any particular regret. 'I've given up as a matter of fact. Boys will be boys after all, I always say so anyway.'

'He has deteriorated,' agreed Christina.

'Hasn't he just,' replied Minnie, surveying her son's uncouth physiognomy as if analysing a specimen of a type quite unrelated to herself. 'He's a proper horrible boy.'

'Can't his father knock some sense into him?' asked Christina with quiet horror, as the youth scored a goal into the back of the settee.

116

'Eggs him on, see,' said Minnie. 'As you know, Albert hasn't a lot of patience with me and Alison. He don't mind Sam causing a bit of trouble around the house, to exasperate me and keep me on my toes.'

Florence's father stood up.

'Now you stop that, boy,' he said. 'You come over by here and sit with your uncle, and behave yourself to your mother.'

Sam looked mildly surprised, but did so. He accepted the half-crown Jim gave him to go and get a haircut at the barber's. He'd buy Woodbines with that, he gloated to himself, warming the coin in his palm. For the duration of the visit he sat up close to his uncle, squeezing the half-crown lovingly and occasionally staring vacantly into his uncle's face. Hazily he recollected how, in the period of his extremest need, before he had finally elected on the consolations of a career of hooliganism, an airman with that face had come back from the war, wearing a jubilant smile he could have worshipped; who rumpled his hair; whose kitbag he sat and kissed.

'Does he suffer from nits?' asked Christina.

Florence briefly dwelt upon this question, and the unoffended way in which her aunt with the screw loose accepted it. She dimly remembered the restrained and melancholy joy with which her grandmother welcomed Christina, admired her, fed her eyes upon her; but muted, as if she had to keep reminding herself that she must not show, and therefore seem to ask, too much affection. Dreamily she watched her grandmother's rheumatic, reddened hands poking at the fire to bring up the blaze. She had no prior memory of the grandmother, the house, the tiny back yard overgrown with brambles, the town or the spire that dominated it. But she felt interested in the grandmother. Her cheek when kissed goodbye was more silkily soft than anyone's Florence had ever experienced. Her accent was dark and magically strange. Florence wondered why her own voice was without the soft, chalky burr studded with chips of flint, which the Salisbury family shared. Could it really be the case that she spoke in a superior way, as her parents told her, and that a local accent was a mark of coarseness?

'But you have traces of it in your voice, Mummy; it's beautiful. I don't think it's nasty at all.'

They were on the train for home. Christina had begun to relax, but now her mouth went anxious, as before, and she enunciated carefully, not looking at Florence, 'I don't speak with any accent.'

117

'Your mother speaks perfect English, Florence, Queen's English, and you can't do better than copy her speech.'

'I prefer your Welsh then,' muttered Florence, who embarked early on a course of mutiny against the incomprehensible forest of negatives with which she was hedged round.

'Does this particular grandmother have a grandfather to go with her,' she asked. 'Or did she come on her own?' She had no memory of such a person.

'There was a grandfather, naturally, but he was old, and died,' said her mother matter-of-factly.

'Poor Granny.'

'Oh no, she's quite happy. Old people don't feel things in the same way.'

'What was he like?'

'Who, darling?'

'Grandfather.'

'Oh – well, he was just an ordinary sort of man. Quiet, you know. Betted on the horses. Liked his pint. He was just a man of his time, not much you could say about him. Shouldn't you go and wash your hands and freshen up before we get in at the station, Florence? I bet you haven't thought about it. It won't do, you know. Cleanliness is next to Godlinesss.'

Cleanliness next to Godliness? Really? Florence always translated things into visual images. She forgot about Grandfather in the effort to imagine the two neighbours, God and Cleanliness. The one was a black-cassocked prelate advanced in years, looking out of a stained-glass window into the next-door house at whose bathroom window stood his sterile partner, Cleanliness, who brushed his teeth with vigorous circling movements so that he might keep them forever and be a credit to the neighbourhood.

Florence's love for her mother had begun in a passionate outpouring of devotion whose abandonment was demonstrated in the torrent of chattering with which she encountered the world as soon as the code of language was broken, to unseal her nature. She had power over her mother, and used it: she reigned and revelled, the springs of her spirit bubbling over into an ever-widening resource of vocabulary, sensually fluid. Until the age of five, her idyll remained inviolate. Her noisy ego drowned out the surrounding absence of voice. Then she encountered the silence. The more she stopped talking and listened, the more she heard it and could not put a name to it: a void, an absence, reflected in her

118

mother's coercive silence. The moment she caught the echo, she became afraid. It seemed like an intelligence test she could not match up to, the reason for her mother's saying of 'No', her angry turning away into the ice of reserve. They were nomads in the Air Force world of postings and evacuations: Singapore, Aden, Kinloss. Their dwelling place and landscape were one another. They knew no place of sanctuary, moving between the drab interchangeable married quarters with the brown linoleum and the inventory of thick white china, and a drawer of staple cutlery. At each station, loved and valued as she was, Florence got more suffused with this fright. Christina's 'No' gained in power as the daughter cringed, the riddle of it all like a chip of ice stuck at an angle in her heart.

Florence invented an arrogant manner to cover the fear. She spoke back, precociously, and Christina felt obscurely threatened, even betrayed. She never knew what Florence would say to her next; what dreadful question or accusation would rise unjustly to her daughter's lips. She had to be on her guard. She had to be vigilant. When letters from Florence's grandmother came, Christina hid them away in her handbag for months at a time before quietly incinerating them in the stove as out of date. Florence, poking about in the fascinating depths of the handbag amongst powder puffs and nail files, would secretly chance upon these letters.

'Dear Florence,' one read. 'I think of you so often, remembering early days, how you would play with Grandad's pipes and put them in neat rows, and fill his pipe from the pouch, do you ever remember that by any chance I dare say you were too young and now a busy clever little girl. Your mother has done very well for herself in life and so kind sending money to poor Minnie whose brain is no better and I am sorry to say her Sam is on remand for breaking and entering he has gone quite beyond since his dad's made away with himself, so drunk though I daresay he didn't really know what he was doing. That's Albert and your Grandad gone by such a means in this generation alone. But all is for the best you know so proud of you as ever your loving Gran.'

As she read, the hairs on Florence's neck and back rose; her body was all gooseflesh. She sat with the rifled handbag on her knee, holding the letter, and shivering with chill as if she were going down with flu. Experience had not prepared her for this betrayal; nor how to cope with her own criminality, rifling through the contents of another's life. She was an officer of justice, rightfully liberating and appropriating what was her own. She stuffed the letter back in the bag, into what she vaguely remembered to have been its original place. She replaced the black leather bag on the sideboard. Then, crimson to the roots of her hair, she re-opened the bag, pulled out the letter and hid it up her cardigan sleeve. Shortly, the door latch clicked, and Christina was back with the shopping. Florence hurried to the kitchen and began to help unload, but with a look of such fixed and neurotic anguish that Christina bent to her and said,

'Is everything all right, darling? You don't have to help with this, you know. Go and get on with your own things. Anyone can unpack shopping. It takes a special person to play the flute. Go on, skip off. I'll bring you a drink when I've finished.'

This was the mother to whom Florence's heart yearned, for whom she would have died. This was the one who was not only tender but also, uniquely, left you alone, to get on, because she knew the distinction between what was important and what was trivial. She was the mother no one else had, who gave you automatic advantage in life by saying that girls need not cook or sew but ought to better themselves by becoming explorers of the Orinoco and Chancellors of the Exchequer. Florence felt a worm for rifling through this mother's handbag.

'No, I'd rather help you.'

'*Are* you all right, my love? You don't look yourself at all.' She puzzled at Florence's flushed, darkly frowning face, and felt her forehead. 'You do seem rather warm.' Florence doggedly stacked the tins of fruit, beetle-browed with anger at her own corruption.

'You sit down, Mummy. I want to do it. Not you. You always do everything. Sit. By order.' She was learning the propitiator's art, the tokenism of an ersatz love offered to placate the goddess. Yet the real love survived, fresh and whole, beneath the substitute version, but troubled and churning. The crust of guilt and anger was beginning to set hard.

It was not for some weeks that Christina detected the disappearance of the letter, and feared the worst. Florence was essaying a Mozart *adagio* when her mother burst in. She had forgotten the letter, more or less, so that her innocent air was unfeigned.

'Have you been in my handbag, Florence?'

Florence paused, the flute an inch away from her lips with the embouchure still on them, looking bewildered.

'Well,' she said, thoughtfully. 'I did try to climb in but I'm just that bit too large nowadays. No – of course not.'

'Very funny,' said Christina, retreating. 'Well, don't go searching through other people's handbags in future, Florence. It's a very ill-bred thing to do.'

'But I didn't.'

She pursued her researches periodically in her mother's absence. She was in the handbag, sifting through drawers, sorting out the objects and papers in the great wooden trunk which carried their earthly goods from continent to continent like a covenanted Ark. She quarried, she archaeologised, to come at clues to the things Christina would not say. There was so little. Although Christina was a hoarder, she also had a knack of throwing things away, as if with her left hand. Florence widened her attentions to include a study of waste-paper baskets, where fragments of torn-up letters could often be turned up, shredded very small, which Florence took to her room and glued together as jigsaw puzzles. Often the finds were a disappointment, old bills and shopping lists, Air Force chitties, the detritus such as gathers in disused storepits in archaeological sites, from which experienced diggers might make deductions, but which the layman scorns as rubbish. Then Florence would give up in boredom, and get on with her real life for several months until it occurred to her to undertake a fresh scavenge. The trouble was, she was growing up volatile and capricious, prey to sudden bursts of directed energy which suddenly petered out. She was not the patiently durable type with the vigilance and staying power to accumulate evidence about the riddle of the past, and make final conclusions about the self. In fits of violent desire she stormed the guarded past; when the impulse spent itself, she gave up, and let things through. She knew she must be missing things in this haphazard way, letting unique opportunities slide. She knew this most graphically when she happened upon the torn-up photograph of a baby in her mother's arms.

Downstairs they were resting after lunch, listening to Forces Favourites on the wireless. Father was nodding off with his feet up; mother was knitting, counting the stitches. They would not bother her for at least an hour. Cigarette smoke filled the house. She shut herself into her bedroom with the picture. The photograph was in eight pieces. The dismembered aspect of her baby self had, to her, a grisly look. One eye gleamed widely in the flash-bulb's beacon, a startled cyclops on its own shred of paper. The other eye was partly torn through, and when reunited with its partner presented the appearance of an ironic wink. The past derided her with its grimace. She quickly had all the parts of the photograph back together again on her bedroom table. She studied it hungrily, since there were no pictures of her extant till she was a toddler, the reason for which she had understood to be the inaccessibility of film in the war. Her parents often lamented it, going through the album where her father assembled the family photographs with methodical pride. Now here was a unique print, black-and-white and very small, certainly, but still a record of that prehistoric time when there was a Florence who did not know there was a Florence, and could therefore not take stock and make assessment. Had her mother, so shy and self-conscious a creature, perhaps taken exception to the likeness of herself and torn it up because it was unjust to her own beauty? This could be a reason. Florence addressed herself to the task of reconstituting her mother, seeking to gauge how good a photo it might be. But the mother's image was even more sheerly cloven than the baby's. She had ripped her own face apart twice, from top to bottom, from side to side. Florence's busy, deft fingers could make nothing more telling than a cross of tears in place of features. The suspicion of a smile underlay the cross, the implication of pleasure and pride in the upright carriage of the head and the way the hands bore the infant up for the camera's eye. Florence tried to discover where the picture might have been taken, by studying the background. There was no clue in that circumscribing black void. It could have been – Florence's inflamed imagination worked – down a coalmine or in an air-raid shelter. Somewhere underground, and dark, and cold. She had gone shivery, her throat being crammed with tears. I'll bolt, she thought, I'll take the bits and show them to Daddy, and he'll tell me why she did it, he will. He will denounce her. He will condemn her. He will say, 'Out of my sight, thou Serpent', and she will creep off and hide in the wardrobe. Then he will sit me on his knee by the fire, and explain, because he must know. He knows everything, in actual fact.

Instead, she went to her mirror, and stared at her own reflection. Quite often she came up here and kissed her own mouth, and smiled at herself winningly in the glass, or held a dignified wordless conversation with her likeness, making apt responses, authoritative, sympathetic, pouting, gesticulating. At other times, she and

122

her reflection swayed to the music of their one flute, so charming one another that they seemed to inhabit the secret world of the Blessed Spirits. Now Florence stood and looked herself in the eyes. The unity of her real image reassured her; the pale blue eyes maintained an air of fortitude and composure; the strong chin defined the oval face as unlikely to be robbed of identity. The dark blond hair with streaks of gold which her mother vainly tried to curl on pipe cleaners lay in a shoulder-length mass of resolute straightness. The endangered sensation had passed. She combed her fingers through her hair and let it flop back again. It did what it liked. She did what she liked.

In place of the sense of threat to herself came a sensation of the sadness in her mother. It was an acute sadness. It was a sadness as big and heavy as all their bags and baggage when they packed for a move. When Florence felt sad she cried, buckets, seas. If no one took any notice, she had final resort to the tantrum of earlier childhood, drumming her heels and making a loud noise. When her mother was sad, Florence now saw, she did not cry. She tore something up, jettisoned some relic as junk. And the grief swelled inside her like a terrible egg, like a pregnancy, like a tumour in her secret body. And this was why she hoarded food, Florence saw, so that while the waste-paper basket contained scatterings of documentary evidence, the kitchen cupboards were crammed with tins of peas, tins of peaches, tins of steak-and-kidney, as if there was never a time when she could feel secure of the family's having enough to eat. Yet Christina's own plate was always meanly supplied.

Florence sat down on her bed and thought about their meal times, her mother serving up, passing plates through the hatch. It was like the Three Bears, with the significant variation that although Father Bear's plate came through mountainously piled with roast potatoes and gravy, Baby Bear's greedy helping has superseded Mother's penitential ration of the fattiest meat eked out with a most speaking scarcity of vegetables. In the mother country there is famine, there is dearth. Together and with speed, her father and Florence ladle some of their own superfluity on to the deserted plate, as if they have been challenged and must instantly rise to the defence of the self-starving victim. They have to do this before Christina arrives from the kitchen bearing the covered dish of extra potatoes. Otherwise it is:

'No, you *mustn't* put your food on my plate. I had plenty before.'

It is a voice of real anger. 'And look, Florence, you've spilt gravy on the cloth. Now, I really must ask you both to eat the food you're given, and not redistribute it.'

'Come on Chrissie, you can't survive on that. You're just being a martyr.'

'I'm not being a martyr, Jim. I just don't know why you keep saying this. Have your sprouts back. I only want three.'

Redistribution commences. Father loses his temper.

'Now stop this bloody martyr business once and for all, woman. Once and for all. Let this be the last time.'

Florence never knew what it was all about. Yet the satisfaction her mother derived from coercing her husband and child into force-feeding her was manifest. It appeased the ghostly judge presiding over the tribunal of Christina's consciousness who pronounced her not fit to eat; not fit to live; and who had set her feet upon the treadmill of guilt at some early and indeterminate era of history.

Father was a show-off. He clowned around like a little boy, and made her mother ache with laughter. His high spirits were glorious excess of sunlight; he had so much to spare. His enjoyment of the present moment was intense. Nobody enjoyed simple pleasures so heartily. Plain food was sensuality to him; a landscape was a vista of heaven. But he was inarticulate, unlettered, and ashamed of his lack of hold on language. He thought there was a correct form of language which his inheritance had failed to father on him. His highest term of approval was 'well spoken'. He lived in time, purely. When he died, there would be nothing left of him. His power to love the few he trusted was so deep it shocked him as unmanly; he tried many stratagems to conceal it, failing. When Florence was sick in the night, he cleared up the mess. When she was poorly, he sat up with her all night. If she wept, he wept with her.

Father was hot tempered. He often shouted at them both. He thrashed Florence's bare bottom ritualistically with his slipper for her unladylike naughtiness. He often seemed surprised that this failed to prevent her from sitting down in puddles in her best dress, sliding down the coal hole, and joining with the children of their fellow 'Other Ranks' in vilification of the officers' children, who dwelt beyond the wire netting in the opulence due to their caste. Florence would not play with the other girls. She toured the camp on a boy's bike she 'borrowed', and her father thrashed her for it.

124

The next day she went swimming in the local pond, and got thrashed for it.

'Why do you do it, girlie?' he asked, one night when they had forgiven one another, and he had tucked her up in bed. His face was intemperately loving, genuinely puzzled, as he asked it. He was holding both her folded hands in the one of his that was so warmly protective, the one that had hit her.

'Didn't you ever do things when you were young, Daddy?'

'Oh aye, of course I did. I was a holy terror.' He laughed indulgently at the reminiscences evoked. 'But I was a lad. You're a girl, and girls are better behaved aren't they? Don't you want to grow up like your mother?'

'No, I want to be a flautist in an orchestra and be extremely famous.'

'And will being disobedient to your mother and father help you to attain that end?'

'I honestly think it might, Daddy.'

'You don't really want to be a hooligan though, girlie, do you? We think so much of you. You're the only one.'

Florence wondered why they didn't have another one then, as an insurance, who might turn out to be a paragon of maidenly virtues. But she was glad they didn't. The turbulence of their nomadic lives – father's ranting, mother's silences – disclosed to her, daily, nightly, an underlying stillness and tenderness within their home. She lay in the bath, soaping herself, rinsing the lather off, soaking, adding more from the hot tap when the water cooled. It was a balmy spring night, and she could hear the voices of her parents ascending from the garden, where they were exclaiming together at the beauty of the crocus, snowdrop and daffodil, piercing the clay soil of their Cornish quarters. The voices rose each with its own lilt and flavour, in delicate recitative. She caught the music of the dialects rather than particular words or phrases. Her father made an observation, her mother responded; they laughed, they paused. Florence imagined their twin fingers bending to inspect the flowers. The continuing rhythm of their answering voices constituted a music: Florence felt as though she were receiving not random notes from a score but a complete section from the whole music. She half slept in the amniotic warmth of the bath water. The voices were still there, lyrical, ordinary. But time was gone. The voices wove and unwove their singular theme out of time altogether. She used to feel cut out, cut off, from the continuum of

125

her family's mutual history. There was a thing – a place – a person –
she used to feel, and it was hers, and somehow in her travels she had
lost it. But within the dialects, their accents unguarded now into
the approximation to standard English for which they inde-
fatigably strove – the lilt of the Welsh, the brogue of the Wiltshire –
there the secret lay by which she sought to be clarified. Finally, she
heard them go indoors together, as the evening light deepened grey
blue. She opened her eyes; put down the small grey lozenge of
pumice which had come, her father said, from Mount Vesuvius
years ago. I've been asleep, she thought, and dreaming.

Two

Christina sat in the bedroom of the first home they had
ever owned, beside the sleeping body of her husband. She had not
wanted to return to Salisbury to live, but he was so ill that she could
not deny him anything. Besides, it no longer mattered where they
lived, if he was not going to be well. Relatives came and went, and
she seemed to speak to them, but they were ghosts merely. She set
no store by their reality, though she accepted their gifts of tomatoes
from the greenhouse and the sweet new potatoes her sister Lilian
brought from her smallholding, a whole sackful expressive of
sympathy. Lilian, Minnie, Mother, George, they all came by, with
spouse or brood; they all departed. It did not matter. They
impinged like brief whispers in a cave of silence. Jim lay on his side
of the double bed and suffered, and that was the only reality. And
he was only fifty. He was in the full vigour of his prime, though
mellower in temper, since the operation last summer. He was too
young for any of this; and brimming still with humour, and
interested in life, and wanting to live; and it followed that this
disease (her only reality) she refused to believe, she discount-
enanced it, and that left her no reality of any sort. She lived among
the shades.

Night and day she nursed him. It was like having a newborn

baby in the house, bringing him home from hospital, bringing him semi-solid food in bright-coloured dishes to tempt his appetite, rushing to him when he cried out. But such a heavy load this baby whose Christian name was Death. All her strength was wanted to turn him in the bed, she fought him to shift his bulk from the dirty sheet to the clean sheet, and his pain cried out from where it ate at him unreachably beyond the deadening curtain of morphine. It cried out against her. 'For God's sake, Chrissie,' he howled as she pushed with all her weight against his shoulder to lever him across. 'For God's sake Chrissie leave me alone. You're killing me Chrissie you're killing me.' He flailed his still powerful arms at her.

And because he sounded like a tiny boy, shouting out for his mother's help – and because the mother is as perishable and impotent as the child she is supposed to protect – and because he was Jamie for whom she would have died, and she needed him to help her in this crisis, she left him lying there on the open sea of sheets, drifting far out with his mouth open. She crossed blindly to the wall by the dressing table, laid her head against it, and cried like a little girl. Florence would be coming home from Leipzig this evening on the London train. She would have to take over the nursing work. It was the only hope. (Lilian had said she would come in and help. She was almost in the door and rolling her sleeves up, revealing the great biceps, the hard-skinned hands. 'Come on, our Chrissie, you need me. I'll fetch and carry.' But Christina would not accept that help. He would not like to waken in the arms of an Amazon, to the sight of Lilian's large and fleshy features. He would be humiliated. 'No, Lily,' she said. 'I'll manage for myself.') Even now she did not class anyone else as family, only the three of them, Jim, Christina, Florence. We are all in all to one another, she thought. We are three-in-one. We don't belong anywhere but with each other, and in each other.

She was going crazy with the sleepless nights, the indoor world, the nightmare vision. Present and past were becoming indistinct, even to her scrupulous inner eye which combed her own con-sciousness to rid it of the burrs of memory. I am forty-two, she said to herself, only that. But no, she seemed younger, half her own age, and halve it again, she thought, and so on: no age can express this infinite sense of being a lost child wandering on the boundary-less plains of time. She sat again by Jim's sleeping head, and stared at the wild flowers Minnie's boy Sam had picked, and handed mutely through the door in a jamjar. He was a bad boy; had been in prison for small thefts graduating in his twenties to larger thefts; but here he stood with the jamjar muttering about having been up Wilton way picking for Uncle. He kept his head low, and looked up furtively from beneath his cap; and though his eyes were dark and rather sly, she recognised in them the gentleness belonging to her father's. She recollected him as a small boy, all his clothes in undarned holes, his hair a grubby mass of curls, standing at his mother Minnie's side, his worshipping face wizened like a little monkey's stupid with the wish to please. And as she looked at him, receiving the jar into the unreality of her home, the older Sam who had gone to the bad in fact became the younger Sam at the outset of his pilgrimage; and the sweetness in his eyes metamorphosed into the shyness of her own father's pale eyes; and she wanted to shout out now to her long-buried father, 'Oh I want you now! Please please come back!'

'Thank you, Sam,' she said, and closed the door on him as he turned on his heel.

The flowers stood on the bedside cabinet just behind Jim's head. Looking at them from where she sat, it appeared that they sprouted from the head itself. The curve of the forehead, where the hair was so thin but gossamer-soft and the skin was shiny, was the sphere of the globe, from which the veined harebell and shimmering celandine transiently drew their fragile life and silken colours. She had used to love to press such flowers, it was her hoarding instinct, she could not let them go. Her mind's eye looked down upon her own girlish fingers separating out the violet and the cowslip from the green world, setting the blossoms within paper and pressing them in a book. The imagery was so clear that it assumed a more substantial reality than that of the wild flowers only just beginning to die at a tangent to the circle of the sleeping man's mind. Her body jerked convulsively as one does on the verge of sleep. It was the old family Bible, of course, that she was thinking of, the locked book which put a latch on the past and bound up into itself their shared mortalities. There they all lay retrieved with the brittle flowers of outlived springs. The book was under the bed now. She would not read it.

Jim began to stir. He turned his face slightly toward the direction in which she sat, the direction of the dawning light. The morphine was beginning to wear off but the pain was as yet only creeping nearer to the surface like a slow snake gliding upwards from an underground hole. His hands appeared above the counterpane,

128

still the great hands which evoked for her the sensation of overwhelming safety. He had been a rock; the rock of ages, all she knew of God. The hands played and plucked above the sheets, at some imaginary object. It looked as though he was knitting; or sewing some tear in the ripped seam of his world. Then they went still, and he continued to sleep. Florence would arrive in the evening. Florence would raise her flute to her lips perhaps, and blow, and then magically Jamie would awaken, whole and healed; he would raise himself upon one elbow with the old laugh in his eyes and ask what all the noise was. Florence must take on the nursing. Florence must cope. For she was going out of her mind. 'Oh Jim,' she wanted to say. 'Wake up and help me.'

Instead, she must have lapsed out. She awoke to the sound of an awful thump; she looked at the pillow and he was not there; she screamed. He was lying on his side up the corridor outside Florence's room, with one arm outstretched, the fingers grazing their daughter's door. It was impossible. He could not have done it by himself. Wasted away to a skeleton, a man with only inches of healthy lung tissue left, so weak he could scarcely move an arm, who had not eaten for weeks and weeks: how could he have got there? She put her hands over her mouth and screamed again. Then she went to him, where he lay unconscious at Florence's door. She implored him again and again, kneeling in her nightgown, to wake up; to put his arms round her neck and be put to bed. Tears poured down her face, soaking her neck and breast. They fell upon his poor face, and ran into his eyes. Finally she managed to hoist his arms round her neck, and he unexpectedly took hold and squeezed. With her whole strength she pulled them both to a standing position, face to face, and inched him – like the slowest of slow dancers waltzing body against body – back to their bed. She sat him down on the edge, with his head hanging forward and his eyes still shut. He let her lay his head down on the pillow, and lift his legs into bed. She tucked the blankets in tightly; she kissed his clammy forehead repeatedly. 'Oh my darling, oh my darling,' she kept on saying, as if to a baby. 'Whatever did you think you were doing?'

His mind cleared, he awoke.

'Chrissie,' he said. His voice had been eaten away long ago by the cancer, so that only a whisper remained. 'Did I just get out of bed, or have I been dreaming?'

'You did. I found you at Florence's door.'

'I thought it was the war, I was home on leave, and Flossie was a baby. I thought she was dead because I couldn't hear her breathing. I had to get to her. Is she all right?'

'Fine, she's fine. She's coming back from the concert tour this evening.'

'That's good then.' He rested, breathing hard. It was more than he had said for weeks. And although he looked more like an inmate of Dachau or Auschwitz than ever, Christina had the irrational feeling that he had reached a turning point; was going to get better after all. He lay with his eyes resting upon her face, seeming quite at peace.

'My mind keeps turning on the war, Chrissie, for some reason. I'm often certain it's still going on. I hear the Spitfires taking off from Sarum, or I imagine I'm eating corned beef in the desert with the lads from Five Squadron, or I see the smoke go up from Vesuvius – the molten rock fizz in the sea – the women with the ash in their hair.'

She had to bend her head to catch all that he wanted to say.

'There isn't any war on, Jamie. It's all over. It's peace now. You're going to get better. It's just a very bad do. We'll go to Italy like you always said, and see the sights.'

They had never admitted to one another the fact that Jim was dying; had never once named the disease. The word was worse, a million times worse, Christina felt, than the concentration-camp suffering in which they now existed. Without the word, they might survive. With the word, survival was ruled out. She kept the word at bay. How bravely she fought it. In their mutual shyness, growing over the years, speech had become less and less possible. But love lay ever more vast like an ocean beneath an ocean, and beneath that another ocean, floorlessly, on and on, but landlocked behind the languageless peninsula.

The morning sun was gaining on the mists outside. Very pale shafts of light filtered in, pooling at the foot of the bed. Suddenly Christina knew that she had been here before, at a place named Missing Presumed Dead: Golgotha, the Place of Skulls. She had seen the landscape of this obscene grief in its totality. Now she was a nineteen-year-old girl again, and the war was forcibly weaning her baby from her breast, the milk dried up, and she had consented, in her sleep, to a most unpardonable crime; and her young husband was lost in a foreign geography, mutilated, parted from himself. And what indeed was the difference between this war of cancer, and that, of bombs, the young self and its child, the older self?

Jim's lips were parched, the skin cracking. She moistened them with water from his glass.

'Are you in pain, my darling?'

He mouthed 'No'. He frowned in concentration, for his mind seemed to be sucked away again, spiralling anti-clockwise back down into that stifling darkness where it perceived all but could communicate nothing. He stared fixedly at the shaft of sunlight in which a vast population of specks was dancing, each mote burning like a firefly with reflected glory, journeying in large upward or downward circles until each passed out of the lit throng into invisibility. He wanted to say some things before he too passed out of the company of light.

He called her face closer with his eyes. There were things that ought to be said, and he had them on the tip of his mind, but what were they? Here was her beautiful, appalled countenance, close up to his, hardly any grey in her hair except at the temples a trace, large violet-blue eyes full of unshed tears, high forehead wrinkled in anxiety; and a sense of blessedness centred in her, the way found home through a street map of infinite complexity: so that he should speak now. He must. He must say the uncommunicated things, moving toward the statement of 'Goodbye'. It was possible. But here, on the other hand, was the lava flow of pain bursting from the crater. Here was the first shower of the more minor agonies like voided stones fizzing into the cold of the sea; and the laval flood became perceptible, black but at its margin the golden ripple of fire, which was the cauterising line of pain, running nearer with every second, the barrier of morphine ebbing before it, leaving his mind exposed. When the flow gets here there is nothing to say. They broke my ribs to get at the lungs. I hear them crack now under the scythe edge of pain. They ran their threshing blades amongst my bones and left me like the fieldmouse shattered in the wheatfield. Which enemy and whose army?

'Who – are – we – fighting?' I can ask her in a whisper, this blessed one who has stayed with me, who is me, or was, when I was anyone.

'There isn't a war. We aren't fighting,' she bends to me, tears flowing. Her tears scald my parching face.

I cannot remember what there was to say. The streets of Herculaneum blocked with volcanic mud, hardened to stone. I saw that. Pompeii and the little girl caught running; the famishing people, the children drinking sea water, the women selling their bodies for food, incommunicado. Love has nothing to do with any of it, it is the exchange of the healthy and well fed. I saw the end then: I arrive now at the end I saw. No, but there is still something to be said.

'I'd – do – anything – for you – and you'd – do – anything – for me.'

She bends her head now beneath my terrible words and her body shakes with sobs. Her hands are covering my hands. She cannot defend me. My mother could not. But on the verge of Jordan she is all there is: the first milk, the first bread.

'Tell Floss . . .'

'Tell her what?'

'Tell . . .'

'What, Jamie? What am I to tell her?'

'If I don't last till evening . . .'

'But you will. You will.'

'*Tell* her.'

'But I don't know what.'

'Paper.'

She brought paper and biro. With shaking fingers he drew a frail cartoon of a man peering over a wall, a question mark upon his head. He looked as though he were inwardly chuckling as he laid it down on the orange quilt, even as the final wave of pain, high as a house, broke upon his entire body.

Christina discarded the paper on the bedside cabinet. She saw he was drowning again. She got the bottle of pain killer and poured a measure. Levering up his head, she managed to get some into him. After a while his body began to quieten; he ceased to howl. But his breathing appalled her. Sometimes it came rattling and snoring out very harshly, full of voice. Then it appeared to encounter a hitch, and no breath came at all for what seemed minutes. The rhythm of silence and noise continued throughout the morning. At noon the district nurse arrived. Christina clung to her. She willed her to speak healing words. The nurse was a down-to-earth girl who dealt in plain speaking. She felt the poor old bloke's pulse. He was a goner.

'Won't last another twenty-four hours, this one. If that. He's had it all right.'

Christina winced as if she had been struck with a whip on the mouth. 'No,' she said tremulously. 'He's been like this for a long time. There's no change.'

The nurse was putting her things away with a deadpan expression. 'No point in giving the bedbath at this stage. Messing him around for nothing. He won't wake up again. Lungs all gone, see?'

'It's not true. You don't know.'

'I've seen enough of them to know, all right.'

'But what can we do? There must be something we can do?' She clasped the other woman's arm, tightening her fingers to commandeer her skill.

'Look here,' said the nurse, quite kindly. 'You don't want him lingering on in this condition, now, do you? Let him go, nice and peaceful.' She reopened her bag and gave him a lethal injection of morphine, after which his body lay perfectly still, and his breaths grated less loudly.

Jim's mind divided into two equal halves, and whilst one half remained anchored to the body on the bed, crammed from eyes to toes with solid pain, the other floated free and high. With his floating mind, he witnessed it all. He heard the nurse crucify his wife upon the nails of her plain speaking. He watched his wife continue to sit beside the body on the bed. He watched her heart die within her. He wanted to call down, 'Chrissie, it's all right my love, I'm here, things are not quite as you see them,' but this was impossible. Because he was not really up there, his tongue could not really call out, even if what he had to say was real. There was no time at all, levitating up there. There was a kind of levity. He wanted to laugh at the thought of being, at the very last, an airman. Invalid *me* out, he thought: we'll see.

When Florence came charging in, twilight falling, he was still there, and could register the meeting of mother and daughter. He noted with interest that Flossie didn't cry. She sat down beside his body, took its cold left hand in both of hers and let out a stream of talk. She went on and on. She called him by all the most loving names, and spoke of the places they had seen together. Again and again she told him how much she loved him. 'He can't hear you, you know,' said Christina.

'We don't know though. He might be able to catch some of it,' said Florence.

'No, he's past hearing anything. *You* don't know, Florence. *You* haven't been here to cope.'

133

With that mind which rode in the thin air of the heights above them both, Jim discerned the two turning fractionally away from one another. His aerial view encompassed his daughter's head bending nearer to the body on the bed; the mother turning her back on the *pietà* that had supplanted her own courageous posture, holding her temples between the thumb and forefinger of one hand, turning toward the mirror of her own despair. Yet his sensations as he watched the split begin were tranquil. And though he would have liked to say to Christina, so that she would remember it when he floated clear altogether, 'Look here, my beauty, it's all a mistake. I am just at an angle to you. Round a corner in time. Crosswise to your existence, transverse. And not to worry. It doesn't matter. It's funny really. I could make you laugh about it if I had use of words still.' Though he would have liked to pass this message down so that her brow would unfurrow from deep pain-ploughed wrinkles, he did not passionately wish it. He looked at his own body lying down there beneath him with an equivalent disinterested curiosity. The massive hands lay still on the quilt, surrounded by white daisies imprinted on the cotton cloth, as on a marvellous field of orange light. The hands were quiet, one of them being encased in both of Florence's; and she was stroking it with her thumbs, over the old war wounds, the carbuncles. The head of the body lay with its eyes shut like a warrior's effigy upon a sarcophagus, the intense air of puzzlement it had worn since this illness began being soothed into an impression of pure monumentality. The body itself no longer appeared as shrunken, its waste of flesh being covered in voluminous bedclothes. Its feet rested upon a pillow Christina had placed beneath them to comfort the soreness of their chafing. 'The poor old fellow,' thought his hovering mind. 'So this is what he's come down to. You can't help thinking he's well out of it really.' He thought of the baby beginning its voyage in its mother's lap, trussed round with lace-edged shawls, its head capped with a tight bonnet, its feet tied into boots of knitted wool. He thought of all the fuss, the mess, the incontinence and work; and he was glad the poor old chap was out of it, all things considered. He wished he could induce the body's hand to give Florence a parting squeeze, but so choked and blocked with pain the body was, the nerves could pass no signal down. The pain was a sediment hardening to stone. It had finally set adamantine through every passage of the body.

Between the processes of labour, a stage is reached which is called transitional. The baby's chamber has dilated open far enough to allow the head to begin its expulsion. This is the volcanic stage of labour; madness and turmoil are discharged in body and brain. It is the end of the beginning and the beginning of the end. Christina remembered this suddenly, as her stricken eyes watched the eyeballs beneath her husband's closed lids flickering as if he dreamed; and the grinding breaths seemed to stop altogether. For some reason she remembered a boy-baby; the maelstrom of his coming. She and Florence, with bated breath, waited for the next breath to come; or not.

Now his free mind descended to rejoin its partner in the body. The air had thinned; and thinned again, as it might for a mountaineer approaching the summit of the highest alp. Only a thread of oxygen was reaching the remaining inches of his corrupted lung; the dark wine of the bloodstream soughed its precious trove more and more slowly to the brain. His brain was starving of oxygen, it was famishing.

In the famine was liberation. He had no choice but to travel along the passage out. His head was caught in the soft jaws of the canal through which he must be evacuated. The passage contracted upon his head, rhythmically, biting him softly, squeezing him along. He was a boulder in a cave; the cave was dark as a mine, coal dark, tar dark. The cave must expel the blockage of his identity.

He had turned his back upon the vision of wife and daughter. They no longer existed. He remembered no such irrelevancies. The babble of their language did not approach him in the deep enclosure. There was no air through which might be transmitted the murmur of audible human claims.

They were in the future but he was going back. They were confined there like travellers on a railway station who roam about at the edge of the platform and gaze back up the line. But he was the train that is already deeply engrossed in the return journey along the tunnel cut through the mountain. His journey was as beyond recall as yesterday.

Darkness deepened, solidified. Night was substantial. Night was incorporated in the ribbed walls which, surrounding his head, urged it onward. Now the oxygen was almost all consumed that was carried in his blood, and his blood was heavy, torpid in the veins. Now he saw that the tunnel had an opening, and that he was drawing closer. The walls relaxed their hold and allowed him to slip helplessly along the remainder of the passage. His body was light; gravity in abeyance, as though the weightless lunar atmosphere received him. In the brilliant light which was turned on as if with an electric switch at the opening of the passage, he gauged that he had travelled a distance of just over fifty years.

It was a garden of viridian light. A woman in her prime was standing, musing, in the dappled light beneath a tree. She stood at an angle to him, lost in thought, her chin in her hand, her forefinger on her lips. She turned her head slowly toward him and her eyes suddenly smiled in recognition. She saw her child, he saw his mother. She had been waiting in the garden. She is here. She takes me back. It is warmth, it is ease, it is homecoming.

She opened her arms to him, and drew him from the passage complete. They cut the umbilicus and threw away the afterbirth. Seas of golden water flooded out after him. In the halcyon bliss of release, he fell sound asleep.

'He's gone,' said Florence, with her listening head upon the heart that now failed to stammer.

Three

The undertaker's men removed the corpse that evening, but they did not do it tactfully. They made clattering noises, and discussed in loud voices the strategic difficulties involved in manoeuvring the stretcher round the bend in the stairs. Florence had removed her mother into the sitting room, but the house was so small and the walls so thin that they could not help hearing every bump and expletive. The undertaker himself was hard to shift from the premises. He seemed to want to enliven the occasion indefinitely by discussing choices of sepulchral arrangements and itemised payments with the dumb-struck women. In the end Florence urged him to the door by walking straight at him. She seemed to push his condoling, wheedling voice physically along before her. 'Don't hesitate to get in touch,' he called back from the street. 'It's what I'm for.' She stared at the pin-striped person under the street lamp with astonishment. The world had opened to admit all sorts of grotesque foreigners, to do awful things to their most intimate lives. As she closed the door and glanced up the stairs, she saw that the removal of her father's body had been so clumsily done as to have left a trail of black marks up the wall. She fetched a cloth from the kitchen, and tried to rub them away, but the shadowy stains would not budge.

'What are you doing up there?' came her mother's voice.

Florence felt hot and faint, as if with shame; as if she were being accused. She wished she could hide all the evidence away from her mother, for it was as if she had been left responsible. But it could not be done. The marks were impossible to touch. The bed needed stripping and making up. The medicines had to be thrown away, so that her mother should not be exposed to the sight of them. But here was Christina insisting on advancing out of the safety of the sitting room, enquiring, 'What are you doing?' The desecrated house was an inventory of horror.

'Mummy, go and sit down. I'll get you some tea, and then I'll clear up a bit. Will you? Or shall I take you round to Gran's?'

She tried to lead her mother by the arm into the sanctuary of the room where the horror of the past months showed least.

'No, Florence, I must see to it myself.' She was tying on her pinafore. Her face was white and fixed.

'You don't have to, darling. I'm here now. I can do things for you. You're not alone.'

Christina jerked her arm away. 'Oh yes, you're here *now*, Florence. But where were you when you were *really* needed? Who helped me then? Not you. You were swanning off round Europe if I remember rightly. Making noises on that flute and getting clapped for it. Don't go on about how you'll help and I won't be lonely. It's too late for all that now, Florence. Daddy wanted you and you weren't there. *I* had no one.'

She was on her way upstairs when her eye registered the black marks, and she recoiled. 'What's that mess?'

'Won't you let me take you round to Gran's or Auntie Lilian's, Mummy? You'll be better there. I wasn't swanning off. It's my job.'

'Oh yes you were swanning. Your job was here. But you weren't doing it. What are those marks, Florence?'

'I don't know. I think I might have made them with my case

137

when I came in. We'll paint them out if they won't scrub. Won't you go round to Gran's, Mummy? Please do.'

'Get your hands off me for God's sake. Get them off, you hateful girl. You arrogant girl, I wish I'd never seen you. I wish I'd got rid of you when I had the chance and kept the boy instead. At least he'd be some use to me now. Not like you, you useless abortion. You made me keep you. You did. And this is what I get in return.'

Has she gone completely mad, Florence wondered. Why, with my father three hours dead, are my mother and I standing on the stairs in the dark and she's calling me an abortion? Resentment, incomprehension and pity tussled in her mind.

'And don't you keep saying that about Gran. That's not my home. It's not yours either. You and Daddy and I are all the family we need.'

'Why are you so angry with me? We shouldn't be angry at a time like this.' She was afraid now to put out her hand to her mother: it would be slapped away. She held on to the banister and fought her tears.

'I'm not angry. I don't know what I'm saying.' Her mother's voice came small and defeated. 'Let's go upstairs and clear things up.'

Here was the empty bed still crumpled from where his suffering body had lain, the skewed pillows, the blankets in a heap at the bottom of the bed where the undertaker's men had dumped them. Her father's glass of water had been knocked down, and its contents were spilt over a piece of paper on the bedside cabinet. Without a word, Christina removed the sheets, brought new linen and began to remake the bed. She threw the windows open, and the warm night air came in loaded with balm and pollen to displace the sickroom smell. They worked in silence, bundling the old sheets out into the corridor and emptying all the medicines and pills into a plastic bag. Christina was businesslike. She began saying sensible things.

'The chemist can have the unused cotton wool and paper sheets back, Florence. It would be a shame to waste them. Put them in a pile here, love. That's right. We'll have the blankets dry cleaned.'

'You've been incredibly brave. You really have.'

'He was brave. I wasn't brave. He did this drawing for you earlier today. It seems to have got rather wet. He told me to be sure and give it to you.'

Florence took the indistinct cartoon over to the lamplight. A

138

querulous little man in blue biro was poking his nose over a wall. He wore a question mark upon his bald head, and tears dripped from his eyes.

'What is it?'

'It's a Mr Chad. Don't you know what that is? It was a cartoon they had in the war, to satirise the shortages. The Chad is peering into a shop and saying "Wot, no –?", meaning no beer, or no fags, or no sugar – whatever was in short supply at a particular time.'

'Oh, I see. And he really meant it for me to have?'

'Yes, he said so.'

'But what does it mean, do you think?'

'I wouldn't know, Florence. Of course, if you'd been here at the time, you could have asked him yourself. But as usual you were a bit late in coming forward.' The storm was rising again, Florence could hear the murmur of a lifelong suppressed anger focusing on herself, in lieu, she supposed, of other victims. She took the picture to her desk, and locked it in a drawer. None of it seemed real. Her spirit needed to express its grief at her father's loss; to begin to know its wound, and instead found itself surrounded by tidal currents of venomous fury, and reduced to a sensation of childish unease. She sat down on her bed, setting her fingers on the handle of the unopened case, as though she could spring up and run away with it, back to her London flat, to be on her own with a grief that could be as simple and natural as it surely ought to be.

Once Christina had started to throw things away, she found she could not stop. Everything to do with his illness had been jettisoned. But late in the night, staring round the house which had been nothing more than a sick bay throughout their occupancy, she became aware of the herculean task that waited to be done. On the dressing table lay Jim's hairbrush and his comb, a matching tortoiseshell set, tidily set out ready for use. In an oval wooden box lay his mother-of-pearl studs and an Air Force tie pin bearing the badge of the eagle and the crown. She had not cried at all. Her eyes were dry and gritty as if they suffered from conjunctivitis, and each object they saw seemed to scratch upon the sore membrane. She sat at the dressing table rubbing her eyes, leaning on her elbows with her downcast face quite close to the mirror, so that when she raised them she was looking into the reflection of a face not her own; a face strange and pale as a lunar landscape. The features were each one unfamiliar. You could not compose them into a harmony of named relationships, like a map: you could not say, 'This is my nose, these my eyes, mouth and all the related etceteras, such as are usual and expected in human faces.' Composite normality failed; it broke down, snapped apart. The pallid collection of features looming like a planet was not Christina. Christina departed from herself, as all objects departed from their uses; the alphabet divided into twenty-six unmeaning signs; and the vertical and horizontal rejected their ancient treaty.

Swaying on the heaving floor of the bedroom whose floorboards shifted like planks on the deck of a ship, Christina focused on the brush and comb, the studs and tie pin. They would have to be got rid of. When she picked them up to dispose of them into bags, the brush and comb were lead heavy in her hands. The pin was a magnetic weight. His watches, travelling clock and the fob watches he had inherited from her own father, when lifted from the drawer where he had lovingly laid them, bound in felt, started ticking with being jarred into wakefulness; and the ticking beat with echoes the tattoo of time, each clock at its own rate. She threw the golden fobs into the bag, and followed them with pairs of spectacles, in their cases or naked; and the little bags of coconut sweets which he kept by him to eat during the night in case he woke; and his false teeth; and his nail clippers; and some fluted scallop shells he had brought back from Naples with him in the war, wrapped in handkerchiefs. After a while she arrived at his shoes in the cupboard, all lined up with a gleaming, military aspect; and his beautifully pressed shirts, his hand-knitted jumpers, suits and ties. It all had to go. There had been so much detail to him. Would she never get to the end of him? To her exasperation, in the bathroom she found his shaving tackle forgotten on the shelf; and flannels, toothbrush. She pitched it out. For all these things were lies. These evidences would kill her outright with their deceit, if she let them stay. Finally she remembered the biggest lie of all: the most cunning of the cheats that had been practised on her. On her knees, she dragged the great family Bible from under the bed, and with the deepest satisfaction added it to the pile of waste material. Then she could weep. The tears came flowing, to comfort her wounded eyes. She climbed into the bed, took his pillow in both arms and, kissing it repeatedly, soaked it with her tears. She lay thus in his place, not asleep but not quite awake either, entirely still, through to morning, the helpful tears oozing out from between her closed eyelids.

Florence had been sitting up in bed listening from behind her closed door to the racket of breaking glass and chinking of metal.

Once she crept out to see what was going on, and there was her mother framed in the doorway of her parents' room blindly emptying the contents of a drawer into a black dustbin bag. Florence was afraid. She stood in the corridor in her thin nightgown, cradling her own bare arms; and wanting to speak; but nothing came out. Her mother did not notice her at all. She felt as if she would not be recognised if she did approach. 'Who are you?' would demand the solitary, dementedly active woman. 'And what do you want?' Florence's life had always assumed a posture of triumph. Her nature was yeasty, vagrant, strong willed. The alcohol of innate egoism which had washed buoyantly round Florence's bloodstream since birth, protecting her from all failure of nerve, was beginning to falter. Her constitutional high spirits, resounding throughout her twenty-three years of life in a chatter of self-celebration, were failing her. She loitered uncertainly, then went back to her bedroom. She's throwing away all his things, she thought; all the precious remnant of his personality. I'm not letting her do that. Her will came down hard against her mother.

With first light Florence crept out of her room and rummaged through the dustbin bags lined up outside the front door. Christina was not stirring. It was a beautiful sunlit morning, with an edge of tingling cool. The world was awash with surplus oxygen. The birds were shouting their music from one to another, it volleyed and ricocheted around the unpeopled spaces. The air was pure, astringent on her face as she knelt in the long shadow cast by the house to begin her work. She could not credit that they had really taken their death blow, yet this jumble of rubbish that only yesterday had constituted necessitous objects seemed to prove it. She worked with methodical, swift industry. She seemed to recollect the art from a period now long past. But a new terror and pathos were added as she pursued her work of salvage. Some deeply-buried memory was being stirred and dragged to the surface: what was it? She tried to name it, this obscenity seen once and packed down into the quicklime of the unconscious. It was Germany – Dachau, the museum of the Holocaust – and her father's obsessive insistence that she be taken to view it, as a representative of her generation, to be educated in the horrors committed by her species, so as to avoid repeating them in the future. And Christina said to him, 'She's morbidly sensitive already, Jim, she doesn't need that kind of knowing.' (Doubtless she knew they'd be up with their daughter's nightmares for months afterwards.) But Jim did not seem convinced that the child of the war could claim exemption on the grounds of temperamental disaffinity with mass murder. She saw it all now, being driven through the iron gates in their Volkswagen, and being shown the gas chambers, the burial trenches and the huts, the gallery of photographs of the victims and their fates. He made her look at them all. 'It's best you should know.' The grass had been newly mown in the camp, and sunlight on the shorn blades released drifts of sweet vapour-like incense. Gipsies had moved into the prison huts and hung their washing out; their children tumbled and shrieked outside, wearing red scarves tied round their necks. 'Not nice for you, girlie, but it's best you should know, don't you think so?' She refused to reply. She was angry. She remembered his hands flat on the driving wheel as they came out of the camp, the anxiety in his voice. She wondered if he had ever killed anyone in the war as she considered those hands, and whether it was his own bloodstain that induced him both to appease and implicate herself. She would not speak for the rest of the day, but turned her head obstinately away when spoken to. She was bitter in her mind, as if she had been assaulted. It had nothing to do with her. She did not want to know. She overheard her father, crestfallen, in the hotel that night, asking her mother, 'Did I do wrong, Chrissie? *Didn't* she have to know?'

Now she knew, all right. Now he had educated her properly. This knowledge came to everyone sooner or later, she saw. Sorting through a bag containing a beloved person's false teeth, shoes, empty wallet, you soon got the idea. She sifted out three chubby golden fob watches, some identity papers, all sorts of precious things, and soon had a pile big enough to fill a bag of its own. The last thing she retrieved was the family Bible. The great hasped, metal-bound book was not something with any associations for her. Indeed she couldn't remember having seen it before. But you couldn't possibly get rid of a thing like that. She did not, however, unlock and open the Bible. God was out of the question, and Christ and his mother, and the raging prophets and the mellifluous words of sacred anodyne in the parables, the Sermon on the Mount. The forces of darkness had overrun the forces of light: the war was over: not to admit surrender must be hypocrisy. But the book made a personal claim on her affections, aside from its theology. She stroked its cover of flaking leather; it needed to be kept. Therefore she stowed it as a Book of Remembrance with her various other

142

spoils at the top of her cupboard, packing them all round with a spare blanket.

Together for three days they fought over proprietorship of Jim's absent spirit. His ghost was stretched between them, and they kept grasping and snatching at it with avaricious hands, tugging it this way and that. Sometimes Christina had hold of it, sometimes Florence pulled at a rag of his garment and tore it out of her mother's grip. Yet even when one of them had hold of the ghost, possession brought no solace, for his nature was made of air, and went to nothing in their hands. They argued about who had loved him most, which of them he had loved more. Their competition, unlike that between the true and false mothers at Solomon's famous show trial, was irresoluble by the abdication of the genuine lover, for each love had its legitimacy; and each loved him in the other. The child could not be salvaged whole in a world whose heart had fled away to chaos and scattered into multiplicity.

'Well, of course, you knew him for twenty-three years,' Christina would begin, meaning well. 'And that's a long time to know someone. You're bound to feel it badly.'

'But you knew him for twenty-four years,' replied Florence, also meaning well. 'So that must be worse, I suppose.' There's something wrong with the logic of this, she thought. 'But for goodness' sake, he was my father. So it doesn't matter how long it was in years. Does it?' She stared at her mother in bewilderment and irritation.

Christina grabbed the hem of the ghost and tweaked him back towards herself. 'But you can't know the love that a husband and wife can have,' she said evenly. 'That's not within your realm of experience.'

'No, that's true. But I don't claim to. What is our discussion really about? What are we arguing for?'

'Well, you see, *you* don't know about that kind of love because you're – for want of a better word – promiscuous. He was the only one for me, for twenty-four years.' Deny *that*, she thought.

'I'm not promiscuous!' Florence flared up. 'Why do you say so? And even if I were, what difference would it make? He's still my father.'

'You do sleep around, Florence, I think that's the phrase. You made no bones about it. It made Daddy very upset, but he never said anything to you about it because he never wanted to hurt you, only protect you. But the fact remains, you did blight his closing years.'

'Just because I can't find the one single person I need doesn't mean I – doesn't mean I didn't care. I didn't do that – what you said – did I? Make him unhappy?' She felt like a child caught out in wickedness. But it isn't like that, she thought. Yet now the thought of being in bed with Tim, the images she tried to focus on, to save her from this morbid world entombed in their home, didn't seem so nice. She saw herself coupling with him as the struggle of insect bodies trapped writhing under a net. She hunched forward with pain and shame, and drew her arms defensively together over her breast. Her mother's face was blank and deadly, like a Fury.

'I don't think a person like you should ever think of having a baby,' said Christina matter-of-factly. 'It just wouldn't be right.'

'I wasn't thinking of having a baby!' gasped Florence. 'But why shouldn't I? What unfits me that doesn't unfit thousands of other people?'

'You're just a certain kind of person. You'd never get up to it when it cried at night (they do, you know) and you wouldn't have the patience to feed it and clean it, and so on. It's better for you to indulge your liking for freedom, and travel round the world. Altogether a better idea.'

It's because I didn't get home in time to nurse him, thought Florence, that she's saying this. She resents me. She never wanted me. She's always wanted a boy instead. I was a let-down.

'If you wanted a better child than me, you should have had other babies. As it is, you're landed with a promiscuous, undomesticated gypsy, and you'll have to put up with me.'

'What would Daddy say if he heard you speaking to me like this, being so cruel after all I've gone through?' The ghost reverted to Christina.

'Well, he can't hear me now, can he? Would you prefer me to go away, if I'm so freakish and generally unwholesome?'

Terror seized Christina; her face worked to keep back the tears. 'No, you can't go. You're all I've got. You're so like him, Flossie. I can see him in your face. I want you to be to me as he was, very close, so that I can depend on you.' She got up and put both hands on Florence's shoulders. She was slightly the taller. It was like being clapped in irons. Florence heard the chains on her future rattle; and an ironic peel of laughter echoed back from the future, as her mother continued, 'I've just thought, Flossie, to seal the bond between us, let's make wills in one another's favour.'

'But Mother, we've never been very close.' The harsh words slapped Christina back. She staggered. The lunatic world was heaving beneath her feet. Words kept coming from her which she had not intended to say, and whose meaning was very obscure. And Florence was being so very cruel.

'How *dare* you say we're not close? How *dare* you?' she shouted in a frenzy, at the top of her voice.

'The neighbours will hear you.'

'I don't care about the bloody neighbours!' Christina continued to shout. She heard her own words with astonishment. 'Let them hear! I'm asking you Florence how you dare to say we're not close – as mother and daughter we've always been as one, like one person.'

Florence's skin crawled. She retaliated brutally. 'We weren't. We never have been able to communicate. You always shut me up. Yes you did. I was closer to Daddy from the day I was born than I've ever been to you.'

'Oh *were* you,' Christina said slowly. 'How little you know about that.'

'Exactly. You don't tell me anything.'

'You have no idea, Florence, how much I gave up for you. I gave up everything so that you could have your life – and your freedom – and you could squawk away on that oboe like a sick duck, and go fluting off around the world pleasing yourself, and living a charmed life.'

'Tell me then. Just tell me what you gave up. *I* can't see what I caused you to miss out on. I never asked you to give things up: you always made a point of it. It was a pleasure to you, martyring yourself. I never asked to be born either,' she ended with a childish sulk.

'Do you think that if you'd had a brother, Florence, you would have been educated as you were, and given all the advantages you were?'

'No, I don't suppose so for a minute. I was my father's only son. I was grateful for that. I am grateful.'

Christina went silent. Her body drooped, limply, and she had to sit down. She could not remember what they had been saying, except that it had been ugly, and stupid, and entirely beside the point. Language was venting itself from her automatically. Words just went on morning and evening speaking themselves from her, without her consent. She imagined language as lying in the depths of her self like a black tarn; the charnel words, thick and black in sound and meaning, kept spilling upwards into the light, like jets of oil from the underworld. When would this terrible exposed place of liquid darkness seal over, she wondered, and let her go back to the merciful silence of her own reserve. Or would she always be like this, mad and out of control, raining corrosives upon the spirit of her daughter, so innocent of blame and so long loved?

The pain of pitying her mother was the really unbearable thing, thought Florence. Christina's face was gaunt; the skin marble white stretched across the high cheekbones. Her expression now resembled the stillness which sculptured the pain of a Michelangelo *mater dolorosa* into its unreachable reserve of virginal beauty. She knelt at her mother's side and took up her folded hands in her own. The ghost between them thinned and fled, having no battlefield to haunt.

'Your fingers are so cold,' she said, chafing them between her own palms.

'I've said awful things to you,' said Christina, turning her eyes reflectively on her daughter, judicious and disinterested, as if judging a case. 'I'm not sure what they were. But I hope you can forgive and forget them, bearing in mind that I seem to have gone mad.'

The night before the funeral, Christina heard the bombers passing overhead. They came in waves, roaring over the roof tops in a long crescendo of noise which died away into perfect stillness. Were they ours or theirs, she wondered? Lancasters from Sarum, or the swastika-bearing Messerschmitts. They seemed to be coming in very low. She sat up in bed as the house trembled under the tempest of sound. She experienced no fear. On the contrary, her mind was calm and clear. Her terror of the bombs had been confronted and purged twenty years ago when the whole of Europe had been blitzed; and the map of the world was buried under heaps of charred rubble, through which the refugees filed with bundles and wagons; amongst them the young women with blank masks for faces, carrying their unweaned babies, separated from their husbands. For then it was the common condition, to be alone, to know destitution, of body, of spirit. In her present dereliction she remembered the details of her old, first loss. When they brought the telegram. Mother gave it me. She'd been washing Florence's nappies and the suds were everywhere. Mother's face, crumpled, guilty looking. When I knew. And how I couldn't feed Flossie. My milk dried up. I couldn't feed her; she sucked and nothing came for her. And didn't she just howl. She howled the place down with outrage. I felt like a criminal. But then he came back, you see. He wasn't dead at all. He was hiding somewhere else, out of time, safe. But still I couldn't feed Flossie, even so. The milk wasn't there. It was useless to fret about it.

She must have dreamed the aeroplanes, she thought; or imagined them. She switched the light out, laying her head on the pillow, to see if sleep might come again. But as soon as she closed her eyes, the murmur began again. From the northern horizon it mounted, and the planes came thundering over the roof tops, formation after formation. The water glass upon the bedside cabinet shook until it tinkled. Some plaster from the corner of the ceiling shook loose and sprinkled down a fine white dust. But were they ours, or theirs? Consumed with curiosity rather than fright, she got out of bed, threw open the window and craned her neck to get a view of the sky. The roar had died away, and the sky was a field of black velvet upon which the stars were thickly massed and very bright. She remained there, drinking in the cool of the night air, letting it wash the skin of forehead and wrists; and all night the aeroplanes kept coming, squadron after squadron, and still she could not tell whose they were, ours or theirs. With the coming of the morning chorus, they ceased; and Christina slept then.

'Did you hear the planes in the night?' she asked Florence, as they got dressed in their new black outfits ready for the funeral, hours early. 'They made a terrific row.'

'What planes?' asked Florence. She was surprised at her mother's calm manner. Christina wore a faraway expression, as if she had heard some news which distracted her from the present dance of death.

'Oh, didn't you hear them? They were very loud. Exercises from Sarum, perhaps. It reminded me so much of the old days; brought all sorts of things back.'

Four

   She meant to try and play a little on the flute, the funeral being over and the burden of their dread in temporary abeyance. Christina had drunk some sherry and was dozing in front of the television. Florence sealed herself into her room, which was filled with orange light from the sunset, burning on the mirror and glowing dimly in woodwork and furniture. She had not practised once for over a week; and she was not a person who could afford to let go for a minute. The 'Dance of the Blessed Spirits' from Gluck's *Orfeo* seemed the obvious place to start. She got out the score and the music stand, and assembled the flute. How cold its metal felt in her hands and on her lips. As she settled her fingers on the keys, the joints twinged as if with arthritic pain. A sensation of dark apprehension invaded her. She blew a few arpeggios, watching herself in the mirror. The tone was thin and breathy; the embouchure made her mouth appear to have assumed an insincere and deathly grin. She took the flute away from the ugly face. The reflection registered panic. She could not play. She dismembered the instrument into its three parts, and shut them away in the box, snapping the locks together sharply.

   The spirit had gone out of her, the force and drive. Her will-power had flown back down a long tunnel and buried itself in solid darkness. She was walled in, miles underground. She could not hope to get in touch with herself. Until today she had never wondered how to play, the spiritual mechanics of it, where the vital breath came from that gave the music its conviction. Florence had early chosen the French rather than the less Romantic American school of flute. Her playing tore at the notes of the bottom register of the instrument, to express a metallic music of harsh beauty. She coerced the soft flute to abandon its femininity; to become its own opposite. In the higher registers the sound was large and round, like a glass-blower's globes. Impersonating the god who first blew the pith from the oaten reed, an element of violence characterised her manner, as though she were trying to force the chamber open, to free as many harmonies as it could yield, at the risk of over-blowing into the next octave. At the top of the register her flute could reach a kind of empyrean where the harmonics seemed to go altogether. She exhibited herself with busy tonguing and reckless vibrato. Yet she could also be eerily quiet and restrained, with the inwardness of a stateless, nomadic searching. She had won a competition at an early age, to find instant acclaim as a soloist. Later she began to be criticised for wilful misinterpretation. Her Mozart was extravagant, melancholy and Romantic; her Beethoven regressively classicist, rigorous and severe. The *Guardian* critic, Gerhard Lerner, had recently written that she did not so much play as betray the music, astonishing the ears of Mancunians with her capricious misreadings. Florence took this as a compliment. She was not so flattered when she read somewhere that she was expected to burn herself out very young. The element of growth was lacking.

Florence knew this, and with part of herself had daily awaited the failure of her nerve, the process of withering. So this, she thought, is it. My voice has been buried with its father. But no, it's just too early for me to start playing again, after all this. It will come again, the power of speech. You don't really lose that. She did not want to consider seriously the fact that she came on her mother's side of an inarticulate people, who – like her grandfather, her uncle – took the earliest opportunity of merging back into the silence of the plain.

A fortnight had gone by, and still she could not play. She stayed at her mother's house, and probated the will, which yielded a mean subsistence for Christina, since James had been too liberal and spendthrift ever to close his fingers round his earnings. She wrote 'thank you' letters in response to messages of sympathy. She wanted to go home to her London flat and see Tim again, and take up the threads of her own life, but could not think of the appropriate words by means of which to communicate to Christina the fact that she was going. She coughed, drew breath prior to uttering her intention, and let it out again falteringly without having spoken. Christina gave her to understand that she did not wish her to mix with the Salisbury relatives. She did not say why, but Florence knew the reason was that they were too common for the likes of the Llewellyns. Christina gave commands with her eyes rather than through explicit directions; and Florence's will to resist seemed to have wasted away. Fear of hurting her mother and fear of her mother rendered her inert. She loitered round the house, which had been put on the market, and went on shopping errands. She spent long periods sitting at her bedroom window looking out with glassy eyes at the perspective of hedges and lawns, registering time like a sundial clocking the monotonous cycle of light and expanding, abbreviating, reiterated shadow. Christina's bereavement eating into her nature like a cancerous tumour was terrible to contemplate. Cowering back from the hell her mother inhabited, Florence did not dare to begin the process of her own grieving. She put it off for a freer time, and lived in a state of limbo.

One morning Christina seemed brighter. She told her daughter she had not dreamed that night, and seemed more rested. She would go out herself, she said, and shop. When she had gone, Florence's mind fixed itself on the objects she had retrieved from the rubbish, the morning after her father's death. She brought them down from the cupboard and laid them out on her bed. Bright sunlight burnt upon her grandfather's golden fobs, and warmed their metal bodies through, so that when she came to pick them up they held the heat, as though they had only just been removed from the owner's waistcoat pockets. She fingered them with poignant joy, opened up the backs and wound the serrated ball to set them ticking. In the body of each, time leapt up like a responsive heart eager to resume the beating out of its own pulse music. Soon there was a concert of symphonic tickings. Kneeling in the band of high-summer sunlight that flooded her bed, Florence felt her own heart dilate with urgency to get on with the business of living. Dust flecks danced in wild animation above her bent, bronze-golden head, as she pondered her salvage.

She kept the great Bible back till last. It excited her by its promise of a locked-in life of marvellous longevity, recording generations of continuous existences. She ran her fingers over the cover with its rough textures of crumbling leather and rusting iron. Then she freed the hasps, which, having rusted into one another, were hard to work loose. The open book released an odour of must and mildew. Its pages were hemmed with brown, where the paper was fast decaying. Pasted within the front cover she found cuttings from local newspapers relating to members of the Gartery family since the turn of the century: a Gartery found guilty of drunk and disorderly behaviour at Winchester Crown Court; a Gartery meeting an untimely end by cycling into a Number 5 bus; a Middlewhite creating history by being delivered of her fourth set of identical twins, in 1903; a Christina Gartery achieving a school prize for Good Behaviour. Florence read every word hungrily. They all sprang to life in her imagination as she read, with a vivacity and enchanting remoteness not shared by the merely living. The company of the dead crowded upon her mind, claiming kin. Turning the pages over, she found the Pentateuch littered with violets, tissue-thin with their dark tracery of veins in petals transparent with age. The pages creaked as she raised them, buckling with damp, the torpid weight of the past seeming to resist disclosure.

Between the Old and New Testaments was inserted a list of Births, Marriages and Deaths, on paper whiter and less elderly than the rest of the book. Florence began to read from the beginning, savouring the Josiahs and Henriettas, Arthurs and Alfreds of the last century, a teeming inventory of infantile deaths and mothers perished in childbirth. As she moved toward the present, she began to recognise names. Finally her eye caught her own name, in her mother's handwriting:

'Florence Sarah Amelia, beloved daughter of James and Christina, born 10.27 a.m., 18th December, 1944.'

Underneath this she read:

'James, beloved son of James and Christina, also born on the evening of 18th December, 1944.'

I was born with a twin brother. It doesn't say he died. It does not say so anywhere. The rest of the page is blank. The blood roared in her ears.

She sat and stared at nothing. Stealthily, unseen presences have packed the room. They jostle and crowd at her, the legions of the unknown. Many possible faces approach and depart. They are an impediment to breathing.

She stared into thin air. Thin air solidified into a wall. It bounds the living and holds out the dead. I hope it is stout. I fear that if I reach out I could put my hand right through. James my father is just behind the wall, loitering mortally near. If I reach out he will grasp my hand and drag me through. I dread him, I long for him.

She read the inscription again. James her brother breaks from the land of the shadows by her reading of his name. He shows himself for the first time in twenty-three years tersely to the light of

151

day. Missing presumed dead, she thinks, you have been. But you could be living round the corner in the next street; or pseudonymously in another country; or dead in some unmarked grave in Devizes Cemetery, long forgotten. His shadow getting up from the page terrified her like an enemy long hidden in a secret trench.

The Chad, her father's legacy, came into her mind. 'What, no father? What, no brother?' enquired the comic little man, topped with the question mark. A brief glance over the wall is all we get, she thought; then the muddled eyes drop back into the dark.

Leaving the Bible open on her desk, she leaned her head against the window pane's cool transparency. It is incredible that the world is going on out there just as usual. Don't they know? Don't they feel the static electricity in the air, the rumbling of thunder on the horizon. Such insistence on normality seems mad. Women cluster round the butcher's van in a hum of chatter. A toddler breaks loose from its mother, sheers off joyously down the pavement and is meshed by the fingers of a passer-by. A cyclist free-wheels. Sunlight forges rainbows through dewy prisms of beads of moisture on the limes in the avenue. This sauntering normality of summer, it is like the Phoney War. They go on reciting their mellifluous tales under the squadrons of darkening clouds.

How sinister it was, this bleaching of reality. When you fell into knowledge it seemed unbearable. I had a twin brother but she never told me. She said, 'I wish I'd kept the boy and got rid of you.' She said that. And yet everyone out there got on with business as usual as though the continuum of ordinary life were still unchallenged.

Florence's body ached with its swelling need to weep for her father. She could not stay indoors with the aching. She put the key in her pocket, let herself out and ran weeping past the butcher's queue.

Five

'Young lady to see you, Mrs Gartery,' the baker called back in. He had been delivering Amelia's small white loaf and enlivening her with his daily dash of conversation. 'A very tall one, a very red-in-the-face young lady. Do you want to see her?'

'What does she say her name is?'

'She wants to know what you call yourself.'

There was a pause.

'A deaf and dumb young lady, Missus,' called the interpreter. 'Possibly of Red Indian origin, judging from her rig-out.'

'Oh send her in whoever she is,' called back the voice. 'Get along with you. And mind you tell the chimney sweep I want him – the chimney's smoking summat awful.'

'Go on through,' said the baker. 'She's quite compos today. Not exactly skipping around, with that ulcerated leg. By the way,' tugging the tassels of Florence's smock, 'Cherokee or Sioux?'

Through a door standing ajar, a chamber pot could be seen glinting beneath a downstairs bed, the upper floor having long been surrendered to the spiders. An elderly draught curtain of greenish velvet screened the sitting room. Florence pulled it aside. The old woman at the fireside sat with one leg bandaged and raised on a stool. Against her charcoal dress and cardigan, the silver-white hair which was abundant and straying, appeared quite luminous. Her blue eyes were clear and spry. Florence advanced.

'Don't tell me now, I'll work it out. I'm sure I know you.' Florence awaited identification. She did not remember Gran at all. In a line-up of old ladies, she could not have picked her out.

'Over my dead body they'll get me out of here. Doctors and daughters and do-gooding busybodies. *Very* unreal they are too. I dream a lot, you know, I see faces of people they keep telling me are dead and gone. Sometimes they speak to me. Confused, my daughters call me. Do you think I'm confused?'

153

Florence shook her head.

'Certainly not. Quite right. Now there's something about the eyes. Something to do with Chrissie, that's it.'

'I'm Florence,' said Florence. The blond child like a little dancing ghost slid straight into Amelia's field of vision. She herself often slipped back into the mother-selves and became one with them, a shadow cast among shadows, a pool of the greater sea. The large girl in guise of an Indian brave now came and kissed her cheek. She found her no stranger than many of her other apparitions.

'You were our baby you know, Flo – your grandad's and mine – till you were about three. We brought you up. A lovely little child but difficult, you see, eccentric. Wouldn't eat. Hair as white as wheat. You're darker now, my love, aren't you. Your grandad thought the world of you. He had a store of mint humbugs in a tin – that round one on the shelf there, go on look up behind you – specially for you, those were – and he'd come up and just pop one in your mouth when you were opening it to give one of your speeches. You never stopped talking for a minute.'

'Was I born with a twin brother?'

'Course you were; our Chrissie had a terrible time with the two of you. Nearly lost her life. No one knew it was twins, see.'

'But what happened to the boy, Gran?'

'Stillborn, Flo. You came out first, safe and sound. Then they found Chrissie was still in labour, but when the second twin came, they found he'd been dead a long time. I never saw him, mind. They had a compassionate attitude and took it away with no fuss.'

'My mother never told me.'

'No, well I think it upset her too bad, more than she would say. Chrissie was always one to bottle up if anything upset her. The neatest girl she was – liked everything folded up just so. She reminds me of my mother . . .'

To be moored at one haven with a death, at the very outset of one's life. To keep company with a creature to whom the nurturing umbilicus was no better than a hangman's cord. To open your sticky eyelids to the light of day, while the carcass of your eyeless equal rots further on his passage out.

'Did my father ever see my brother?'

'Who was your father, dear?' Amelia appeared startled, unwilling to cause pain, but she could not for the life of her imagine who her visitor was. Had she seen her somewhere before?

154

'James Llewellyn, Christina's husband.'

'Oh no, he never knew anything of Florence for months after she was born. He was abroad you see, fighting. Missing in action. Chrissie had to cope on her own. She didn't want him told about any of it. Quite queer she went with all the trouble. Now my own mother –' There was the sound of the front door being opened; shoes wiped with ponderous vigour on the doormat. 'Oh good that'll be Lil, I wanted to ask her something, about my teeth I think it was.'

'Who's this then?'

Lilian in her late forties was a bulky, cumbersome woman, gone to lard rather than seed. Her features were conspicuously bulging, with fleshy nose and cheeks, square jaw. Florence mentally shrugged the intruder off as unimportant as soon as she sized her up. She thought, go away, you hideous woman; Lilian thought, what a ridiculous girl, snooty looking piece. Lilian sat down opposite her mother, hands in her jacket pockets, trousered legs stuck out ahead of her.

'You all right then, Mother? What have we got here?' She stared quite rudely, Florence thought. She flushed.

'I'm Florence.'

'Oh are you *really*. Chrissie's girl. Well well, fancy that, Chrissie's Florence, honouring us with a visit after all these years. Let's have a good look at you, don't be bashful now, come over into the light so that I can see you.'

Manhandling Florence toward the small back window, she stood gripping her niece's shoulders, severely scrutinising her features. The interior of the house was chill and dark, but here a patch of dazzling sunlight illuminated them face to face. Florence turned her head slightly away; she would have liked to shove the woman off; bolt. This isn't what I had in mind at all, she thought. 'Yes, I can see something of our Chrissie in you, Flo,' said her aunt judiciously. 'You haven't her beauty, mind, she was a one-off job in our family, but you've the carriage, and the eyes. And you're a lanky thing, aren't you.' Not much to write home about are you Florence, she thought. For all the fuss they made about you here, you're nothing much, are you, when it comes down to it. Done up in your fancy dress, arrogant sort of face, not a lovely person like our Chrissie was, but even so. A complexity knit itself into the depths of Lilian's consciousness as she assessed Chrissie's daughter, a tilting of her whole dimension, a slight scalding of her

155

eyes, at the remembrance of Chrissie and all she had meant, in the nervy, vulnerable face. I might weep: but I never weep: I am angry at the thought that a thing like you could animate my tears. I'd like to slap your silly haughty face, Lady Muck, she thought, I'd like to sting you with words you'd remember. Florence caught and returned the anger. What right has this odious creature to lay her great fat hands on me? She tried to step back, but Lilian's grip was firm. 'Well, well, well,' said Lilian meditatively. 'Chrissie's girl. We haven't seen you for about ten years, do you know that, Florence? Now why was that then, girl? Too grand for the likes of us were you? Hob-nobbing round the world, I suppose, and never thinking of what you left behind. When you left here your Gran and Grandad cried for days, they did: it finished your Grandad off. But you obviously didn't think of that.'

'I *was* only three at the time,' muttered Florence, scarlet-faced under the attack. Monstrous three-year-old Goneril, she thought, thus to abandon a helpless grandfather.

'Oh well, it can't be helped. You *would* go, and that's that,' responded Lilian with an air of beneficence, as if reconciling herself to the existence of original sin. 'Your mother keeps well, does she?'

'Not exactly. My father's just died.'

'I know that.' But he had died before, your lifetime before, Florence, and I went through it all with Chrissie, I went through the valley of the shadow with her, and drew her (closer than lovers, more one than mother and daughter) gently over the river of death, whereupon your father got up from the grave and said, 'I'm not dead after all, all a mistake', and your mother having inspired me to go all that way with her just left me there to drown. 'Oh I know about your father,' she said with venom. '*We* weren't asked to the funeral, Florence, do you know that? Her own flesh and blood. And what do you have to say about that? After all I've done for you.'

'Excuse me, Aunt Lilian, but just what have you done for me?' She pulled away and moved toward her grandmother, who seemed to be looking for something.

'Oh well you wouldn't remember. You being only a few months old at the time.'

Disgraceful baby, thought Florence, so to consign to oblivion inestimable benefits conferred.

'Then excuse me for saying so, but I don't think I can legitimately be held responsible for what happened before I can remember. If you'll tell me what you did for me, Aunt Lilian, I'll be more than happy to thank you in arrears.'

Lilian grinned, surprisingly. It was another face then, not sour and canting, but strong and cordial.

'Your mother's daughter all right. On your high horse. Don't mind me, our Flo. Don't take any notice of my queer ways. Nobody does round here – do you, mother? Now let's see. You play an instrument in a band, don't you?'

'Yes, I do,' said Florence, and she too grinned broadly. 'I play the pipe in a band.'

'And you're not married?'

'Not likely. I like my freedom and I like my work.'

'Well that's a real achievement,' said Lilian. 'I've had some jobs too in my time, I can tell you. But the end of the war finished all that. The men were demobbed and the women were pushed out of the good jobs. We'd been called up and directed into work, you see, but it was on what they liked to call a voluntary principle – so I took up all sorts of trades – land girl, coalman, plumber, fireman, I was all those – and then when I got fed up with it, I just chucked it in and looked for something else. Oh yes, the war was a great time; the happiest days of my life.'

The end of the war had not only put a stop to Lilian's professional adventures; it had soured her temper and accentuated the bitter streak in her nature, by stamping her a spinster and nothing more. She found herself devalued by the returning armies of young men who swamped the labour market. Domesticity and child rearing were recommended for women, now that they had done their bit. '*I* don't intend to end my life a clucking hen laying eggs in a hen coop,' Lilian had said to anyone who would listen. 'And that's that.' But the world was nest-building then; the fathers and mothers of the new peace were busily flying with sprays of grass and twig out of the public back into the private world, to build. It was the spring of the world. They sang, they mated, they built, they bred. From the vast outdoor theatre of world war the young turned for home, slept with the head sheltered under the wing, in pairs for warmth, for forgetfulness; and they guarded their young. Fertility was everything; the seedbed of the future. Lilian saw the beauty of it, in a frustrated and wrathful way. Part of her would have liked a young man with open arms into whom one might (like Christina) meltingly disappear; Christina, whose story was, Lilian had felt, a classic happy ending such as one might pay to queue for at the cinema. The other part of Lilian scorned the self-engrossed cooing of the couples who flocked like martins under the eaves of houses; and twittered there together, in vacuous togetherness. She took over a couple of allotments, and started to cultivate them. Her ireful spade split into the chalky soil with violent impetus, cleaving worms into wriggling counterparts; she sold produce privately, and finally opened a market garden. She sometimes thought with yearning of the farmer who had claimed her devotion and exploited her labour; and laid her off. It made her hard on weaklings like Chrissie whom she had tried to help. But if Chrissie had turned to her with love and gratitude after Jim had come back in 1945, Lilian would have embraced her, and wept and laughed with her, and forgiven her any amount of happiness. But Chrissie went waltzing off round the world on her married idyll. Lilian was discarded as unnecessary.

But I have my uses, she thought ironically. Keeping an eye on Mother, who was going a bit daft, was one. During the conversation with Florence Amelia had been drifting in her customary trance, staring into the fire, then vaguely looking round. Suddenly she announced,

'Lily! Where are my teeth?' She clutched her mouth. 'My bottom ones!'

'Where did you put them last night, Mother?' Lilian spoke even more loudly than usual for her mother's benefit.

'In the glass next to the bed I *thought*, Lil. But when I woke up this morning, do you know they'd vanished clean away. Do you think a prowler stole them?'

'I hardly think so, Mother. Florence and I will look for them. You sit still and don't cause trouble.'

They searched for the teeth in flowerpots, behind cushions, with great diligence.

'No luck, Mother!' bellowed Lilian in Amelia's ear.

'No what, dear?'

'No teeth, Mother!'

'Oh yes, my love, I've got them in. Not to worry.'

'I give up. I suppose now that we've found your teeth, you'll be wanting to eat. What do you want?'

'No, no, you shoo off now. I get my own dinner. I'm not completely without faculties, I still know how to cut a slice of bread without cutting my fingers. Off you go.' She had forgotten who the Red Indian was. A social worker in disguise, most likely, come to

158

trick her into being carted off into a home. 'Over my dead body,' she said to Florence, darkly.

'Now that I've got hold of you, you might as well come over and see your mother's other sister. She'll want to see you – and your ma don't answer the door, does she, Florence? I've seen her hiding behind the curtains.'

She strode along the sunlit terraces, with Florence half running to keep up.

'I was just asking Gran about my twin brother. I only today found out I ever had one.'

'Oh, yes.'

'Do you know anything about it, Aunt Lilian?'

'This is where the nursing home used to be where you were born, Florence. It was hit by some stray bomb or other, and later it had to be demolished.'

Florence looked at the hole in the world which had yielded her entry into life. They had not rebuilt on the destroyed site, but turned it over to a small civic garden, with green-painted railings and a few rhododendron bushes and fuchsias.

'I was wondering about my brother.'

'Oh, yes?'

They were striding forth again. Her aunt's face was neutral. She kept parroting 'Oh, yes' with a faint air of irritation, as if she were too busy and sensible a woman to go bothering about flighty people's anachronistic fancies.

'Gran said he died at birth. It was a peculiar feeling, that one had been born double as it were, and yet through a fluke of nature come out single.'

'It would be. If you chose to look at it like that. Now, here's where your Aunt Minnie lives, Flo. You wouldn't think you could bring up eight children in such a birdcage, would you – but she did. It used to depress my Dad something chronic, all them children popping out into the world one after another. Even your coming gave him a turn for the worse, the poor old fellow, even though you did become the apple of his eye. He had a Population Problem, did Dada.'

Unseen within the interior of the drab house, someone was singing. The voice was rich and womanly; the words were those of a nursery rhyme:

> Little Boy Blue,
> Come blow your horn,

The sheep's in the meadow,
    The cow's in the corn;
But where is the boy
    Who looks after the sheep?
He's under a haycock
    Fast asleep.
Will you wake him?
    No, not I,
For if I do,
    He'll be sure to cry.

Florence had never, in all her musical years, heard a voice quite like this. It had a fluting, silvery perfection, but it was artless too and candid, and entirely taken up in the burden of its song. The unseen girl sang her heart out on the subject of Boy Blue. It became a matter of anxious concern that the sheep were wandering in the wrong meadow and the cattle were treading down the farmer's corn. Trepidation on the subject of the future swept through the voice as it identified Boy Blue playing truant beneath the haystack. The world was going to rack and ruin as a result of his defection: disorder reigned. But upon the dilemma of whether to risk awakening Boy Blue, the voice became turbulent and divided against itself. After questioning 'Will you wake him?' it paused, as if to work over the problem from every angle, but the 'No' – though clearly the product of personal cowardice – was decisive. Boy Blue must sleep on eternally, for the voice would not dare to arouse those tears. Let the child sleep, it pleaded. It is better so.

The song ceased. Florence looked in at the overgrown garden, thick with grasses, nettles and dock. Slates were off the roof; paint flaked from the window frames. It was the sort of house which neglect and poverty unite to render hopeless. The gate sagged from its hinges, and had to be lifted bodily by Lilian to allow them entrance.

'That's your cousin Alison singing her baby-songs. Daft as a brush she is, but she can't half sing. Problem is, she won't stop half the time, which can get proper wearing on the nerves.'

'I can't imagine getting tired of such a beautiful voice.'

'That,' said Lilian, rapping on the door with her knuckles, 'is because you have the luxury of not having to live with it twenty-four hours a day.'

Minnie had aged significantly, but the bliss engendered by the

160

birth of Alison had not. In features she appeared elderly by comparison with the hardy Lilian. Her body swelled and sagged in every part of the anatomy that permits swellings and saggings. Her small, dark-eyed face had an unhealthy look; her hair was grey and greasy, held at one side by a clip. The house was, as she often remarked, a tip. Nobody bothered to wash the scuff marks from the walls. Spillages on the mats were cursorily mopped and then left to be trodden around. The furniture had been systematically wrecked by eight pairs of children's feet, clambering around on it without reproof. What can any one person do, though, on her own, about the actions of sixteen feet, she used shruggingly to enquire of herself. She took a quietistic stance in relation to the resident mob of children, sealed away in a capsule of self beyond all their havoc, with a small smile on her mouth. She was like a little female Buddha, grounded in the seething world of incarnation and mutability, but not a part of it; listening to her own music. Alison alone of all her children belonged to this intimate world. Alison sang to her, reminding her over the twenty-two years of their mutual life of the gift God had chosen to extend to her, of all people. For Alison recapitulated her first, beloved, dead baby Albert. Alison was the tangible proof that on the Other Side, Someone was thinking of her, working out her good. That, and her widowhood, were her two tokens of election. Nothing else mattered or existed whole-heartedly.

The child who admitted Florence and Lilian was a sulking adolescent in a tiny skirt, flaunting hugely mascaraed eyes.

'Yeah the old bag's in,' she answered Lilian. 'She and Pea-Brain are having a nice cosy singsong in the kitchen. Want to go and join in?'

'Annabel, don't you dare speak of your mother so rudely,' said Lilian without conviction. 'Go and wash that muck off your eyes.'

The girl shrugged and slopped off upstairs, rolling her hips as she went, and leering down on her aunt derisively. The mini skirt was so brief that it demonstrated rather than implied her bottom.

'Quite hopeless,' said Lilian. 'The whole family's neglected, it's a wonder the Welfare haven't been on to them by now, not to mention the Public Health. Hello Minnie, hello Al. I've brought a visitor.'

Alison looked sublimely back at Florence with the placid well-being of a Mona Lisa. Florence grasped the resemblance immediately. It was like walking into a room full of figures, one of whom

161

you suddenly identify not as a person but as a mirror. A distorting mirror, of course, which widened the image, for Alison was as tall as Florence, but rounded and plump; a mirror which subtly changed the relationship of the features. Florence's pale eyes slanted orientally in Alison's broad face, and wore a consistently amiable expression, whereas in Florence they shifted mercurially between fair and foul temper. Both had the dark blond hair streaked with brazen gold which Florence preened as her uniquely crowning glory. No one else in the room appeared struck by the resemblance. Florence's outfit – the embroidered band round her long straight hair and a fringed smock over her jeans – obviously rendered her in the family's eyes an incomparably outlandish figure. Alison perched on a stool in a sleeveless baggy dress, showing plump knees and wearing aged carpet slippers.

'Was that you singing, Alison? What a really lovely voice. Did you have a teacher?'

'My Alison's a natural genius, Florence,' said Minnie, 'though I say it myself. Your mother used to be real proud of you, Flo, but my goodness when I first heard my little girl here start chirruping out her songs, I thought – well, *here's* the special one. Didn't I, my darling?'

'I can well imagine.'

Alison rocked on her stool, smiling faintly. She's a Mongol, thought Florence. 'You must be intensely proud of her. Such a rich voice. I'm very fond of music myself.'

'The sun shines out of her eyes, Florence, it really does. Now, all the others may go to the bad, but my Alison – never.'

How long do Mongols live, wondered Florence. Thirty years? What an awful smell in this kitchen. Rancid fat. Meat going off. Something indescribable. The mini-skirted cousin had flounced in to listen; stared fixedly at Florence with an expression of disbelief. Everything that Florence said she silently echoed, miming Florence's London accent with her brightly painted mouth.

'Behave, Annabel,' said Lilian. '*Why* don't you make an effort to take them in hand, Min? Before it's too late.'

Minnie shrugged, shaking her head indulgently.

'Got any money for chips, Ma? I'll clear off from the big pow-wow if you give me a ten-bob note.'

Money changed hands. 'Goodbye then Mother you old ratbag. Goodbye Birdbrain, that's right smile for the camera, oh what a natural genius it is. Goodbye Aunt Lil you ravishing creature, a right sex-symbol you are ain't you. Good*bye* Cousin Florence Aym Very Fond of Myusick May Self You Know Wha Wha. Farewell you boring band of fogies and phoneys.'

'Bye bye Anny Belly,' said Alison. 'Kiss Alison before you go, Belly.'

'Can't you do something about them, Min?'

'It's their lives, that's what I say. Cup of tea, Flo? No? All right then. Mind you, Lil, I am a bit surprised at my Sam – the eldest, Flo, four years older than you. Apparently he's starting beating up his wife, little Cressie – would you credit it? She came round here with a bruise on her eye the size of a cricket ball – but I said, I can't believe it of him, Cress, I know he's been in and out of the nick but basically he's a good boy. There's no history of violence in our family.'

'Minnie, how can you say it! Your Albert used to punch you in the eye as soon as look at you.'

'Never.'

Minnie looked scandalised. She drew herself up to her full five foot three inches. Widowhood had settled around her a mantle of forgetfulness. After the years of beatings and fright, rapes and childbearing, his suicide had given rest and solace, time to dream and the possibility of rewriting her personal history from scratch. In Minnie's scrupulous revision of the past, Albert had assumed the character of a gentle, reticent man, a lover of children, a lover of nature, thoughtful and kind hearted. The death of Albert, in this Revised Version, had come as a dreadful blow, which she assuaged by the daily invention of new hoards of treasured memories.

'My Albert lay a violent hand on me! He was a lovely husband in every way, God rest his soul, the kindest gentleman. No, Sam never got his vicious ways from my hubby. It must be in his nature, that's all, he never was quite normal, still not to worry.'

Lilian tapped her forehead to Florence, who had listened with perfect incomprehension.

'Sam was all right. Uncouth perhaps – not the cleanest boy I could wish to meet – but he loved you when he was a little chap as if you were the last woman on earth, Min. It's convenient to you to forget all that. It was only when you wouldn't take notice of him that he started breaking birds' legs off and pilfering from Woolworth's. Anyway it's a hopeless task, Minnie, trying to talk to you about it.'

'Mum is lovely, Mum is dear,' said Alison, protecting Minnie

163

against what she understood to be her aunt's critical attitude. She rubbed Minnie's hand with vigour, and smiled encouragement into her eyes, face up close. 'Sing a song with Alison, Florence?'

Florence and Alison stood in the centre of the filthy, chaotic kitchen, singing nursery rhymes. Alison held Florence's hand and swung it to the music. Her heavy tongue, over-large for her mouth, by some miracle of effortlessness managed to imply the syllables which were so hard for her to shape intelligibly in normal talk. Two hulking schoolgirls in a playground, thought Florence, that's what we are like; the biggest boobies in the school. But the audience listened spellbound as the voices rendered 'Dance to your Daddy' as a joyous anthem; 'Little Polly Flinders' as a tragi-comic lament for the fate of children; and 'The Grand Old Duke of York' as a mutinous satire on the military. Florence stopped wondering what freaks they must be looking, and started to sing, really sing. Alison's commanding simplicity, softly powerful as a wooden flute, brought out her own voice, not as original as her cousin's, but positive and clear. She tried a descant to Alison's, and found that her cousin could hold a tune against her. She began to taunt Alison's voice by elaborating the counterpoint. Alison held out yet more strongly against the challenge. Her voice did not deviate from the central tune; it sustained the melody as the dominant theme upon which Florence was dependent for her variations. Alison's voice was faithful: Florence's wandered. She is the pattern, and I am the distortion, she thought. I reflect upon her reality. She let her voice play outrageous tricks with the songs, sheering up and down the harmonic registers, holding out aloof from the sanctuary of Alison's tune. They filled the tiny kitchen, and the house, and the garden, with mutual sound that, for the time being, reconciled the dissonances of their history, and forgave its delinquencies and illusions. Florence clean forgot to ask her Aunt Minnie for memories of her twin brother before she left for home.

Six

Lilian left her niece at the corner of St Christopher's Road, meaning to return to Gran's and enquire further into the teeth situation. So that was Flo. That long-haired hippy with the flighty smile and the high-class accent, and the willingness to sing with poor half-baked Minnie's half-baked girl in the middle of a filthy kitchen. That was the Flo about whom so much fuss was made at her birth, you'd have thought it was the Second Coming at the very least. All done up like a Sioux warrior, the only thing lacking being bow and arrows (as I told her straight out: 'Come and have a pow-wow at my place, no peace-pipe though: I *hope* you aren't one of these young people who takes drugs now?') Looking for her brother.

Shall I tell, or let sleeping dogs lie? I could crush Christina like a thrush's egg between finger and thumb. Just like that. Just by opening my mouth. Nobody has ever really taken me seriously, thought Lilian. No one would ever credit me with knowing a secret and keeping it to myself. Lilian is just a joke to people – half woman, half man – bit of a dinosaur, good for work, surplus to requirements. Marital status: Spinster. Status: Nil. The war was incomparably my best time, not that they took me seriously then of course either but my God I was an asset to have around.

What I do have, she thought smugly, lingering at the railings of 'The Limes' public gardens, is a sense of reality. Feet on the ground. Pragmatism. That wild look of Florence, searching, quick with her eyes, nothing in the world would be just ordinary for her. Everything too intense, full of mystery: a mystifier. Now she thinks there might be a brother at large, off she bolts in pursuit of this long-lost prey. Larger than life; character from a myth. What if the brother doesn't want to be found? Is leading a nice stable life with wife and children, and in bounds a long-lost sister with hectic spots of excitement on her cheeks, and sings her song at him; hits the

165

flawless note that shatters a glass? Disturbs the ordinary man by wanting to have him extra-ordinary? Now, for instance, I've a brother: George. Railway worker like our Dad. Has there ever been and will there ever be anything to say about my brother? No. Because he's ordinary – solid as a rock, dull as water, featureless as Salisbury Plain. I couldn't even describe him if I tried.

A dust layer like a sifting of very fine ash lay over the waxen dark surfaces of the rhododendron leaves. It greyed the petals of the daisies in the fumy air. Lorries thundered past, splitting into the old peace of the town. Not that Salisbury had ever been much of a sanctuary for the poor and needy. In a sense the Cathedral was an illusion, she had always thought so, though its aspiring beauty dumbfounded her some mornings, and she turned in her tracks to stare. But the citizens had always hated the clergy; they fought them in gangs to punish the audacity of their fluting. moneyed voices so that some king or other had to build a wall round the Close, with a portcullis, to defend the Cathedral against the people's righteous indignation. Clicking their well-shod heels on sacred ground, wagging their tongues telling us what to do, wearing dresses as if they were as good as women, living off the fat of the land: it's all one can do not to stick out a well-timed leg and send them sprawling as they finick past. Although I made use of the Cathedral one time, she thought.

She went through in her mind the time when she had found out about Chrissie's giving away the twin boy. It was a full ten years after the war. She was out at the market with her produce, at crack of dawn, and a most beautiful sunrise, she remembered: it had been pouring all night and then the sun came up and lit the wet pavements like a sea. She tramped up with her crates, and there was Polly Cornwell, the orderly at the nursing home where Florence was born (this very patch of air I'm inhabiting now, come to think of it, she thought, looking round at the shabby garden). She had finally bought herself out of the WRENS where she was nursing, and come to market with her Dad. A furtive little piece, and a blabbermouth, I never could stand her. I tried to pretend I hadn't seen her but she pursued me, wheedling. I accidentally stood on her toe.

'I know about your Chrissie,' she said to me.

'What do you know about Chrissie?'

'*Don't you know?*'

'Know what, for Christ's sake? Are you all there, what's the

166

matter with you?' I gave her a baleful look, and elbowed her out of my path.

'I know what she did in the war. To her baby boy. *I know*.'

'She had a girl, not a boy. Now I'll get on, if you don't mind.'

'No, Lily, she had twins. At "The Limes" Nursing Home. I was working there. I saw it all.'

'The boy was born dead. Shut up and clear off.'

'Oh no. The boy was alive and kicking. She gave her boy away, to be adopted, like a common bastard. Ever had second thoughts, did she? Ever try and see it again? I tried to awaken your Chrissie's natural maternal instincts, I did, but she didn't seem to have any. She wouldn't hold it or look at it or feed it. Funny how these lah-de-dah highly superior people with the affected Lady Muck manners aren't even as good as normal when it comes down to it. I put that boy in her arms, and I begged her to love it, but she let it slide down on to the floor, might have cracked its skull. That crooked matron sold it, she did, to some folks down in Exeter. Didn't you know that, Lily?'

My blood ran cold. I knew at once the little bitch was telling the truth. I could have throttled her, the beetle-eyed malicious tart. That was when I made good use of the Cathedral. Marched her snivelling up to the high altar and made her swear on the Holy Bible never to tell a word of it to a living soul or I'd break every bone in her weasel body. But she'd had a bastard at the Home herself, and disposed of it; didn't want that put about. It was a bargain.

Lilian sat reflecting on the garden seat between the ashen rhododendron bushes, traffic roaring past her. Somewhere in this space, this patch of empty air so long evacuated by human business, my Chrissie had a girl and a boy, and gave the one away and kept the other. For some reason known only to herself. I loved her and helped her when Jim was missing, she could have confided, I would not have blamed. But when he came back from Italy she swooned away toward him, forgetting me. I became paltry and negligible, I was discarded. They seem to think I have a hide like a mastodon, a rind or cuticle where they are soft and sentient. Having the power of the secret, I could hurt Chrissie by telling. It could be her death blow. And they don't take me seriously?

'Consider Lily,' she said once. 'Look how she toils and spins. Even Solomon in all his glory was not arrayed like one of these.' The tenderness she forced from me half-killed me, it was so without reserve: could it be unholy, outside nature, I wondered, to feel such passion of concern just for a sister? I saw how undecided she was in spirit, how she couldn't count on herself. When we were young she used to be jealous of me, I saw it in the chilly turning-away of her head. 'You're a tomboy, Lily,' she warned me, because my boy-self threatened her. But even so there was a bond. I remember her hands as a child arranging sweet peas in the tumbler; the pastel colours; the ache of scent in the air; her saying 'They'll die indoors but aren't they so lovely Lily while they stay?' No, I won't wake him. Let him sleep.

Florence took to her heels, to work off some of the excitement at having discovered so many long-lost people, unearthed so much that was fascinating and extraordinary. Her path lay along the gentle downward inclination of the Blake's Brow estate, a criss-cross of unpretentious suburban roads, very green and quiet at this time, when everyone was indoors having lunch. As she ran she could see the spire of the Cathedral giving direction to the whole town like a magnetic needle, at eternal stasis to the Pole. Through a gap in the houses she glimpsed a walking figure, two or three streets away, recognisable immediately as her mother. Rounding the corner and zigzagging back up the next street, she again caught sight of the figure through the houses, nearer now; but always she was running tangentially to the figure, obscurely at angles to her direction, her view intermittently blanked off by the houses. They were in a maze together, travelling each within her own loneliness between the hedges that bounded individual vision in the silent, childless streets. The midday sun beat down ruthlessly as Florence ran, her loose blouse stuck to her skin and her hair was hot and damp. Did she actually want to catch up with her mother, though, and what would they have to say to one another? Some scalding bitterness perhaps would come out, to the effect, 'I've seen our past, you know, the one you kept from me – I've met my family, the roots you cut me from.' Or a retention of these facts and feelings, behind laboured small talk just as death-dealing, and the iron bands of pity hooped tight round her rib cage.

She reached the final bend, and there was her mother half way down the road. She was walking with measured pace, her head carried high, her spine straight. She was walking through the world totally alone. She was doing so with upright bearing. Florence saw how slender and young her mother's figure still was, in the blue

168

dress, her camel coat discarded in the heat, carried neatly over her left arm. She looked like a young person, gentle and vulnerable seen from behind, if one knew of the extreme self-consciousness with which she had to meet each moment. Now there was no Father to guard her shyness with his own, to turn inward to her and create a private room wherever they two were. Momentarily Florence conjured the form of her father into being, to walk alongside her mother. At once the heart lifted. Christina walked protected, in shadow, less visible in the lee of the taller figure so dapper in blazer and trilby, shoes shining with a military gloss. He would grasp her arm at the elbow when they wished to cross a road, and precipitate her across quick-march. Christina quite liked that: it freed her from responsibility. Florence used to scowl and jerk her arm away. And he would usher them through a door with insistent courtesy. Florence flounced ahead, cross at the bullying. Christina was made happy by it. Now the ghost faded away from Florence's retina. Her mother walked alone, unbefriended, through a world that was made up of eyes; only of eyes. 'Oh come back and bully us – come back and annoy me till I could scream – come back and care for her!' she cried out inwardly to the ashes of the mutilated protector she had scattered at Old Sarum. The truancy, the defection of God struck her afresh. She started to run toward her mother.

Intense heat throbbed. Breath came in tearing gasps. The tarmacadam had melted and softened, and its heat burned up through her soles. Everything was slow. Her limbs were heavy and inflexible, unable to cover the ground between them although she put all her remaining energy into it. The gap seemed life-long. She was like the egg in the womb initiating its odyssey; the conception that is not yet seen or known but whose gathering force creates momentum to split the sac of the past and burst into the future, overtaking the conceivers as it charges into time. The stop-watch of her eye ticked out the seconds. She laboured up the dead-still, airless road through mirages of heat haze, till she had nearly closed with the figure of her mother. Here was deliverance, the brief moment of communication before the young pitch forward on their headlong dash into the future, and the spent mother is left behind to fall back into the common twilight.

Christina turned, and realised that the galloping footsteps belonged to her offspring, crimson in the face, perspiring and grinning.

'Hello you great lumbering thing. What are you doing hurtling round town when you know perfectly well you ought to be indoors practising your flute. I haven't heard a cheep out of you for weeks. No, don't stop – *I* don't want to be seen walking with a fright like you for company. Get along home, put the kettle on, and I want to hear something a bit musical coming from the house when I arrive.'

'I'm all in. Let's walk together.'

'Oh no you're not. Off you go. You'll be off on tour soon. You don't want to be out of training, my love, do you. I don't want to hold you back.'

'I'll put the kettle on. See you soon.'

Florence ran on ahead. She had passed through the barrier of effort, and ran lightly, airily. Christina had done that for her. She had given her breath. At the crossroads she looked back and waved. Christina was a smaller figure now, coming on at her own pace. She no longer appeared as excruciatingly vulnerable, nor as childlike, as she waved Florence on again; but more grown-up somehow than she had ever looked.

'Tea or coffee?' she hollered.

'Tea. And stop yelling, you horrible girl!'

At home, she passed the 'For Sale' board with barely a glance. By the autumn, they would be gone from Salisbury. That was good really: they had never truly lived in this house. She had no idea where her mother would settle. The seaside perhaps, where the retired go idling along the front, in couples or singly, in an attitude of waiting; peering out to sea. She had said, 'You'll be off on tour soon.' Christina had accepted it, then, her own singleness. Florence too would have to accept hers. The Bible, with its misleading message of a lost boy, still lay open on the table. She latched and buried it at the back of her cupboard, shrouding it in blankets. It was not such a great event, after all, this business of the boy-twin. It happens in nature all the time: natural waste, deaths, miscarriages, spontaneous abortions. The boy-child could not have been much more than a foetus. It just got trapped in there when its time was past. Nasty for my mother but not as significant as I took it to be. I'll take my pipe down there and accompany Alison one of these days. People will wonder which is the voice and which the flute.

Putting the kettle on the gas ring, low so as to give Christina ample time to catch up, she splashed her face and arms with cold water. Then she opened all her windows and assembled the instrument and the music stand. This should wake them up a bit, she thought, the dozy lot around here. The flute felt so good, its clean, cold weight balanced along her hands. She had plenty of breath. She was relaxed from the running. It was like having taken a drug; nothing could go wrong to inhibit the music.

It was Debussy's *Syrinx* that Christina heard as she neared the house. Florence used to play the unaccompanied solo as an encore at concerts, using the stage as if it were a private room in which the dark music could most deeply meditate upon itself. The notes floated out of the window like rows of bubbles. Christina stood by the beech hedge in a brilliant sea of green and golden light, mutely listening, flooded with sound. She heard her daughter's breath forcing at the flute, commanding it to open out, to be flute no more, but protest itself as music purely. She took in the angry energy of her daughter's account of how things stood, as the dark tide of beauty poured through the severally wounded sides of the flute.

Coda

The young man was on a tour of the West Country in his mini station-wagon. He slept in the back, and cooked his own meals on a primus stove, so his holidays were dirt cheap, and as frequent as he could make them. Though his work was that of a solicitor's clerk in the family firm in Hereford, his love was archaeology. But he said that your love should be a private matter, in which you should neither invest your livelihood nor your sense of duty, so he had not wanted to study for a degree in history; nor in anything else for that matter. He said he was more than happy to plod along as a clerk in the firm. If he took a degree in law, that might entice him to take the whole thing more seriously. Too much like getting married, he said. His father tore his hair, wrath mingling with tenderness till both were indistinct. 'But you'll inherit the business! Don't you want to be able to carry it on?'

'I'm too easygoing, you know that. I'd mess it all up. I'd only want it for you, for love of you – and that's not good business policy, is it? Leave it all to Jeannie; she's more cut out.'

His father shook the tall young man, then embraced him and fiercely rumpled his shock of pale brown hair. Both Eric and Jeannie were adopted children, much the same age, but he had naturally wanted the boy to inherit.

They had not told the children of their adoption until their eighteenth birthdays. Eric and Jeannie seemed so genuinely their own: children of their choice, of their passionate need. Accidents of birthplace, of genetics, had seemed irrelevant to that love, fostered since the matron brought first Jeannie, then Eric to them, wrapped in long white shawls against the winter cold, outside Exeter station; and they handed over the cash; and bought so cheaply the right to love two strangers' children, casualties of war. Jeannie was very shocked and disturbed at the news. She shot back into herself as if she had been scalded. When they spoke to Eric about it, he took the news matter-of-factly, seeming more concerned to assure his adoptive parents of their reality to him than to enquire into his random origins.

'If you *ever* feel you need to know more about your real mother, will you let Dad know, and he will do all he can to trace her,' said his mother, her eyes slightly averted, but speaking in her most spirited voice.

'I'm pretty sure I know her already,' said Eric, fetching her in to a huge friendly bear hug. 'I don't require any parents extra to those already in being, thank you very much. One of each is more than enough to put up with.'

On his present holiday he had dimly thought, now and again, passing through the villages of the Plain, 'I wonder if it was here that I came from?' but his major interest was devoted to wandering round ruins, henges, churches, barrows. There were so many objects of fascination in this area that (since he could never resist stopping off at any relic of even minor interest) he was viewing places all day long, and recuperating at evening in pubs drawing out local people, chatting and listening; and slept dreamlessly all night. It was a winter holiday. He was hardy and stoical, and pleased with himself for being so: no weather could deter him. He slept in a balaclava helmet, three pairs of socks, long woollen sack-like garments knitted by his mother, zipped into a sleeping bag; lulled to sleep by taped music, of all kinds, jazz, rock, classical. He was omnivorous about knowledge and experience, and it was axiomatic with him that no subject was in itself intrinsically boring.

It was on the second day of December, a fortnight or so off his twenty-fourth birthday, that he reached the hillfort of Old Sarum, two miles north of Salisbury. He had already visited Silbury Hill, and Avebury, and Stonehenge which had been enlivened by a parliament of hippies gathering early for the Solstice, celebrating Peace and Brotherhood, casting for ley lines, and fortifying themselves against the cold by keeping high on cannabis. They lay in the circular ditch and sang their songs of love. 'Don't get trench foot now,' he called back as he left. 'Love and Peace, Love and Peace!' their chanted refrain echoed its fragile illusionism on the frosted air. It was impractical weather for making love, not war, he thought as he drove away; but they were not bad people at all. Old Sarum would be his last hillfort before he turned for home.

When he awoke and opened up the back of the car, he realised that the misted windows were not just the product of the overnight condensation of his own breath, but that a thick mist had packed itself round the car, wrapping it up tight in freezing blankets. A deep frost lay on the ground; individual grasses creaked and snapped beneath his feet as he clambered out. He had parked in the lee of the hill, quite near, but nothing of it was visible through the murk. He brewed up quickly in the aching cold, heated a can of baked beans and shut himself in the front of the car to eat his breakfast, tearing hunks of bread off a loaf to mop up the baked bean juice from the dish. Nothing ever tasted as good as these boy-scoutish feasts of plain food, eaten salted with lovely isolation from the human community. He stared into the mass of violet-grey mist sealing the capsule of the car. It was going to be another tremendous day.

He got out. Two feet from the car, and the car disappeared. The mist flowed straight in behind him and barred his vision back. But as he walked in the general direction of the hillfort – waded, rather, through the heavy bank of air – the sky cleared for a moment toward the south and the rising sun showed like a torch of white light. In its transient beam, the mound of the hill fort was located for him as a blob of darkness. He saw the hill upon the hill, enclosed within the concentric circles of bank-and-ditch. He meant to see everything, spend the whole day browsing round the Early Iron Age structure, the Norman fortifications, the eleventh-century cathedral and Bishop Roger's palace ruins. A treat, a feast: he could have jumped with his customary joy at the thought of the rich day ahead of him. But the mist could take hours to clear. He stumbled up the bridge over the inner moat, and on to the round high centre of the hillfort.

It was like stepping out on to the pupil of a great eye directed at the heavens: a strangeness. He caught it immediately. The whole place was so quiet, a fund of mist and frost, but straight above him the sky was transparently clear and excessively blue, with a white morning moon one-third full hanging above the fort. First it was like being on an eye. Then it seemed to him like being in an egg, or the uterus itself, the path he had scaled between the high grassy banks being the birth passage: yes, this last, and he was here microscopic as a seed at conception, back in the natal chamber. Thoughts of the Normans, and their Bishops, and their fortifications, were driven away. They could not have been further from his mind as he began his passage round the inner circumference, looking out to the plains extending in every direction indefinitely, a sea bed for the oceanic grey-blue mists that rolled and drifted in his aerial view to every horizon of the earth. He went on slowly, as if with pain. The enormous landscape cancelled his thoughts; returned him languageless to source.

Nobody had been there before him. The virginal frosted grass crunched beneath his light tread. He was all eyes, all ears. At its margins the world was clouded grey and pink. Far out on the flowing tides of mist dark clusters of trees voyaged like vessels adrift, and seemed to rock upon the waves. He stood on the rim of the hill looking out south toward Salisbury, the New Sarum. His hands were perishing cold, his face scalded with it. The sky over Salisbury was slate grey, with a fluted, scalloped edge of brilliance to the cloud where the sun caught it. He thought he could make out the spire of the Cathedral, needle-thin in the grey darkness over there; but it vanished under his stare.

He turned his eyes away from Salisbury, and went on walking round the perimeter. The chirrup of birdsong from many miles away travelled to his ears across the acoustic plain. The mist was quicksilver here, with the density of cold fluid metal flowing against the membrane of his eye. Then, like mercury, it ran away for a moment, it slid down between the barbs of the surrounding hawthorns, it drained away leaving him enveloped in a sac of light. Drops of dew were hanging from the joints of bramble sprays and hawthorn boughs. These airborne globes of water reflected the tree that held them, as if a tear should enclose an eyelash. They hung out their mirrors from ivy, nettles, old seed pods, and shimmered above the whited grass, illumining the old year clinging on barrenly round the sides of the hill in a thorny wilderness. It was like being behind a vast and shining bead curtain, strung with glassy, light-gathering pearls of moisture. Each single drop how perfect, how worthy of consideration. Every common transient thing seemed miraculous, out of the ordinary, before the returning mist obscured it. The light was gone but the sensation not, the sense of seeing as if it were a kind of touch. It was like being a baby again, before the conjunctive membrane toughens on the eyeball, before the font-anelles close over the sealed self. They crowded on the lens of his eye, the beaded worlds of water, and refused to be blinked away. In normal life you could not afford to see like this; the eye must be killed by its own rage of sentience. He turned from the path.

In the bowl of the hillfort the mist was cupped. His feet travelled down the rounds and delves of grass, its soft irregularities, until he

178

was submerged in the whitest mist of all, and added to it the white of his own breath. He hardly glanced at the Norman remains of the castle, which would normally have intrigued him. The Normans were late arrivals, day trippers. He ignored them scornfully, immersed in the obscurity of the inarticulate, prehistoric centre.

Now time and space were at a loss to know each other. The disassembled moments could not track each other down. Is this my mouth, these my eyes? Now he was in the central high basin of the fort, now he found himself on the rim of the great outermost earthwork, but the interval between was lost. He could not recall his name without effort. He could not put a label to the place. Migrainous shadowed mists came down, his vision spun, then they cleared. He was on the shell of the egg, the lid of the eye; now he was in the black vortex of the pupil. At times the mist seemed thick as candyfloss, he could have plucked a handful out of the air, it would stick to your fingers like white wool. At other times there was no mist at all where he stood, but he was within a globe of pearly light, swimming about lost like a minnow in a bowl. Perhaps there are two of me, he thought, I am at the centre and I am at the edge, we brush past each other in our polar journeys. He felt quite drunk, he laughed out loud, he went on.

But the sun was breaking through in places, to disclose the bare boughs of bramble and thorn, the blood-red of rose hips round the chalky path, striking and poignant, like the sacrifice of one who has bled beads of life's blood. The hips stood in clusters of two and three upon the boughs; and near them blackberries shone for a moment, glossed with wet. Wild barley bowed down its head at the tips, saffron yellow. When each particular had been truly seen, the mist rolled back in again and cancelled it. Beyond and around the plain went on for ever, pooled mist on a sea of halcyon quiet. He stood on the outermost rampart near the uterine opening, facing inwards. Before him the cloven earth dropped sheer away into a great ditch. The strangeness deepened; deepened further, deepened. He was on his knees on the frost. It was agony of cold, it was killing but it was homecoming. He cried, he was going mad, he wished for the safety of foreign parts. The sun broke through in a laser beam of white light, disclosing nothing but itself: it blasted the air like nuclear fission. Then a paler light of neutrality, of normality began to show.

His hands were covered in soft chalk. He saw a white flower in full bloom. He saw the face of his watch, and it was eleven o'clock.

Three hours had vanished. The mist came in again, but not so dense now, clammy rather than freezing. He went on walking, round and round, not really knowing what he was doing; but his heart was soaring, it seemed, as if it sailed far above his own head. It was a joy at odds with his habitually genial and cheerful good temper. It denied his customary unthinking cordiality. It took in pain, void, loss of being. It was like being in a dream; and he would never know or be able to say what it was he dreamt.

But the sun was gaining, definitely making headway. Time was burning in to the mist; and in the vast blue ceiling he occasionally glimpsed, the moon had certainly paled. As the sun broke through, it caught the barbed-wire boughs of the naked hawthorn, the stab of its innumerable spear heads; and near it a cluster of rose hips gleaming with wet in the burning sunlight; and behind them a coincidental robin perched, with his wounded breast. It seemed a long time that he stared at the blood berries of Sarum, and at the entrance of his eyes took into himself the harvest of the ancient mother-sanctuary.

The mist had almost cleared. It was all very picturesque, but he was too tired to appreciate it any more, and jaded almost, as if suffering from a hangover. This is not like me at all, he thought. I'm not myself this morning. Perhaps I'm coming down with flu. He did not like intensities or raptures in other people. They were embarrassing. He didn't go in for them himself, but went round the world steadily enjoying its miscellaneousness, trying to understand as much as possible, not worrying too greatly about what he couldn't grasp. But as he came down the hill now toward his car, he had a peculiar sensation not so much of having elected to leave as having been expelled. He turned and looked back. Other people had come in – the Wiltshire yeomanry in capes and boots walking their labradors, calling out to one another in friendly voices through the clear air of this loveliest of mornings. He had been superseded. He had been squeezed out; it was all over; he was discharged. What was all over, he could not conceive, but a surge of inexplicable melancholy took him over completely, and a helplessness, as if in himself he could not hope to find sufficient resources to manage his life. He got in to the driving seat, and sat huddled up, staring at the sunlit hill, cold to the marrow. He felt like a baby. He would have liked a companion to be there, to embrace him and hold him, and cuddle him into a state of wholesome, self-forgetful warmth; to pour him out hot coffee from a flask; to crack jokes with. He would have liked to cry.

He lay down in the back of the van, bundled up in his sleeping bag, and slept. When he came round, the car was like a furnace from having stood in the full sunshine so long. He felt fine, completed, restored. He climbed out and looked back at the hillfort, which was peopled with tourists now, and seemed a smaller and more comfortable place altogether than in the mystifying weather of early morning. Its roundness pleased his eye, like the contour of a breast. But he didn't want to go back in: too claustrophobic a confinement. He was eager for the journey; couldn't wait to get going. All that he saw fed his eye with pleasure: the milky light, the yielding, open, sensuous countryside. His legs still felt a bit wobbly from overtiredness; and he was hungry. He fed himself, put on a tape, and set off for Hereford. As he passed the RAF station at Old Sarum, he glimpsed the monolithic hangars with their double-domed roofs, and their great metal sliding doors sealed. All the glass and metal in the buildings was glistening in the sunlight; and the airfield lay quite still and deserted, with a look of peace across the expanses of grass and concrete. No planes were flying that day, but if they had been, Eric – having turned the volume of the music up to maximum – would probably not have heard them.

Janet Frame
Living in the Maniototo

Winner of the Fiction Prize, New Zealand Book Awards, 1980

Janet Frame again offers us a richly imagined exploration of uncharted lands. The path is through the Maniototo, that 'bloody plain' of the imagination which crouches beneath the colour and movement of the living world. The theme of the novel is the process of writing fiction, the power, interruptions and avoidances that the writer feels as she grapples with a deceptive and elusive reality. We move with our guide, a woman of manifold personalities, through a physical journey which is revealed to be a metaphor for the creative process – on which our own survival depends.

'Puts everything else that has come my way this year right in the shade' *Guardian*

Fiction £3.95
ISBN: 0 7043 3867 X

Joan Riley
Waiting in the Twilight

When Adella, a talented seamstress, moves to Kingston,
Jamaica, life seems to promise much: a respectable career and
the chance of professional status. Instead she falls for a young
policeman who leaves her with two children. She is befriended
and married by Stanton, a carpenter, and sails for England to
join him. But Stanton too deserts her, for Gladys, Adella's
own cousin.

She resolves to buy a home of her own, but is forced into
sub-standard housing; in the end even this is taken from her by
the council.

Now a grandmother crippled by a stroke, Adella waits
patiently for her husband to return. Haunted by memories of
the past, she assesses what has been achieved. Her life,
apparently bleak, is sustained by her own generous love, and
the warmth of her children.

This is the moving story of a woman's struggle for dignity
against a background of urban racism. Riley pulls no punches in
her effort to portray 'the forgotten and unglamorous section
of my people' within a system which 'openly and systematically
discriminates' against them.

Joan Riley's first novel, *The Unbelonging*, was published by The
Women's Press in 1985.

Fiction   £3.95
ISBN: 0 7043 4023 2

Caeia March
Three Ply Yarn

'The blitz on the London docks got my mum. My dad died in Burma. That's when Dora and me first took to cuddling. Behind the hay barn, while Nellie collected eggs.'

This passionate story is narrated by three women, Dee, Lotte and Esther, as they struggle to take command of their own lives in a world they have not made.

The three choose different paths. Lotte marries for money, Esther seeks education and politics, Dee loves women and learns, through her relationship with her lover's black daughter, about an oppression different from her own. Yet their lives increasingly intertwine, and their realisation grows of the importance of other women to each of them.

Full of the realities of working-class lesbian experience, *Three Ply Yarn* is an absorbing read from an important new writer.

Fiction £3.95

ISBN: 0 7043 4007 0

JoAnne Brasil
Escape from Billy's Bar-B-Que

'There were lots of Post-War Babies and Hippies in our building, it turned out...they were always offering to baby-sit; but Betty Baines wouldn't let them because they might smoke reefer and start asking 'what is real?' and stuff like that or start reading *Finnegan's Wake* out loud even though they said they didn't get it at all...'

After High School, Cecyl escapes from the racist society of Phoebus, Virginia, to the 'liberal' North of Boston. Yet her encounters with the Post-War Babies, a group of South American musicians, and an assortment of room-mates, leave her perplexed at the barriers raised by class, sex, race and by people who won't 'treat each other normal'.

Utterly convinced that everyone else knows something she doesn't, Cecyl possesses that uncluttered honesty which sees right to the heart of human contradiction and hypocrisy.

Fiction £3.95
ISBN: 0 7043 4046 1